Three Weeks
Last Spring

Happy Reading

Victoria Howard

Victoria Howard

DEDICATION

For my Goddaughter Suzanne, who, for one
so young has faced so much and always with a
smile.

ACKNOWLEDGMENTS

To Daphne Rose, Lesley Dennison, and Dorothy Roughley for their encouragement, support, and tolerance in reading every page as it came off the printer. I could not have done this without you and I am honored to call you my friends.

George Bennett, a published author in his own right, deserves my thanks for his guidance and generosity in showing 'the new kid on the block' the way. This book would never have been completed without your help and guidance.

Finally, to Stephen, my thanks for his patience, support, and belief that I really could write this novel.

CHAPTER ONE

England April 1999

Skye Dunbar stood by her kitchen window and waited for the transatlantic phone call to connect. She was going back. Back to try to make sense of the biggest heartbreak of her life. Foolish, she knew, but she needed some type of closure.

She gazed at the meadow beyond her home. After the heavy rain this weekend, everything looked gray, wet, and cold, cold as the heart that beat inside her breast.

The phone rang and rang. Was she calling too early? She glanced at her watch and calculated the eight-hour time difference between London and San Francisco. She hoped she wouldn't wake Debbie. Her friend would be irritated enough that Skye was planning a trip to Seattle instead of visiting her.

After a while, a sleepy American voice answered.

"Hello?"

"Debbie? Did I wake you?"

1

"Not really. I was lying here thinking about getting up. Talk to me, Skye. You sound anxious."

Skye took a deep breath. "I've decided to take a month's sabbatical. I've contacted British Airways and have an option on a flight leaving in a week's time. They're holding it for twenty-four hours."

"Why, that's great. You need to get away, and you love San Francisco."

"Actually, Debbie, that's why I'm calling. I'm not flying to San Francisco. I'm going to Seattle."

"Skye, you can't possibly want to spend a month there, not after all that happened last year."

"I can't explain why, but I need to go back." Skye twisted a strand of hair between her fingers while she waited for Debbie to respond.

"You're right, I don't understand. Please, come here and stay with me. We can visit all our old haunts— Fisherman's Wharf, Chinatown. We can go for a drink in the *John Barleycorn* and listen to that folk singer you like so much. If that doesn't appeal to you, then we could hire a car and drive along the coast. You haven't seen the Marin Headlands or Monterey yet. Or we could meet somewhere else. How about Vermont? If you wait until I get to the office on Monday, I'll see if I can beg for some vacation time."

"That's a lovely thought, Debbie, and I do want to see Vermont, but in the fall. Please, save your vacation time. This is something I have to do on my own. It sounds crazy, and I don't expect you to understand. Just give me your blessing and tell me that if I need you, you'll be there for me. Okay?"

"I really do worry about you, Skye. You have to put what happened behind you and move on. So, where are you staying?"

"I've rented a cabin on the San Juan Islands."

"You've done what? No one visits the San Juan Islands in the middle of April. It's too cold for one thing, and Friday Harbor will be deserted. What will you do in that little town for a whole month?"

"I plan to relax and catch up on some reading, go walking, and enjoy the scenery."

"If you ask me, the last thing you need is to be by yourself. As you've made your mind up, I guess there's little I can say to dissuade you. Promise me, though. If you get lonely, you'll catch the first available plane to San Francisco. Deal?"

"Deal. And, Debbie," Skye hesitated before continuing, "thanks for understanding. You're the best friend anyone could ask for. As soon as I finalize my plans, I'll let you know."

Skye replaced the receiver and turned once more to look out of the window. Was she being stupid for returning to the Pacific Northwest? What would her visit achieve? Would it put her mind at rest? They were questions she couldn't answer, yet in her heart she knew she was doing the right thing.

She had met Michael while visiting Debbie last year. She'd been roller-skating in Golden Gate Park, when suddenly she was knocked to the ground. He helped her to her feet and insisted on buying her a coffee. Coffee turned into lunch, and before they realized how much time had passed they had spent the whole afternoon together. Skye was due to fly home the following day and Michael asked for her address. She had given it to him, but didn't expect him to keep in touch. Six weeks later, returning home after a particularly fractious day at work, she found his letter on her doormat.

Michael's initial letter, and those that followed, had been read and re-read, the words feeling as if they were engraved on her heart. Finally, in January he wrote and invited her to visit.

Skye pushed the thought of him out of her mind. She had so much to accomplish that she couldn't stand and daydream all evening. Her flight confirmed and the cabin booked, she concentrated on clearing her schedule. Then all she had to do was pack a suitcase and get on that plane.

The following week passed in a blur. Each day she arrived at the office early and brought her files up to date for John, her business partner, to take over in her absence.

They met at university shortly after her mother's death. John had been a graduate teaching assistant when Skye started her degree course. At thirty-nine, he was five years her senior. Six feet tall, with brown eyes and unruly curly hair, he had a smile that could melt the iciest of hearts.

When Skye graduated, they set up business together. Years of long hours and neglected vacations finally paid off, and their services were in demand by major corporations all over the world. Despite the success they experienced, their relationship never passed beyond friendship.

Skye's friends knew she was a high-level executive, but as she didn't talk about her work, they knew none of the details. In another few months, she and John would be making a presentation to government officials in the hope of securing an exclusive contract—top secret, and most the most demanding of their respective careers.

The day before Skye was due to leave, she scheduled a meeting with him.

"What are you going to do with a month's leave? You'll be bored by the end of the second week, and you know how busy we are. There is still a lot of testing to do."

"I realize that, but you said you could handle it. The code is complete, so you really don't need my input."

"This has to do with what happened between you and that Navy guy last year. I wish you would tell me what brought you scuttling back two weeks earlier than planned. I told you not to trust a guy in uniform, and in particular a sailor, but you didn't listen. What you need is a real man, not one of these military types who still play with action figures they had as a child."

"And just who did you have in mind? Yourself?"

John ignored her comment. "You've been a scared rabbit ever since you returned. You've become a recluse. You never go out; you spend every waking hour here at the office. Just what did Michael do to you?"

"I not going to discuss my love life, or lack of one, with you. What if I do spend all my time here? At least the work gets done, and we're ahead of schedule on one or two projects."

"Look, love, I know something happened, and it must have been something major to have affected you this way. You have to pick up your social life. You can't bury yourself in your work or it will make you ill. You will meet someone else, and I promise you if he really loves you, he won't hurt you. If you're frightened of being left on the shelf, you can always marry me."

"I appreciate your offer, John, but you're not the type to settle down. So, just leave it there before one of us says something we'll regret. Now about the Jones account—"

"Before we get down to business hear me out. Professionally, you are one of the most logical people I know. You have an eidetic memory and know instinctively when a project is about to go pear-shaped. You're also shrewd and a ruthless businesswoman. You even have a temper to match the color of your hair, but then nobody's perfect. But having said all that, you're just a big softie at heart."

Skye smiled. Only her voice betrayed her mild annoyance. "Thank you for the character analysis. Remind me to return the favor one day."

John reached across the table and gave her hand a reassuring squeeze. "Why you couldn't see that guy was trouble, I'll never know. If you must go on this idiotic trip, will you at least allow me drive you to the airport on Sunday?"

"I am capable of organizing a taxi, but if you feel you must take me, then I will accept your offer. Check-in is at noon."

"In which case, I'll pick you up at nine-thirty."

Sunday dawned warm and sunny, and although early April, the daffodils were already in bloom. As she showered and dressed, Skye wondered if this was the new beginning she was seeking or whether she was just being stupid.

A short time later, she heard John's car pull into the drive. She took one last look around the house, picked up her suitcase, and opened the door.

"Ready?" John asked. "Have you got your tickets, passport, and packed everything you need?"

"I think so." Skye snatched her purse off the hall table.

"It's not too late to change your mind. Debbie thinks you're slightly crazy for taking this vacation," John said.

Skye stopped in her tracks. "You talked to Debbie behind my back?"

"Actually she called me. Now, don't be annoyed with her, she's concerned about you. Besides, Seattle wasn't the happiest of places for you, now was it?"

"I wish you two would accept that this is something I need to do, instead of hounding me to change my mind. I don't expect you or Debbie to understand. You're both good friends and I know you have my interest at heart, but please allow me to do this and don't tell me I told you so if I come home in tears."

John put his arms round her diminutive frame and gave her a hug. Skye seemed so small, so vulnerable, and yet beneath that very feminine exterior there was a strength and stamina that defied her appearance. "I don't want to see you hurt again, that's all."

"I know. But if you don't put my suitcase in the car, I'll miss my flight."

They hardly spoke during the forty-minute journey to the airport. John collected her luggage from the trunk, walked round to the passenger side of the car, and opened the door. They entered the terminal, where Skye completed the check-in formalities for her non-stop flight to Seattle. John accompanied her as far as passport control. He gave her a hug, and then kissed the top of her head.

"Have a good journey, Sweet Pea. Get some rest and lay that ghost, then come home and be prepared to do some work," he said with a grin.

Skye smiled at his use of her nickname. He'd called her that all along because she reminded him of the delicate flower. "I'll do my best." Without a backward glance, she showed her passport to the official and went through to departures.

She chose a seat close to the gate, and took out her book, but found it difficult to concentrate on the words. Instead, she amused herself by watching people in the terminal, wondering where they were all going to and the reasons for their journey.

Time passed quickly, and soon her flight was called. She found her seat in business class and settled down for the long flight, fervently hoping that the seat beside her would remain unoccupied. The last thing she wanted was to spend twelve hours next to someone who wanted to talk all the way to Seattle. Luckily, her wish was granted, for within fifteen minutes of boarding, the flight attendant closed the door, and the aircraft pushed back from the ramp. As the plane taxied towards the runway, she suffered one last moment of self-doubt, but knew it was too late to turn back. Seconds later, she felt the increased tempo of the Boeing 747's engines as it thundered down the runway. After what seemed like an eternity, the huge plane lifted gracefully into the air.

Skye spent much of the flight reading and watching the movie. It was late afternoon when the plane touched down in Seattle. The terminal buildings looked as gray and uninspiring as they had a year ago. Having completed the immigration formalities, the delay at customs was only mildly annoying. She hired a car, and within minutes was driving out of the parking lot and down the ramp onto the Interstate.

Rather than drive to Anacortes that evening, she stayed in a hotel close to the airport. Her room was on the third floor, and looked down on an atrium garden filled with wildly colored tropical plants. Tired from her journey, she rang room service and ordered a burger, then brewed a carafe of coffee in the bathroom. When she finished eating, she took a shower and crawled into bed.

Over breakfast the next morning, Skye consulted her road map, tracing her route north. The hotel receptionist told her that it would take roughly two hours, depending on traffic, to drive the seventy or so miles to Anacortes.

As she had time to spare, she decided to spend the morning sightseeing. She found a parking place near the ferry terminal on Alaskan Way. She stopped to admire the fountain before walking along First Avenue to Pike Place Market. Many of the shops were empty, and she browsed at will. When she reached the Westlake Centre, she caught the monorail to the Space Needle. The weather was kind to her, unlike her previous visit when the sky had clouded over. Today, there was hardly a cloud visible, although it was a little on the cool side.

The panoramas from the observation deck were stunning—well worth the white-knuckle ride in the express elevator. Far below, a state ferry steamed toward one of the islands in Puget Sound. A few small sailing boats were out on Elliot Bay, taking advantage of the fine weather. She gazed across the bay, thinking about Michael, until a seagull's cry snapped her out of her daydream.

Annoyed for allowing Michael into her thoughts yet again, she rode the elevator down to ground level. She quickened her pace and walked down Broad Street to Alaskan Way, past the Aquarium and Omnidome until she reached *Ivar's* restaurant on the waterfront. She found a table overlooking the bay and ordered a bowl of clam chowder and a pot of coffee.

After her meal, she returned to the car and drove out of the city. According to her guidebook, the bustling port of Anacortes was founded in 1877. Shipyards, seafood processing facilities, and tourism all contributed to the local economy. Spectacular panoramas, combined with exclusive real estate, yacht charters and marina facilities brought residents and visitors alike to the area. Judging by the number of expensive cars that she saw in the town, Skye had no doubt that the book was correct.

The ferry to Friday Harbor left at eight the following morning, and the travel agent had recommended that she stay at the inn close to the terminal. Tired from her drive, she ate a solitary dinner in the hotel's dining room before calling it a night.

A short time later, she slipped between the cool white sheets of the queen-size bed and settled against the comforters. She was weary, bone weary. Sighing deeply, she wiped a surreptitious tear from her eyes.

"Where did we go wrong, Michael? Why couldn't you talk to me? Why did you have to hurt me the way you did?"

CHAPTER TWO

The following morning dawned cold and gray, the cloud level so low that the majestic mountains of the Pacific Northwest were completely hidden from view. Only a few cars waited for the ferry, and appeared to belong to locals and business people. The tourists would arrive later, when the weather improved.

Skye locked the car and climbed the stairs to the main deck. The aroma of coffee drew her towards the small cafe. She purchased a beaker of coffee and carried it outside to the observation deck.

As the ferry steamed towards the islands, the cloud base gradually lifted, allowing the sun to filter through here and there. Amazed by the panorama unfolding before her eyes, she wondered why anyone would want to lie on a sun-drenched beach all day, when they could enjoy such scenery.

Friday Harbor soon came into view. It was much smaller than Skye imagined, and she was surprised by the numerous sailboats with their impossibly tall masts that filled every berth in the marina. The San Juan Islands were a Mecca for tourists, whether they arrived off the ferries from Anacortes or Canada, or on their own yachts, sailing into the picturesque harbors that dotted the islands.

Skye found the realtor's office in a side street, just up the road from the ferry terminal. The formalities completed, and with the key to the cabin in her pocket and a detailed map in her hand, she once more set out.

The roads were deserted, and the only vehicles she passed were trucks carrying fish from the north of the island to the ferry terminal. Skye found driving in this backwater much easier than in Seattle or on the Interstate. Her exit came into view, she moved across the highway and signaled her turn into the private track.

The cabin was all she had hoped for and more. Constructed purely of timber, it stood some two hundred yards from the shoreline and a mile off the highway. A path led down from the cabin to a small wooden dock. Eager to explore, Skye dumped a bag of groceries on the kitchen table and made herself a quick cup of coffee. The rest of her luggage could wait. She wanted nothing more than to breathe the fresh air and savor the view before unpacking and settling into what would be her home for the next month.

Draping her jacket over a kitchen chair, she carried her steaming cup down to the dock, and sat down. She slipped off her shoes and was about to dip her toes into the deep blue water, when a very masculine voice called out.

"I wouldn't do that if I were you. The water is pretty darned cold this time of year."

Startled, she turned and scanned the trees. The voice seemed to emanate from the very depths of the pinewood. She squinted into the early afternoon sunlight, and watched a man emerge from the trees. He was tall, well over six feet, with raven black hair and the slight shadow of a beard. She couldn't see his eyes, but she had a feeling they would be hard and blue, like glacial ice.

A chill ran down her spine. The cabin was isolated. She considered her options as the tall figure approached. If he proved difficult, she could always push him into the sea, and run back to the safety of the cabin.

The stranger halted a mere foot from her, forcing her to look up.

He grinned. "Sorry to startle you, ma'am, but I wasn't sure if you were planning on taking anything else off besides your shoes."

Skye's mouth opened, but she didn't utter a word.

"Because if you were, you'd only last thirty minutes before hypothermia set in. And being a gentleman, I would feel duty bound to rescue you. That would be a shame, because I'd planned on going home and cooking this fish for lunch."

Coughing and spluttering, Skye choked on her coffee. A fish was more important than saving someone from freezing to death. She inclined her head to examine him more closely and saw that she had been right about his eyes. Here was a man who didn't suffer fools gladly. Well, he could just go back to where he came from and take his fishy friend with him!

"I have no intention of removing anything other than my shoes. The thought of going for a swim hadn't entered my mind, but now you mention it, it's not a bad idea. As for you rescuing me, I'll take a rain check. Not, I might add, that what I do is any business of yours. I understand this is private property. May I ask what you're doing prowling around and scaring the life out of people?"

"My, my, we're mighty touchy. What happened? Someone wake you up too early?" The icy blue eyes flashed. There was a trace of laughter in his voice.

Feeling at a disadvantage, Skye stood up in one fluid movement. Not one inch of her five foot five frame gave her any more confidence. She barely came up to the man's chest—a chest that some women would feel comfortable snuggled up to. Close up, he didn't appear quite so intimidating—'impressive' was a better adjective. In fact, she could think of a number of adjectives to describe him, including handsome, rugged, not to mention offensive and arrogant. This guy would stop traffic in London, but there he would be completely out of place. Here in the rugged mountains of the Pacific Northwest he was totally at ease.

Skye revised her estimate of his height. He was at least six foot four, possibly more. His eyes were deep set, and she was right about the color. He had a scar over one eyebrow and a smaller one on his chin. She wondered how he had acquired them, but had no intention of asking. He was dressed in black jeans and a navy-blue check work shirt worn open at the neck, revealing a tangle of dark hair. He held a fishing rod in one hand, a fish in the other, and looked for the entire world as if he had stepped out of the pages of her guidebook.

Skye stiffened. "I'm sorry, but I didn't catch your name, and at this particular moment, I don't wish to know what it is. I've had a long journey, and I'm tired. As far as I'm concerned, you're trespassing. I would appreciate it, if you would leave by whatever means you arrived and allow me to finish my coffee before it goes cold."

"Wow. That's some temper you have. I suggest you take a deep breath, calm down, and enjoy the day. I'm just giving you some friendly advice. I won't disturb you any longer. For future reference, the name is Walker. Jedediah Walker, but everyone just calls me Walker." Abruptly, he turned and strode along the dock. He continued along the pebble beach in the opposite direction from which he came.

Skye smothered a giggle. "I can see why!" What did he mean future reference? Hell could freeze over before she chose to cross his path again.

Her first thought was to call the realtor and complain. They had promised her complete privacy. She had been most insistent on that when booking the cabin. She didn't want noisy neighbors destroying the peace and tranquility of this wonderful place. No campers, no boaters, and especially no screaming children; just her own space in which to do as she pleased for the next month.

Then logic kicked in.

The San Juan Islands attracted fishermen and women from every corner of the planet. The guy had probably moored his boat somewhere along the coast and followed the shoreline until he found a suitable place from which to fish. No big deal. However, now that the cabin was occupied, she hoped he would respect her privacy. Other than the mailman with the occasional letter from Debbie or John, she had no wish to see anyone during her stay.

Skye picked up her cup and shuddered in disgust as the cold liquid hit the back of her throat. She retrieved her suitcase from the trunk of her car, and carried it inside.

The cabin was very well equipped with cable TV, VCR, and an impressive stereo system. Skye could live without a television, but music was a different matter. The centerpiece of the main room was a huge stone fireplace. The polished wooden floors were scattered with native Indian rugs. A large leather couch sat invitingly in front of the fireplace. Full-length windows opened onto the deck, where the owner had left wicker chairs so visitors could sit and admire the wonderful scenery.

Skye carried her suitcase into the master bedroom and started to unpack. The room had full-length windows, which opened out on to the deck, a king-size bed and an open fireplace. A hand stitched quilt with matching comforters covered the bed. She ran her fingertips over it and marveled at the hours of work involved to complete it.

Once settled, she would telephone Debbie to let her know she had survived the journey. Without wasting anymore time, she set off to explore the cove and surrounding woods.

***

After terminating his conversation with the woman, Walker followed the trail through the trees to the lodge. He hadn't expected the cabin to be occupied so soon, and was surprised when he saw the small, solitary figure on the dock. He vaguely remembered receiving a letter from the realtor advising him that a tenant would be moving into the cabin, but for some reason had thought the occupant was male.

Screened by the treeline, he'd watched the woman stroll down to the dock. She was dressed in a pair of black trousers and a baggy red sweater. He had a feeling the sweater hid a soft and curvaceous body—the sort of body a man could bury himself in, until he forgot who he was. The gentle breeze lifted her thick, shoulder length auburn hair, which made him think of the color of leaves in fall. He imagined it would be soft and silky to the touch. Unable to tear his gaze away, he had continued to watch as she sat down at the end of the dock and took off her shoes. She appeared so sad, and for one heart stopping moment, he'd feared that she might do more than dangle her toes in the ice-cold water.

Damn it, he didn't need this sort of distraction now. He knew someone was using the cove at night, and now it would be difficult to prove it. He just hoped that he hadn't placed this unwitting stranger in any danger. It was one more thing on his list to worry about. His first priority was to discover who was poisoning the fish around the island. The second was to discover who was hacking into his computer. He rested his fishing rod against the wall of the lodge and unlocked the door.

Walker had purchased the lodge and twenty-five acres of prime waterfront five years ago. It was a place where he re-charged his batteries after investigating some of man's worst atrocities against nature. The lodge was far too big for him, and normally he stayed at the cabin. Over the years, he had come to call it home, and now someone was trying to ruin it, but not if he could stop them first.

Going straight to the laboratory he'd installed in one of the bedrooms, Walker proceeded to dissect the fish. He was meticulous in his sampling, and in the preparation of the slides for the microscope. Only when satisfied he had everything he needed did he discard the carcass. It was a magnificent salmon, but if he didn't find out what was causing dead fish to wash up on the beaches, the salmon might not be the only thing lying on a cold slab.

Four hours later, his suspicions were confirmed. The fish contained a mixture of toxic chemicals, which had it been eaten, would have put someone in hospital. He went into his study, picked up the phone, and called Joe McCabe at the Department of Fish and Wildlife on his direct number.

"I can tell from your voice, Walker, that I'm not going to like this."

"Five gets you ten on this one. The latest samples prove the fish are contaminated with lead, mercury, cyanide, and other substances I have been unable to identify. I'll send the samples to the main lab in Seattle for a more detailed analysis. The results should be back in three or four days."

The voice at the other end of the line let out a stream of expletives. "For once, can't you give me some good news?"

"Joe, it gets worse. Fish have started washing up on the shore in front of the lodge. I want to nail whoever is dumping this stuff. Eventually someone is going to get sick. Very sick. What's new your end? Have the police come up with any leads yet? Someone must know where these chemicals are coming from."

"There are five plants in the state. Any one of them might be responsible. This is unconfirmed, but it's possible they are coming from the plant belonging to the waste management consortium that applied to build a new facility in Anacortes a while back."

Walker frowned and rubbed the back of his neck. "They were refused consent. I sat on the committee. In fact, I recommended their application be refused."

"I realize that. I understand the present facility is unable to cope with demand. The police interviewed some of the employees, but no one would talk. We need firm evidence before we can move on this, and so far no one has found any."

"So what do we do? Wait until someone ends up in hospital or worse, in the morgue? Is that what you're telling me?"

"I'm as annoyed as you are, Walker. I have to do things by the book. You know that."

"I know, but it doesn't make it any easier." Walker slammed the phone down.

After graduating from university as a marine biologist and biochemist, Walker worked for the State Department. His main area of expertise was the environment, and the effect mankind had on diminishing fish stocks. After years of dividing his time between sitting behind a desk and collecting water samples, he'd set up his own company, Walker Environmental Research. Now, after ten years of hard work, his company was well respected. Governments all over the world had sought his advice, and he had investigated several major ecological disasters.

Several months earlier, his old university friend, Joe McCabe, contacted him. Joe asked Walker to help investigate the incidents of dead salmon washed up along the coast of Puget Sound and the San Juan Islands.

At first, they thought the problem was caused by the large oil tankers plying their way between Alaska, Canada, and the rest of the USA. Many of the ships' captains were not averse to flushing their tanks before sailing into open waters. A detailed analysis of the dead fish revealed they were contaminated with a lethal cocktail of chemicals, and not crude oil. However, there was no consistency. One week, fish would wash up on the north coast of one island,

and the next they would wash up on the west coast of another. The changing tides could not account for such discrepancies, which meant only one thing—someone was deliberately dumping toxic waste. Two weeks ago, carcasses had appeared on Walker's land, and last week someone had hacked into his computer. Suddenly, the fight had become personal.

***

Skye spent two hours wandering along the trails, and now as the sun dipped toward the horizon she returned to the cabin. Apart from breakfast and the odd cup of coffee, she had eaten nothing all day. No wonder her stomach rumbled. She carried her supper plate and glass of wine onto the deck to watch the dying rays of the sun.

Once again, she wondered if she had done the right thing. Four weeks in a cabin, alone with her thoughts, when permanent sorrow seemed to weigh her down, why on earth had she come? Suddenly she longed to be back in her house in London, except she felt just as lonely there. The minutes ticked by, during which she fought for control. She clenched her jaw, determined not to give in to the self-pity.

After she finished eating, she rang Debbie's number and wondered where the tall, dark stranger had disappeared to, for she had not seen any other properties on her walk.

"Hi. Remember me, that crazy Englishwoman?"

"You sure timed that right. I've just walked through the door. Obviously, you reached the cabin in one piece. How was the journey?"

"I took some time to visit the Space Needle while in Seattle. And despite having to drive on the wrong side of the road, the journey was fine."

Debbie laughed. "Okay, so you're a better driver than me, but that's because I don't drive very often—"

"Just often enough to remember how!" They said in unison and then giggled with laughter at their private joke.

"No one in San Francisco with any sense owns a car."

"Admit it," said Skye, "I am just more coordinated than you when it comes to things mechanical."

Debbie laughed again. "How's the cabin? Let me guess, you've paid $2,000 for a wood shack with no hot or cold running water, just an open fire to cook on, and the bathroom's a hut at the end of the garden."

Skye smiled. Debbie always made her laugh. "It is beautiful and very well equipped. It stands in two acres of woodland and has a view to die for."

"Met any of the locals yet?"

"Only one, and he was exceptionally rude. He appeared out of nowhere and promptly gave me a lecture on how cold the water is at this time of year."

"My, he certainly got your hackles up. What did he look like?"

Skye closed her eyes and described the stranger. "He's about six foot four, has dark hair, is unshaven, and wears a real nasty expression."

23

"He sounds interesting. Are you planning to see him again?"

"Not if I can avoid him. Besides, he's got a fishy friend to keep him company on long lonely nights, while I have—"

"While you have a computer and your music, I know. I'm not sure either is a substitute for a real man, and from your description of your mystery man, he could be just that. Maybe I should come up for a long weekend and look him over for you."

"Debbie, the last thing I want is an affair. You of all people know that."

"Just teasing. Apart from your encounter with the natives, have you settled in?"

"Just about. I'll call you again in a few days."

"Sure, speak to you soon. Oh, and Skye—"

"Yes?"

"Behave yourself with the tall hairy guy," Debbie said and broke the connection before Skye could think of a suitable response.

It was close to midnight in London, and Skye's phone call to John ran into his voicemail. She assured him she had arrived safely, and all was well, then cut the connection. From now on, if she needed to contact him, she would use the payphone in Friday Harbor. She knew he would be eager to use the new software to its full potential in an attempt to find out exactly where she was staying. That was the disadvantage of working at the cutting edge of technology, and having a business partner who was her self-appointed 'big brother.'

CHAPTER THREE

For the first time in months, Skye felt truly relaxed. She had been traveling for the best part of forty-eight hours and now, with the firelight flickering around the room and the mellow sound of a saxophone on the CD player, her thoughts drifted back to Michael.

His letter inviting her to visit had arrived after Christmas. A whole month in his company was more than she hoped for. They continued to write and talk on the phone until the day arrived for them to meet.

From the moment she was assigned her seat in first class, the flight had been fantastic. She recalled being nervous as the plane touched down at SeaTac Airport. The arrival hall was relatively empty with only a few people waiting to meet the passengers. She anxiously scanned the faces for Michael and felt concerned when he didn't appear to be there. As she walked towards baggage reclaim, he came running off the escalator. Before she knew what was happening, he pulled her into his arms, and spun her round and round. The smile he gave her set her pulse racing. One hand traced the line of her cheek while the other circled her waist. He lowered his head to hers and kissed her.

Skye remembered that first kiss in the weeks that followed. Soft and sensuous, his tongue gently probed until she opened her mouth to him and allowed the kiss to deepen. At that moment, she knew she wanted him with every fiber of her being.

The traffic on that sunny Sunday afternoon in May was light, so the drive into Seattle took just over an hour. They parked the car and walked along the waterfront before finding somewhere to eat. Skye had no recollection of the meal. The only images she could recall were those of sitting opposite Michael, holding his hand and watching his face intently. She memorized each line, each expression, the way one eyebrow raised at a question, and the way his face lit up when he smiled, his hazel eyes crinkling at the corners.

Michael had reserved a suite in one of the large hotels near the naval base so he could be close to the ship should he be required onboard. His gaze held hers as he told her how he wanted to make love to her, but didn't want her to feel under any pressure. How, if it didn't feel right for her, he would understand and book another room. Skye blushed and reached across the table to take both his hands in hers. With faltering words, she softly said that she wanted nothing more than to sleep in his arms.

They left the restaurant arm in arm and joined the queue for the ferry to Bremerton. While most passengers left their vehicles on the car deck and climbed the stairs to the lounge, Michael and Skye had sat in the circle of each other's arms, neither of them able to believe that being together could feel so good, so right.

That first night, Michael made love to her with such tenderness that Skye thought her heart would burst. His whispered thoughts ignited the fire inside her until her body ached for release.

Their first two weeks together passed in a blur. They spent the days exploring the Kitsap Peninsula and the nights making love. Twice, Michael was recalled to the ship, leaving Skye to explore on her own. On those occasions, she caught the ferry to Seattle or Port Orchard and visited the usual tourist venues—Pioneer Square, Pike Place Market, and the Space Needle. While she hoped these where places they would have explored together, she understood that the Navy had first call on his time.

One afternoon, Michael showed her around the 'mothballed fleet,' the resting ground of some of the US Navy's most famous battleships and destroyers. He painstakingly explained the names of the various parts of the ship and how a sailor's bunk was called a 'rack.' She found it hard to comprehend how five thousand men and women could cram together on an aircraft carrier and call it 'home' for six months. Her admiration for Michael, and what he did for his country, grew by the hour. Although he never introduced her to his fellow officers, Skye hadn't thought it particularly strange. It was only much later, when the sorry category of events unfolded, that she understood why.

The cabin was completely dark save for the glow of the embers from the dying fire. Brushing her hair from her face, she felt tears. Would she never forget him? Would Michael always be in her thoughts, her dreams?

She felt for the switch on the table lamp and turned it on. It took several seconds for her eyes to adjust to the light. Nothing seemed out of place. Perhaps the sound of a log disintegrating into ashes in the grate had disturbed her. She placed the guard in front of the fire, making it safe for the night.

One window was slightly ajar; she crossed the room and closed it, then reached to draw the drapes. She had the strange feeling that someone was watching her. Don't be stupid and paranoid, she told herself. You're a country girl at heart. Remember? It's only the breeze in the trees, or maybe a neighborhood cat out on a nightly prowl.

***

From his hiding place deep within the wood, Walker heard the sound of an engine backfiring. By the time he reached the track, the vehicle responsible had vanished into the black of the night. The woman in the cabin must have heard it too. Walker watched the slim figure close the drapes. He stepped back into the shadows afforded by the trees. The bedroom light flicked on, then off. His tenant was going to bed.

He trudged down to the shore to see if there were any tracks, but found nothing. His tenant had obviously spooked whoever it was, just as she had spooked him earlier that day. An owl hooted nearby, no doubt in protest at having its nightly hunting raid disrupted.

Somewhere out on the water a ship's engine throbbed as it made its way through the strait. He'd heard the same vessel earlier that evening as it rounded the headland a few miles south of where he now stood.

Shivering in the cool breeze, he returned to the lodge. He was tired and frustrated, but also angry for allowing the realtor to rent out the cabin. It was too late to cancel the booking; he would have to work around the situation.

He flicked on the percolator in the kitchen on his way to the study. He'd been in tighter spots than this over the years, so why was this beginning to make the hairs on the back of his neck stand up? Part of it, he knew, was the feeling that this case of illegal dumping was personal, that someone was getting back at him. That didn't surprise him. He'd closed down a number of companies over the years, so he guessed it was payback time. The question was who and why?

The other part of the problem was the woman, that small vulnerable figure who brought out the protector in him, even if she did have the temper of a wildcat. He wasn't one for short vacation affairs, although he had to admit she did have a certain appeal. The 'love them and leave them' attitude of the beach lothario was not his style. Besides, he preferred his companions to be less fiery and opinionated.

Although it was after midnight, he wasn't ready to sleep. He sat down at his desk and waited for his computer to boot up. He intended to make a list of every company, corporation, and individual who might want to nail his hide to the mast for closing down his or her business, even for one day.

While his PC hummed and whirred into life, he poured a mug of black coffee. He had a feeling he would need it, and a stronger feeling that the list he was about to make was going to be long. Very long. Twenty minutes later, he took a swallow of his now-cold coffee and reviewed the list. There were seventeen names on it.

Leaning back in his chair, he cast his mind back to a particularly difficult and unpleasant case. He'd been working in South America at the time, but the corporation involved was headquartered in Anacortes. He rubbed the pulsing knot at his temples. The name was in the far recess of his mind, if only he could remember what it was.

Walker pointed his mouse at an icon on the screen and opened up his Internet software. The modem clicked and hummed as the software connected with the server in his Seattle office. His password accepted, he accessed his firm's vast database and located the files he wanted. They started to download when suddenly a jumble of images replaced the text on the screen. He quickly tore phone line out of his laptop.

The latest anti-virus software was installed on his machine, and he had recently changed his password. The server was also protected, yet someone had hacked into the system once more. Only two people had the access codes to the main database—his IT specialist and himself. Everyone else within company had limited access. He hoped that whatever had corrupted his computer hadn't destroyed any other files.

Stopping the hacker was beyond his capabilities, and he suspected the police would be no help either. He needed to call in a specialist firm, but whom could he trust? Perhaps Joe would have a contact he could use. He checked his watch and decided to crawl into bed for a few hours sleep before contacting his friend.

After a long hot shower and an early breakfast, Walker put through his call to Joe.

"Hey, McCabe?"

"I knew it had to be you, Walker. Only you would call me at this ungodly hour. Okay, spill. More bad news?"

"Yeah. Someone was using the cove again last night, only I was too late to see who it was. If—"

"What do you mean you missed them? I thought you were out there all hours, playing the Navy SEAL."

"I was, but I got distracted. I forgot someone was renting the cabin. When I found my new tenant sitting on the dock dangling her toes in the water, I got the surprise of my life."

"Her? You're telling me you're seeing water nymphs now, is that it? You're hallucinating. When was the last time you slept?"

"Joe, I'm serious. My tenant arrived yesterday. I met her on my way back to the lodge. I camped out in the woods last night and heard a truck. I went to investigate, but whoever it was, also disturbed my tenant's beauty sleep, so I had to wait until she retired for the night before looking around."

"She's not a water nymph, but Sleeping Beauty. Make up your mind; this isn't a fairy tale, you know. Why don't you admit you fell asleep on the job?"

"Okay buddy, have it your way. Something else happened to make me think this is aimed at me."

"Go on."

"Let's face it. Over the last ten years, I've shut down enough corporations to upset a few folks. I made a list of everyone who might want to see my company go to the wall. So far, there are seventeen names on the list. As soon as I tried to download the relevant information on each of them from my company's database, my computer crashed."

"Nothing unusual in that my friend, mine does it all the time."

"Yeah, but you're just ham fisted and computer illiterate."

"Give me a tablet of stone and a chisel any time. So, what makes this unusual?"

"Joe, I've spent a small fortune on security and anti-virus software. I can't be sure until I get to the office, but I think someone has hacked into the server. It's not the first time it's happened either. This is way out of my area of expertise. I need to speak to someone who can give me an insight into what damage hackers can do and whether it's possible to trace them. Do you know anyone who might be able to help me?"

"Quit worrying. It was probably high school kids out for kicks. If it will make you any happier, I'll ask around. We're talking about cutting edge technology. I'm not sure the FBI has the ability to do what you're asking. Then what would I know; I'm only a humble servant of the State department. When do you want this?"

"Yesterday will do just fine."

"I thought so. Give me a few hours and I'll see what I can do, but no promises. How do I reach you?"

"Try my cell phone or the office. I'm planning on taking the seaplane over to Seattle and should be at my desk within a couple of hours."

Walker hung up. He grabbed the overnight bag he kept packed in case of emergency and his laptop then strode out of the cabin. He questioned whether he was alert enough to fly. These days he functioned on a mixture of pure adrenalin and caffeine. He climbed aboard his single-engine Cessna and took off.

Less than fifty minutes later, he arrived at his office. Although modest in size, it offered commanding views of the Seattle waterfront. Shortly after sitting down at his desk, the IT technician knocked at his door.

"I hope you've got good news for me, Johnson."

"Sorry boss, but your laptop is toast. In all my years working with computers, I have never seen anything like this. I can't tell whether you downloaded a virus or whether you tried to fry the circuits. Either way, the best place for this is the trash."

"Can you salvage anything? What about the other computers?"

"Nope, can't save anything on your hard drive. As for the server and office computers, we certainly have problems, although to what extent I'm not sure. It depends on what you try to access. I've run every check I can, including updating the anti-virus software, changing the passwords and security levels. I don't know what's causing these glitches. On the surface, it looks like a virus, but it doesn't behave like any virus I've seen. We need specialist help, and I've no idea who to call."

"All right, Johnson, it's not your fault. Let's wait and see what develops. In the meantime, no one—and I mean no one—is to have access to the system except me. Is that understood? I don't care if the secretaries have to go back to using typewriters. Oh, and while I think on it, better get someone in to check the phone lines. If they can hack into the computers, you can be sure they can bug the phones too."

"I'm on it."

As the technician closed the door, the phone on Walker's desk rang.

"My contact informs me there are a number of people doing research into tracing computer hackers," Joe said. "However, the guy leading the field is based in England."

"Great, just what I need to hear. We have no one in the States who can handle this. What about the universities, the FBI, the CIA, or even the NSA?"

"Not that my source is aware of. I can only pass on what I've been told."

"What's this genius's name and how do I contact him?"

"The guy you want is called Ridge. Dr. Ridge."

"Dr. Ridge? That's it? No first name?"

"Sorry, no. Apparently, he and his partner recently finished developing some software that can trace every computer back to its owner each time they log onto the Internet, visit a web site or attempt to hack into another computer, as well as trace every so-called anonymous email sent."

"Wonderful. A way to track all the junk email I receive each day."

"I wouldn't be so skeptical if I were you, Walker. I understand this guy's company is negotiating a contract with the British Government and their armed forces. Rumor has it the Pentagon is interested too."

"Is this information one hundred and ten per cent reliable? It seems a little farfetched to me."

"Yeah, it is. The Pentagon offered him a job a few years back, but he declined. Now, do you want those contact details or not?"

Walker thought hard for a moment. "Let me buy you lunch at *Ivar's*. You can give them to me in person."

"Sure. One-thirty suit you?"

"See you then."

Of all the countries, Walker figured that the good ole US of A would have some geek able to solve his problem. He hoped to keep things close to home. If Joe's information was correct, and he had no reason to doubt it, then he would be placing a transatlantic call in the hope that Dr. Ridge could discover who was making his life hell.

He left his office and walked the short distance down to Alaskan Way. *Ivar's* was buzzing as usual. This early in the year, it was office workers who filled the tables. In another month or so, it would be crowded with tourists. He found a seat at a corner booth and it wasn't long before Joe joined him.

They placed their order with the friendly waitress, and after their meal and drinks arrived, Joe commented, "We haven't had lunch in a while."

"I guess not. Either I'm out of the country or we're both too busy keeping the paperwork down. Mind you, with all this going on, I don't have much of an appetite," Walker said, pushing the food around on his plate.

"What's the idea of meeting here? I could have given you the details over the phone."

"Let's just say that I don't trust email, computers in general, or telephones at the moment."

Joe laughed. "Hey, if I didn't know you better, I'd think you were developing some kind of a complex about all this."

"Paranoia I can deal with. Industrial sabotage is a different matter, especially when it involves my business. How do I reach this guy Ridge?" Walker picked up his beer and took a long swallow.

"You'll have to do some research. Ridge had the idea for this software while at Oxford University, but never took it any further. It was only when he and another computer geek set up business together that he developed it."

"Interesting, but how do I contact him?"

"My contact doesn't know the exact name of the outfit he owns—Ridge and Something or Something and Ridge, which isn't much of a lead, I know. You could contact his old university. They might have a handle on where he is. Anyway, he's probably listed in the phone directory." Joe passed a manila envelope across the table. "This is all the information I have. It should be enough for you to locate him."

Walker slid it into his jacket pocket. "Thanks. I really appreciate this. I guess I'll owe you big time if this pans out."

"Nope. I want to catch these bastards as much as you do. I don't like illegal dumping, especially when it's on my patch. Just be careful out there. I don't want to lose the best environmental scientist I know, nor do I want to lose my best friend, call in the tough guys if things turn nasty. Okay?"

"Joe, I hate to tell you, but things have already turned nasty. I have no idea who I'm up against. They obviously have ample resources to bribe folks do to their dirty work, and if they can discredit my company along the way, that's even better. Whoever it is, I must have them seriously worried. However, someone is going to get sick very soon, and I want to prevent that happening. Once I have proof of who is dumping these chemicals and targeting me, I'll shout long and hard for justice."

Walker dropped some bills on the table and left his friend, but didn't return to his office. He set off at a brisk pace to walk the short distance to Pioneer Square. He turned the collar of his coat up against the cool April breeze coming off Puget Sound. On entering a small Internet café, he ordered a cup of strong black coffee and paid the small fee to use one of the computers. He sat down at an empty desk and set up an email address with one of the many web-based services.

He called up one of the main search engines and looked for any reference to a Dr. Ridge. Ridge may have done postgraduate research, but he had broken all ties with his former colleagues. In desperation, Walker emailed the bursar's office at Oxford University but didn't expect an immediate response, given the time difference between the west coast USA and England. He spent the next twenty minutes searching various on-line newspapers and journals to see if Ridge had written any articles. As expected, he drew a blank. His coffee cold, he finally logged out and deleted all trace of his activities from the computer. On his way back to the office, he stopped and purchased a new top- spec laptop.

There were no new developments since his lunch with Joe. Although Walker planned to return to the island that evening, he decided to tackle some of the paperwork on his desk. Then he would get some sleep. Over the last few days, he'd had very little, spending most of the hours between night and day watching the cove.

His apartment overlooked Elliot Bay. Sparsely furnished, it felt cold and uninviting. In the past, he stayed there whenever in town. It was useful for entertaining, and the view never failed to impress the occasional date. Since his last failed relationship, he'd not used it. With property prices high, it would be a good time to sell. He could always use the executive suite at the office in future. If he had a future.

CHAPTER FOUR

The sound of bird song roused Skye from her dream. She glanced at the clock on the bedside table, and was surprised to find it was after ten. After a quick shower and breakfast, she set off to explore more of the island. The sky was gray and heavy with the threat of rain, but she was determined not to let the weather spoil her vacation.

Rocky inlets and small, sand and gravel beaches dotted the coastline. It wasn't easy walking, but after many hours spent traveling, she relished the prospect of a long exhilarating walk. She strolled down to the beach then followed a narrow path through the woods. Many of the trees were covered in lichen, she noted, as she zigzagged through the woods. The scent of pine and damp earth filled the air. Just as the first drops of rain began to fall, she came across a path leading inland.

Badly overgrown in places, more than one thorny branch snatched at her trousers. Stumbling through a particularly dense patch of lush undergrowth, she found herself in a clearing. The sound of hammering drifted over the cool morning air. Built of pine log and pole, the property was long and low, with windows stretching from floor to roof. Surrounded by a wooden deck, it stood in magnificent manicured grounds. The rooms looked out over a small bay, toward the mainland and the snow-capped mountains beyond. A truck was parked outside, the name and telephone number of a contractor painted on the side. Scaffolding obscured one wall and it didn't appear as if anyone was living there.

Not wishing to trespass further, Skye retraced her steps. Walking quickly, she tugged the hood of her jacket over her damp hair, and stuffed her hands into the pockets against the chill of the rain. Moments later, she tripped over an exposed tree root and fell into strong male arms. She gasped, and wiped the strands of wet hair out of her eyes.

"You!"

"Yes, me," replied Walker. "My, but aren't these trails becoming busier than a downtown sidewalk?" he muttered under his breath. He raised a dark eyebrow. "Expecting to meet *Goldilocks and the three bears*, or did you have someone else in mind?"

"I think you mean *The Big Bad Wolf*," Skye retorted angrily. "Are *all* American men as sarcastic as you?"

"Are *all* British women adept as you at turning up at the wrong time?" Walker replied. He stood over her, hands on his hips, boldly intimidating.

Skye stiffened and glared at him. "I wouldn't know. I'm not meeting anyone. Even if I were, it is none of your business. I was told this is private property and yet every time I step out the door, you're there. You leave me no choice other than to report this matter to the realtor and the police."

Walker watched the anger in her face with slight amusement. "Sorry, lady, you're the one who's trespassing, not me. So, before you start playing the indignant tourist you'd better get your facts straight."

"Look here Mr.—"

"No, lady, you listen," Walker butted in. "The owner is a friend of mine, and I have his permission to be here. Calling the realtor and the sheriff will make you look a fool. Go back to the cabin, enjoy your little vacation, and stop wandering through these woods. Otherwise, I'll be the one making the calls."

Before Skye could gather her thoughts to give Walker a piece of her mind, he'd brushed past her and was rapidly making his way along the overgrown trail. His tone aroused and infuriated her. No one, but no one spoke to her in that way. No matter what he said, she didn't believe him.

She jogged back to the cabin. The rain, almost horizontal at times, stung her face and eyes, sending an icy chill through her body. By the time, she opened the door she was soaked to the skin, shivering, and as mad as hell. No, hell itself couldn't possibly ever get *this* mad!

VICTORIA HOWARD

She paused in the kitchen to turn on the coffee machine, and then stomped into the bathroom, stripping off her wet clothes along the way. As the hot water streamed over her lithe body, she gradually relaxed.

As she dressed, she thought about Walker. His attitude puzzled her. If he knew the owner, then he must know the cabin was occupied, so why was he annoyed by her presence? Wasn't she doing his friend a favor by renting it out of season and at such an exorbitant fee?

She put a match to the logs in the grate then phoned the realtor. In a calm voice, she related her encounter with Walker to the disinterested woman at the other end of the phone. The owner of the cabin, she was informed, was a businessman who traveled often. Skye shouldn't worry, as everyone on the island was friendly.

Needing to hear a friendly voice, she phoned Debbie.

"Hi. I'm sorry, but I can't talk for long. It's been a God-awful afternoon. I didn't expect to hear from you until the weekend. What gives?"

"Just another run-in with the guy I told you about. There's something spooky about the fact that he's always hanging around the cabin and the woods. He's so rude. I thought all Americans were polite."

"Skye, be sensible. The islands are a popular tourist destination. You can't expect to be totally alone. I'm sure there will be other properties nearby. If you wanted complete peace and quiet, maybe you should have rented a desert island."

"I did find another property, but it appears unoccupied," Skye conceded. "It has water frontage the same as this cabin. There's a boat moored to the dock."

"What's the weather like? I bet it's raining and you've been stuck indoors. If you're that bothered, why don't you come here for a few days?"

"It is raining, but that's not the problem, Debbie. As for visiting San Francisco—I'll pass for now. I don't feel up to the hustle and bustle of a city. You could come here. There's plenty of room. We could explore the island together. Think of the fun we would have. There's a charter service from Seattle if you want to fly, or there's the ferry."

"I can't drop everything and come up there. Can you keep yourself occupied for a while longer until I can re-organize my schedule? In the meantime, relax, take a whale-watching trip, take up knitting, or something. It's only a suggestion, but stay off the trails for a while, too. Then maybe Sasquatch will leave you alone. Who knows, perhaps there's a reason he's hiking the trails around the cabin. He could be an arboriculturist. Whatever it is, I'll bet there's a reasonable explanation. So, quit worrying."

"You're right, I'm over reacting. I didn't expect to bump into an obnoxious Neanderthal every time I step out the door. I know it's difficult for you to get away at short notice, but it would be fantastic if you could."

"Hey, what are friends for, but to support each other? I really have to go now. I have a conference call on my other line. Have a good afternoon and think on what I've said. I'll call you soon."

Skye listened to the static on the line as Debbie disconnected their call. Their conversation made her realize she was behaving like a school kid. She was a grown woman, so why did she feel intimidated by Walker? The sparks certainly flew whenever they met. Could there be an element of attraction between them? She shook her head, now she was being ludicrous.

***

By the time Walker reached the lodge, he too, was soaked to the skin. In a foul mood, he was relieved to see that the builders had packed up for the day. He had no desire to discuss the finer points of the restoration with them.

While he dried off, he placed a call to the realtor. Curious about his tenant, he was more than a little uneasy about her sudden appearance. The tourist season didn't start until the end of May when the weather improved. Although the realty company provided him with the dates of the rentals, he rarely, if ever, concerned himself with the finer details.

Most people planned a trip to the islands months in advance, especially if they were traveling from overseas. Yet, Ms. Dunbar had rented the cabin ten days before her arrival. Was it a coincidence that she arrived at the same time fish around the islands were dying? Normally, he got to know a person before forming an opinion about them. Innocent until proven guilty, wasn't that what everyone believed in? Under the circumstances, he wasn't taking any chances. It was about time they became better acquainted. He just needed a reason to act neighborly.

He turned on the radio and listened to the weather forecast. It wasn't good. Heavy rain, and storm force winds, which would result in an abnormally high tide and rough seas. As no one was likely to dump chemicals in those conditions, he decided to catch up on some overdue sleep. Joe would call if there were any new developments. All he could do was sit back, wait for the reports to come in from the lab.

The early spring storm came in fast from the northwest. The wind howled through the trees. Every now and again, there was an explosive 'crack' as a branch snapped and fell heavily to the ground. Walker wasn't worried. He'd ridden out worse storms and often at sea. Both the lodge and cabin were safe from falling timber. A slow smile crossed his face. He hoped his tenant liked storms, because this one was going to get a lot worse before the night was over.

He knew there would be power outages, so quickly checked his email. His mailbox was full of unsolicited mail, and a couple of requests for his company to give advice on certain matters, but there was no reply from Oxford University.

He dragged on the heavy waterproof he kept in the kitchen, took a torch off the shelf then stepped outside.

Struggling against the wind, he checked his boat was securely moored to the dock. Once back inside, he poured a large measure of whisky into a tumbler, and lay down on the couch to watch some TV.

Shortly after nine-thirty, the power lines gave up their valiant struggle against the wind and went down. He knew it would be morning before the electricity company restored power to this part of the island. He swallowed the last dregs from his glass and went to bed.

Thanks to the whisky, he'd slept soundly. He smiled; the storm was the perfect excuse to visit his tenant. He stretched, and sauntered into the bathroom and looked in the mirror. The half-grown beard made him look as if he'd spent twenty days camping in the wilderness. Picking up his razor for the first time in two weeks, he set about scraping the stubble from his chin. Freshly showered, and smartly dressed in cord trousers and green shirt, he lifted his jacket off the stand and headed out to his jeep.

CHAPTER FIVE

Skye woke to hammering in her head. It took her several minutes to realize that it wasn't in her head, but someone knocking on the door. She sat up in a daze, threw the quilt off her legs, and levered her stiff, aching limbs off the couch.

"Okay. Okay. I'm coming. Quit why don't you?" Still befuddled with sleep, she slid back the bolt and opened the door.

"Good morning. Boy, that was some storm," said Walker. "I thought you might appreciate some coffee as the power is still out." He held up two steaming beakers and a small paper bag.

Even without the beard, Skye recognized him. Too stunned to say anything coherent, she mumbled, her voice soft and husky with sleep.

"Why? How?"

"How did I get coffee when the electricity is out? I've been to town. The power company always restores electricity to Friday Harbor first. Outlying property takes longer. I've also got some cinnamon muffins and bagels. If you get dressed, I'll get things sorted." Walker stepped inside and closed the door.

Skye could only stare. Her stomach did a slow back flip. Walker was smartly dressed and smelled faintly of some expensive cologne. An easy smile played at the corners of his mouth. She let out a long sigh and revised her previous assessment of him. He wasn't just handsome; he oozed sex appeal from every pore. She watched him through half-closed eyes, and wondered why he was being so neighborly. Her befuddled brain decided to analyze that thought after the coffee. Conscious of the fact that she was half naked, she stumbled toward the bedroom, snatching the quilt off the couch on her way.

Walker took a deep breath. Skye's hair was mussed, and the T-shirt she wore barely covered her shapely thighs. Fortunately, she was too sleepy to notice his slow appraisal of her body, and he wondered if she realized how attractive she was. He shook his head. If he continued to think like this, he would be in trouble. A hard-on was just what he needed right now.

He set the beakers, muffins, and bagels down on the counter. He waited until he heard the bedroom door shut then took the opportunity to look around. The fact that his tenant had slept on the couch, didn't escape his notice. He crossed the room. A copy of the latest *P.D. James* thriller lay on the floor next to the couch, the corner of a page turned down to mark her place. Apart from a few

CDs on a nearby table, the room was pretty much as it had been before his tenant had arrived.

A door hinge creaked, footsteps padded across the wooden floor. Walker swore heartily, and scuttled back to the kitchen. He grabbed a plate and placed the muffins and bagels on it, as Skye entered. He was right about her figure; he didn't like his women too thin, and she had curves in all the right places. He lowered gaze to the pulse at the base of her throat and wondered if she would shiver with passion if he were to kiss her there.

Mildly annoyed for allowing his crotch to rule his mind, he took a steadying breath. If he kept this up, he'd be taking a cold shower for the rest of the month—no, amend that—the rest of the year. He wondered whether his libido would stand the strain of being so close to this desirable woman for any longer than purpose dictated, but it would be interesting to find out.

He saw the puzzlement on her face and thought fast.

"This place is fantastic, isn't it? I was lucky enough to stay here last year. When I enquired about renting a few weeks ago, they told me that the cabin was booked. I had to rent another property close by." He hated lying, but somehow he thought the truth would be less palatable.

A thoughtful smiled curved her mouth. "That explains how you know where everything is. It's a lovely cabin. I was so lucky to be able to rent it, and at such short notice too."

"I think we got off on the wrong foot. I was out of line in the way I spoke to you. I'd had a rough day at work and had no right to unleash my temper on you. Can we start again and try to be more neighborly?" He held out a beaker of coffee and gave her his most disarming smile. "I'm Walker."

Skye took the cup of steaming amber liquid from him. The rich aroma of the coffee hit her senses. It tasted wonderful and was a much-needed jolt to her sleep-deprived mind.

"Skye, Skye Dunbar. And thanks for this." She raised her cup to his. "I was surprised by your sudden appearance and well, I wasn't very polite either." She broke a muffin in half and popped a small piece into her mouth.

Walker grinned. "Skye. It's an unusual name. And Dunbar, that's Scottish isn't it?"

"I'm from London. My family originated from Scotland, or so I'm told. My parents loved the Isle of Skye, almost as much as they loved each other, so it seemed natural to them to name me after the place where they first fell in love. Do you come here often, Mr. Walker?"

"Its just Walker. I come when other commitments allow, which isn't as often as I'd like. How about you? Have you visited the islands before?"

She watched him over the rim of her coffee cup. His voice was velvet edged and strong, and under different circumstances, would be very seductive. Why was he suddenly taking an interest in her? While he was very attractive, she wasn't interested. She bruised far too easily and took too long to heal to become involved with another man. Michael had seen to that.

"This is my first visit, although I have visited Seattle before. Is there much damage from the storm?" Skye deftly changed the subject to something less personal and penetrating.

"Yeah, some trees are down. None around the cabin, but if you go into town be careful on the roads. It will take the authorities a day or two to get things cleaned up."

"Thanks for the warning."

"Storms like that can take a bit of getting used to, especially if they come down from the north as this one did." He placed his empty beaker on the counter. "I'd best be on my way, and let you get on with your day. He smiled and opened the door. "I'll see you around. Enjoy your vacation, Ms. Dunbar." He climbed into to his jeep and promptly drove off.

Skye shut the door and sat down on the couch. She felt confused by the turnaround in Walker's behavior and the effect he had on her. Perhaps Debbie was right after all; he was just another visitor to the islands, here to relax, fish, and generally enjoy the scenery.

With the exception of John, she didn't trust men, and she certainly didn't trust Walker, that was for sure. If asked why, she couldn't explain. Some would call it womanly intuition. Skye, however, was more logical, and put her lack of trust down to Michael's betrayal.

Michael—the one person she had trusted with her heart, and yet he had almost destroyed her. She recalled the first idyllic ten days of her visit and remembered how things began to change on the eleventh. Over dinner, Michael had asked her to extend her stay.

At first Skye had said no. She had commitments and her business partner to consider, but Michael persuaded her to change her mind. She felt guilty when she rang John and told him she was extending her vacation. They had a blazing row. John was adamant that she should return, claiming the business needed her, and it was unfair to expect him to do all the work. Skye responded by saying that John was complaining because, for once, he was working long hours instead of her. It was the first time they had exchanged harsh words, and the whole experience left Skye ashen, drained, and exhausted.

Michael had comforted her, and said it wouldn't matter, not when she was settled in the States with him. Joy shone in her eyes, she felt blissfully happy. It was what she had dreamed of and hoped for. They talked long into the night, Michael declaring his love for her repeatedly.

They made plans for their future. After twenty-five years service, Michael could expect a reasonable pension, enough to buy them a house somewhere. Skye could continue her career and he couldn't foresee any problems in her being granted a fiancée status visa. Her mind burned with the memory of his smooth words. He'd been so convincing, that it was only with the benefit of hindsight, that she appreciated how easily she'd been sucked in by his glib words and charming smile.

She would never forget the events that followed. At first, it was little things, like Michael's pager going off halfway through dinner. He would rush out of the restaurant, leaving Skye to finish her meal in solitude and to pick up the tab. He became secretive, volunteering little information about why he needed to return to the ship. On Sunday afternoons, he would disappear for hours on end without explanation. There had been other last minute excuses to cancel their plans, like the weekend in Victoria and the trip to Friday Harbor.

When Michael asked about her business, Skye was reluctant to answer, feeling as if she were betraying all she and John had built together. She never discussed her work outside the office, and she refused to break that personal rule. Michael ignored her explanation and questioned her repeatedly. Each time his tone would be civil, but she would never forget the anger in his eyes.

Unable to fathom why her response annoyed him so much, Skye ignored the warning voices in her head. Michael's constant questions were nothing compared to the events that ultimately unfolded.

It never occurred to her that Michael could have a hidden agenda. She had been too wrapped up in her own happiness to realize that anything was amiss. Just how wrong she'd been.

CHAPTER SIX

The bad weather brought little respite for Walker. He stopped at the local store on his way to the airport and purchased a copy of the island paper. His stress level increased when he read an article about the increasing numbers of dead fish that had washed up on the island's beaches. The journalist suggested their deaths were due to the ferocity of the storm, but Walker knew differently.

Barely an hour later, he walked into his Seattle office. Too restless to concentrate on the paperwork on his desk, he thought about the woman staying in his cabin. He was still annoyed with the realtor for renting it out so early in the season. He had enough problems without adding to them with his own stupidity. No more fish had washed up in the cove in front of the lodge, but he felt it was only a matter of time before they did.

He stared moodily out of the window at the Seattle skyline and considered his options. Slowly a strategy formed in his mind. If successful, it could give him the lead he was looking for. His first phone call was to the Port Office at Friday Harbor. He requested the name of any vessel that had passed through the straits, its cargo and heading, along with the time of the changing tides.

His second call was to the meteorological office for details of wind direction and velocity. Finally, he entered all the information onto a large-scale map of the islands, and marked where the latest batch of fish had washed ashore.

None of the ships that had passed through the straits could have been responsible for the new reports of dead fish. They had mainly been cargo vessels delivering containerized stores to small, remote villages in Alaska. Walker studied the map; the lines of concentration furrowed his brow. If his calculations were correct, the chemicals were being dumped overboard somewhere between Friday Harbor and Shaw Island.

He hoped the chemicals were in containers, rather than being discharged like raw sewage. If they were, and the containers were marked, then it might be possible to trace them back to the company from which they originated.

It was a huge area to search, the equivalent of looking for a goldfish in a pond and a pure fluke if they actually managed to find anything. The waters around the islands were treacherous, and even if the containers were lying in shallow water, it would be a dangerous operation to recover them. The current weather conditions weren't favorable for diving off a small boat. Divers weren't the answer, he thought grimly. However, there was another possibility. If he could persuade Joe to involve the Coast Guard or one of the specialist companies in an underwater search using sonar and a remotely operated vehicle, then maybe, he would get lucky.

Walker massaged his temples as he dialed McCabe's number. The stress and lack of sleep made him feel ten years older. He wasn't only concerned about the local salmon population, or the sea otters and seals, which abounded in the waters around the islands, but for the human inhabitants too. Fortunately, none of the hospitals had reported any cases of suspected poisoning. However, once the food chain became involved, there was no telling where this would end.

The seconds ticked away before a somewhat disgruntled voice answered.

"McCabe."

Walker got straight to the point. "Joe, could you organize a sonar survey of the straits, or better yet, have someone send down a remotely operated vehicle?"

"Christ, you don't want much, do you? Have you any idea what you're asking or how much those surveys cost? Let's not leave out the fact that they are way outside my department's jurisdiction. I could easily be kissing my whole budget for the next ten years goodbye."

"Calm down, think of your blood pressure. I haven't asked you to pay for it out of your own pocket. I just wanted to know if you could organize such an operation."

"Calm down? Easy for you to say, you don't have the bean counters at the State Department watching every move you make. Sonar surveys, remotely operated vehicles? What are you planning to do, look for hidden treasure like some perverse pirate?"

"I've been plotting tides and vessel movements. I've narrowed the area down and now have some idea where these chemicals are being dumped. If we could survey the seabed, who knows, we might come up with some anomaly to justify taking a closer look. I know it's a long shot, but I have no idea what else to suggest, unless you've managed to come up with something positive."

"Before I go spending all of Uncle Sam's tax dollars on what could be a red herring, let's see if we can streamline your plan a little."

"What do you have in mind?" asked Walker. A muscle flicked impatiently in his jaw.

"I don't have authority to spend the sort of money you're talking about, that's for sure. I'll have to take this upstairs to get permission for a sonar survey. If anything unexpected did show up then we could justify the need to investigate further. I can't promise I'll get approval for an ROV, but I don't see why we couldn't send down a dive team, provided the water's not too deep, and this damn weather improves. How does that sound?"

"I guess that'll have to do," Walker replied. "Just make sure you tell them that sooner or later it won't be fish turning up dead, but people. When that happens, I'll be the first to say I told you so. Get back to me with the details."

Walker slammed down the phone. Frustrated, he stared out of the window. Not only was his professional life going from sugar to shit, but images of his sexy tenant also filled his mind. Disgusted with the direction of his thoughts, he grabbed his jacket off the back of his chair and marched out of the office.

He walked quickly, glancing over his shoulder every now and again to make sure he wasn't being followed. He entered the first Internet café with a vacant booth, and logged into his web-based email address. There was still no word from Dr. Ridge's old university. His fist hit the desk in frustration. People just didn't disappear without trace, especially not leading computer scientists. He had to find Ridge, and soon. If his request for a survey of the seabed was refused, then finding out who was hacking into his company's computers was his only other option.

He ordered an espresso, and stretched his aching back. After half an hour of searching, he found an interview in a little known computer journal with Robert J. Ridge. It had to be the same person. It couldn't be a coincidence. The article was a few years old, but tucked away at the bottom of the page was an email address. Praying that the gods were on his side, he quickly typed a note, briefly explaining his situation and asking for Dr. Ridge's help. His final request before hitting the send key was to ask for an immediate response.

There was nothing more he could do, other than wait for either McCabe or Ridge to contact him. Ironically, waiting wasn't one of his better traits. He was used to being in control of his own destiny, and for the last few weeks, he'd been anything but. He downed his coffee, deleted all traces of his activities from the computer, and left.

Back in his office, he set about clearing some of the paperwork in his in-tray. Around ten o'clock his private line rang. Few people knew the number, and even fewer knew he was in town. He snatched the handset off the cradle.

"I might have guessed you'd still be at your desk at this ungodly hour."

"Paperwork, Joe. It gets us all in the end. I hope you're calling with good news."

"I need you to send me everything you have so far—lab reports, newspaper articles, witness statements, maps—whatever you've got. And Walker, it had better be convincing."

"I didn't ask you to go out on a limb for me."

"A limb? A mere limb? I've done more than go out on a limb for you, I'm dangling off a leaf at the end of the branch, and I don't want to fall off, and find myself collecting my pension fifteen years early because we didn't cover our backs."

"I hear you, Joe. I'll have everything couriered over to your office first thing in the morning. Do you have any idea of timescale?" Walker's voice was as cold as the water in Puget Sound.

"If your evidence is as good as you say, then within forty-eight hours. I understand the Coast Guard has a suitably equipped vessel on standby, and are prepared to let us have it for a couple of days. My opposite number is already pulling the results of the survey carried out last year."

"I suppose that's something. Want me to go along for the ride?"

"Let the boys in blue handle this. They'll be in touch as soon as the survey is completed and the comparison has been made."

"Okay. But I won't sleep easy until I know the result."

"That makes two of us. I'll give you a call once they've sailed. Will you still be at this number or are you heading back to Friday Harbor?"

"I'll be here. There are a few things I need to check out. Don't worry. I'll keep you informed as to my whereabouts."

"I'll wait for the courier in the morning. Don't burn the midnight oil too much, ole buddy."

"Yeah, old is right. Remind me again, why I let you talk me into taking this on? And Joe, better add this one to my tab, its another favor I owe you."

"Hey, if your tab gets any longer buddy, I'll be collecting 'til hell freezes over, thaws, then freezes over again. Talk to you tomorrow."

Walker worked long into the night, correlating lab results, copying the recent newspaper article, the map he had drawn up, and compiling all the information he had on PCBs, their effects on fish and the food chain. Finally, he wrote his report.

Around four, his eyes burning and no longer able to concentrate, he lay down on the office couch. The masculine, mahogany colored leather couch wasn't built for his tall, powerful frame, but there was no way he was allowing the report out of his sight until he placed it in the hands of the courier. He eased his weary body into the most comfortable position possible in the cramped space, and fell into a troubled sleep.

He woke just after seven. After showering and shaving in the executive bathroom, he changed into the spare clothes he kept at the office for emergencies. He called the local courier company, and arranged to have his neatly packaged report delivered to Joe.

Three days later, he drove out to the airport. A two-hour delay in take-off due to reduced visibility didn't improve his demeanor one little bit. Finally, receiving clearance, he took off, and flew over the straits, on his approach to his landing point at Friday Harbor.

Less than a thousand feet below, the Coast Guard cutter was slowly working lines with the sonar fish. Towing a sonar fish smoothly in deep water in a strong current was not a job for the inexperienced skipper. It would be several days before the survey was completed, the results correlated and compared with those of a previous year.

Walker knew his reputation was on the line. He wasn't confident that the survey would turn up anything significant. If it failed, then all his years of hard work establishing his company as a leading authority on environmental issues would be down the pan. There was no way he was going to give in without a determined fight.

These days his body ran on a mixture of anger and adrenalin. He was tired from the strain, but knew he couldn't rest until whoever was responsible was brought to justice. One thought kept turning over in his troubled mind. There was no doubt this was a personal vendetta against him. They had already succeeded in hacking into his computer. What would be next he wondered, a physical attack on his company? A personal assault?

And where did his tenant fit into the scheme of things?

There was something decidedly odd about Ms. Dunbar's timely appearance on the island, he thought. It was just too much of a coincidence. Perhaps it was time to storm the castle, or rather the cabin, and discover what made the charming Ms. Dunbar tick.

CHAPTER SEVEN

Comfortably settled in the cabin, Skye occupied herself by reading and, between breaks in the rainstorms, visiting the island's museums and window-shopping in the local art, craft, and antique shops.

As for Walker, she felt sure he was somewhere in the vicinity, but was keeping out of her way, and that suited her fine. Debbie had flown up for a long weekend, and they had spent two action-filled days enjoying every tourist attraction San Juan Island had to offer. They even joined one of the many charter boats on a trip to watch the Killer whales known locally as Orcas, and were enthralled by the sight of the huge mammals splashing and cavorting in the protected waters around the islands.

As had become their custom over the years, they decided to spend their last evening together enjoying a sumptuous meal in a prestigious restaurant.

Walker was about to leave when he saw Skye and another woman enter. He'd only stopped by for a meal and a quick drink before returning to the lodge. What a coincidence, his tenant should choose this particular restaurant and bar for an evening out. He ordered another beer and settled down to watch. He had a feeling the evening was about to become interesting, very interesting indeed.

As the waiter showed Skye and her companion to a table overlooking the marina every male head in the restaurant turned to watch them. Their appearance was striking, one auburn-haired and the other titian. They complimented each well. At first glance, they appeared to be of similar height, although on closer inspection Skye's companion was taller by a couple of inches. Skye looked stunning. The calf length jade green dress she wore caressed her figure like a lover, and set off her coloring to perfection.

Caught off guard by the intense feeling of desire that surged though his veins, Walker willed his body to still, but his body was having none of it. He wanted to pull Skye into his arms and kiss her until she was senseless. Why did his tenant have to be so troublesome and so sexy? The first he could cope with, the second might just earn him yet another cold shower.

Skye's companion was dressed all in black, a perfect foil for her vibrant hair and pale skin. Both were beautiful in their own way, although he preferred Skye's delicate features and softer coloring to the more dramatic woman by her side.

To anyone who might be interested, they were just two friends enjoying an evening meal. Walker, however, wasn't just anyone. His curiosity was aroused. Either his tenant made friends very quickly, or she had an associate here on the island. In which case, why had they arranged to meet in a public place, rather than at the cabin, where they could talk without being overheard?

Enquiring from a passing waiter what the two women were drinking, Walker ordered a round of drinks and had them sent over to their table. He watched their reaction in the mirror above the bar. Skye's companion appeared to ask the waiter who had sent the drinks. When the waiter pointed him out, she turned, gave him a dazzling smile, and raised her glass in acknowledgement of his generosity.

"Please don't tell me he was pointing to the geriatric with the walking stick," Skye said as the waiter returned to the bar.

"Don't be silly, with those glasses he couldn't see this far," replied Debbie. "It's the guy on the second stool from the left, the one with the dark hair. He's wearing a sports jacket. One of us obviously attracted his attention, and I doubt very much it's me." She raised her glass once more.

Skye choked on the sip of wine she had swallowed. "Why aren't I the least bit surprised to see him here? That, my dear friend, is none other than the obnoxious and infamous Mr. Jedediah Walker."

"Really? Well knock me down with a feather. He looks nothing like the way you described him. In fact, he's kinda cute." She gave Walker one of her most alluring smiles.

"Cute? You need your eyes testing, Debbie. Or better yet your head."

"I wouldn't turn down an offer to get up close and personal with him. That's one serious hunk of male flesh. I'm going to ask him to join us. I think it would be rude not to, don't you? Besides, what can I say? I'm a woman, and I'll talk to anyone, especially a handsome man like him."

Skye stretched out her hand, but Debbie brushed it aside. "Are you out of your mind? Please don't ask him over. Let's just enjoy our last evening together."

It was too late, Debbie was already gesturing for Walker to join them. Skye watched in horror as he eased his tall frame off the stool and strolled leisurely cross the room, a grin of amusement on his face.

"Good evening, ladies. Thanks for the invitation. I'm waiting for a friend, but he hasn't showed," he lied glibly. "If you've no objection to making it a threesome, then I'd be happy to join you." Before either woman could voice an objection, he dropped down into the chair opposite Skye and signaled the waiter to lay another place at their table.

Skye's temper flared. Debbie was always doing this, but this time she really had over-stepped the line. She forced a smile on her face and begrudgingly made the required introductions.

Debbie returned Walker's smile, shook his outstretched hand, and casually asked, "Are you on vacation, Mr. Walker."

"Sort of. Have you two known each other long?"

"Yeah, we've been friends for a number of years now," replied Debbie. "We don't get to meet up nearly as often as we'd like. The last time was when Skye attended a conference in LA, but that was two years ago. That's right, isn't it?" She barely gave Skye time to nod lamely in agreement.

"That must be hard on your friendship." Walker replied.

"Not really. We talk on the phone and email each other. When Skye told me she was planning this trip," Debbie continued, "I told her she ought to visit with me in San Francisco, but she wanted to come here, so I said I would try and re-organize my schedule. Unfortunately, I could only manage a long weekend, I fly home in the morning."

Skye smiled at Debbie, betraying nothing of her annoyance. She hated being the center of attention, if only she could think of something to say to change the subject and divert the conversation away from herself. Conscious of Walker's scrutiny an unwelcome blush crept into her cheeks. She felt embarrassed.

Debbie was captivated by Walker's charm and his disarming smile. She was in her element flirting with Walker, giving him her most captivating smile, while placing a well-manicured hand on his arm to emphasis a point. If he were to suggest that Debbie walk on water then she was just the woman to have a darned good try.

Walker noticed the strained look that passed between Skye and her friend, and found the situation amusing. He studied the two women. Their personalities were so different; it made their friendship more intriguing. Skye's friend with the doe-like eyes and goofy smile was putty in his hands, and trying too hard to impress him, but he wasn't interested. He found her type mildly irritating and she was no exception. She was willing to talk to anyone on any subject provided she was the center of attention. If only Debbie knew she wasn't the center of his. Her remarks, although innocent, annoyed Skye, but he couldn't fathom out why.

Skye, on the other hand, was charming, polite, and tactful. Outwardly, she appeared relaxed and to be enjoying herself, but Walker was sure it was an act. He sensed her tension. Saw it in the way she held her shoulders and the way her fingers tightened around the stem of her glass. It was particularly evident whenever her friend said something she disagreed with. He was certain that her temper was on its way to exceeding the boiling point and the posted speed limit.

He watched the gamut of emotions flicker through Skye's eyes, and wondered what it would take to make her lose some of her aloofness. He suspected that under the very correct smile, and cool exterior there lurked an incredibly passionate woman.

"It's a pity you're leaving tomorrow," he said for Debbie's benefit. He then attempted to draw Skye back into the conversation. "I'm sure you'll miss her company."

Skye tried hard to control her temper, but her voice was a little too eager, as if her answer was all too obvious.

"Of course I will."

"How much longer are you staying on the island? I hope you won't find it too lonely in the cabin on your own."

"Skye's here for another few weeks." Debbie interrupted, taking control of the conversation once more.

"My plans are flexible. I could change my flight and come back with you, if you wish."

Walker cut in. "I have a suggestion. As the weather is improving, why don't I show you a side of the island that most tourists never get to see?" He offered Skye a smile that even her late grandmother would have fallen for.

"Well, I don't...I mean I..." Skye stuttered like a teenager, a musk-rose flush rising on her cheeks.

"What a generous offer. You were only saying yesterday that you wanted to see more of the island. I'm sure Mr. Walker is the perfect guide." There was a twinkle of mischief in Debbie's eyes.

Walker interrupted, with a conspiratorial wink to Debbie. "How about I pick you up tomorrow—mid morning—and we make it up as we go along?"

"Don't I get a say in this?" Skye demanded. "After all, it is my vacation and I might have made plans."

"What plans?" Debbie laughed. "First I've heard about them."

Skye felt backed into a corner, and knew declining would appear churlish. "Well, if you are sure. I wouldn't wish to intrude."

"Good, that's settled then. Everyone for coffee?" Walker raised his hand to signal the waiter.

They lingered over coffee and liqueurs. "Do you have plans for the rest of the evening?" Walker asked.

Debbie, who had long ago taken the role of chief conversationalist, was quick to reply. "We thought we'd find some live music to listen to, either some jazz, maybe a little folk. If I can persuade Skye, and we can find somewhere suitable, we might go dancing."

Walker noticed the faint blush on Skye's cheeks. He imagined what it would feel like to hold her in his arms, and feel her soft curves molding to the contours of his hard body, as they swayed to an imaginary rhythm. He tried to ignore the sudden flare of heat in his groin.

"There's no nightclub on the island. Unless you ladies can find a party to gatecrash, you're out of luck. There are plenty of places that play live music. Perhaps I should join you?"

The waiter cleared away the debris of their meal and Walker insisted on paying the bill. "It's the least I can do. It's not often that I get to spend an evening in such fine company."

Few diners remained, and although Debbie seemed in no hurry to conclude the evening, he sensed that Skye was. Her wide-eyed look merely screened her anger.

"Thank you for dinner," Skye said. "I'm sure you have better things to do with your time than accompany us." She glanced at her watch. "Besides, it's later than I thought, and Debbie is catching the early ferry in the morning. I think we should call it a night."

"Maybe you're right," Walker conceded. A slow smile spread across his face. He'd better not antagonize Skye too much. After all, her so-called friend had been most accommodating in giving him toehold in the door. He stood and extended his hand toward Debbie.

"It was a pleasure meeting you, Debbie. Say 'Hi' to San Francisco for me and have a safe journey." He tilted his head towards Skye, his eyes holding her gaze. "I'll see *you* tomorrow," he said with quiet emphasis.

Walker was barely out of earshot before Skye turned to Debbie. "Did you have to do that?"

"Do what?"

"You know very well what I'm talking about. Not only did you embarrass me, but you set me up!" Skye banged her fist on the table.

"You could have refused his invitation. Besides, I don't understand why you're annoyed. Walker is perfectly charming, and he obviously finds you attractive. He hardly took his eyes off you all evening. Despite what you say, I don't think you're averse to his charms either. A holiday romance could be just what you need. Your love life's been on hold for far too long, and you know what they say if you go without sex for too long—you become a virgin again."

Skye groaned inwardly. She looked over her shoulder and scanned the restaurant hoping that no one had overheard her friend's embarrassing attempt at humor.

"I'm not interested in Mr. Walker or any man. You of all people should know that. Not after Michael."

"What is *it* with you and Michael?" Debbie asked. "You trot out the same excuse every time a man comes close enough for you to smell his cologne. I know he was a first class rat. He lied, and in your mind that's a cardinal sin. I've got news for you, most men lie at some point about something. It's genetic! It's something you have to accept like the fact that their socks stink, and they snore. Michael was over a year ago, it's time to move on."

"I can't. I've never told anyone, not even you, what he put me through." Skye turned her face to the window lest Debbie see her pain.

"Then tell me now," Debbie said. "Make me understand why you are so averse to having another relationship."

Skye continued to stare out of the window at the lights flickering around the marina. Trapped by her memories of Michael, the last thing she wanted was to rake over old ground.

"I can't, Debbie. I just can't. Drop it, please?"

Realizing that she had said too much, Debbie reached across the table and took Skye's icy hand in hers. She gave it a reassuring squeeze.

"I'm sorry. Whatever Michael did, forget it. And if you can't, then perhaps you should talk to a therapist." When

Skye didn't respond Debbie continued, "I'm sorry if I've upset you, and spoilt our last evening together. You know I would never intentionally do anything to ruin our friendship. After everything you told me about your previous encounters with your Mr. Walker, I was just having some fun with the two of you, that's all."

Skye's temper finally tumbled over the edge. Her head whipped round, and she snapped at her friend.

"Debbie, just stop right there, before you dig yourself an even bigger hole. For once and for all, he is *not* my Mr. Walker."

In spite of Skye's dark looks and the anger in her eyes, Debbie couldn't help smiling, and playfully held up her hands as if to ward off an imaginary blow. She had to have the last word. "If you say so, but what is it, you Brits say? Oh yeah, 'Methinks the lady doth protest too much.'" She suppressed a giggle, picked up her purse, and left the restaurant.

Skye, not trusting herself to speak, followed.

The tension in the car was palpable. Skye concentrated on driving on the unfamiliar road. When they reached the cabin, they quickly said goodnight, the door of Skye's bedroom closing with a resounding thud.

Skye found it impossible to sleep. The events of the evening spun round in her mind, like laundry in a dryer. Debbie was right. She was by no means blind to Walker's rugged good looks, even though he was maddeningly arrogant. When she looked into his eyes, her body stirred with an answering surge of excitement.

As she lay in bed, she took stock. Her life was a mess. Apart from the endless round of work and sleep, she had little to comfort or interest her, not even a cat to welcome her home after a busy day at the office. What spare time she had, she spent in the garden, reading or listening to music. Other than, John dragging her out for the occasional drink after work or entertaining clients, she hardly went anywhere other than the grocery store.

She longed for male company, but turned down every offer of a date for fear of being hurt. She was tired of feeling lonely and confused. It was one of the reasons she had decided to make this trip, a chance to get her life in order and make a new start. Torn by conflicting emotions, she tossed yet again.

Michael had taught her that love brought pain and betrayal. She had no desire to experience those emotions again. Why couldn't she be like other women, have fun, and walk away with no regrets, and without so much as a backward glance? She turned on her side and thumped the pillow in frustration. Her logical mind argued that an affair wasn't the solution. Yet, when she and Walker met, she was acutely conscious of the undercurrents of desire that passed between them. What would happen, she wondered, if they took the time to find out where it would lead them?

CHAPTER EIGHT

The following morning, Skye drove Debbie into Friday Harbor in time to catch the ferry. Their relationship remained strained and by unspoken agreement, neither mentioned Walker's invitation until Debbie was about to board the ferry, when her parting words to Skye were to enjoy her afternoon with the most handsome man on the island. Despite her irritation, Skye laughed. Debbie always managed to have the last word.

Reluctant to return to the cabin, Skye lingered in town for as long as she dared, but there was only so much time she could spend window-shopping and so many cups of coffee her body could absorb. She drove back to the cabin, fervently hoping that Walker had forgotten about his invitation.

She parked in front of the garage and sighed in relief. There was no sign of Walker. She strolled round the side of the cabin to the deck, and found him gently rocking back and forth in one of the wicker chairs. Hands clasped behind his head, his face turned skywards, as he soaked up the morning sun. Skye leaned against the wall, crestfallen. She should have known he wouldn't let her off the hook. She took a deep breath, forced what she hoped was an enthusiastic smile onto her face, and turned to face him.

He stood in one smooth movement, reached out, and caught her hand in his.

"I thought you'd forgotten our arrangement." He grinned mischievously, as if reading her thoughts.

The mere touch of his hand sent a warming shiver through her body. Her brittle smile softened as she lowered her gaze. She took a deep breath then raised her eyes to his.

"I hadn't forgotten. I was unsure if you really meant it. After all, Debbie rather forced us into this."

"I volunteered, and I always keep my word," Walker said. There was warmth in his voice as he continued, "I thought I'd take you over to Lopez Island. But if you've already been there we could visit Orcas Island instead."

Skye eased her hand out of his firm grasp. There was a slight tremor in her voice, as she replied, "No, I haven't. We're too late for the ferry, surely? Perhaps another time?"

Walker nodded towards the dock, his eyes like summer lightning. "No need for the ferry, I brought the boat around."

Skye turned. Sure enough, moored to the end of the dock, bobbing up and down with the swell was a sleek and expensive cruiser.

"Unless there's anything you need from inside," Walker indicated the cabin with a jerk of his head, "we should set off."

Skye could think of a million reasons why she should refuse to accompany him. Short of committing an act of violence on his person, she knew he wouldn't accept any of them. Walker took her small hand in his once more and led her down the path towards the waiting boat. He effortlessly jumped aboard then turned to help her, taking both her hands in his.

Skye watched the boat rising and falling. Confident that she had judged the boat's rhythm, she stepped off the dock, but was surprised when the cruiser suddenly drifted away. She would have fallen into the water if Walker hadn't stepped forward and caught her safely in his arms. Instinctively, Skye's arms wound round his waist, her head fitting snugly in the hollow between his shoulder and neck.

"Are you OK?" he asked.

Filled with a strange inner excitement, Skye colored fiercely. Walker's arms around her felt good. It seemed the most natural thing in the world for him to hold her. His breath was warm and moist against her cheek and felt just like a lover's caress.

"I think so. I'm not used to boats." She felt slightly bereft as he set her loose.

"I'll try and remember that. The water's cold at this time of year. Perhaps I should give you a life vest in case you take a tumble overboard."

Skye laughed as she saw the glint of amusement in his eyes. "I haven't forgotten your earlier warning. I'll watch out for the deck cleats."

She sat down next to the helm and studied his profile as he cast off. Caught up in her own thoughts and emotions, she had to admit that he wasn't as intimidating as she had first thought. In fact, she had an overwhelming desire to be kissed by him. Unbidden, her mind jumped in with a second intriguing thought—what would his kisses be like? Would they be feather-light and teasing or hot and demanding?

Skye shook her head. She was being ridiculous allowing such thoughts to fill her mind. His face was strong, and there were laughter lines around his eyes and mouth, hinting at a softer side to his character. His body was lean, and yet she could see the outline of his muscles under the thick sweater he wore. The warmth of his body was intoxicating, and the degree to which she responded completely unexpected. She tried to rationalize her feelings by putting them down to the shock of her fall, but failed. There was no doubt that what she felt was the flush of sexual desire.

The water in the channel was choppy, but was nothing Walker or the boat couldn't handle. When the wind lifted Skye's hair, he reached out and lightly fingered a stray tendril, tucking it behind her ear. As his fingers brushed her cheek, a shiver of desire shot through him. Good move, he silently chided himself. He wanted her, and if she kept on looking at him with eyes full of unfulfilled passion, then he would throw his rulebook overboard and start kissing her until she begged him to stop.

He rubbed a hand over the back of his neck, and attempted to play the part of the tour guide in an effort to get his mind off his crotch, but failed miserably. When Skye subconsciously moistened her lips, tasting the salt carried on the wind, he held his breath. Although she was unaware, he'd noticed her earlier appraisal of him and had seen the longing in her eyes. If she kept looking at him with those blue eyes and making those sexy gestures with the tip of her tongue, he'd have to start reciting the periodic table, anything to stop from following through on his thoughts.

He knew that the Coast Guard cutter had completed the survey and had returned to Seattle. It would be another thirty-six hours before the results were available. In the meantime, he planned to pump his tenant for all the information she was willing to give.

"How long will it take us to get to Lopez Island?" Skye asked.

"Not long. It depends on how many other vessels we have to dodge. Not feeling seasick, are you?"

"Being on a boat doesn't bother me too much, unless it's heaving up and down and rocking from side to side, at the same time." She smiled and recounted her previous trip in a small boat. "A few years ago, I visited the Small Isles off the West Coast of Scotland." Skye's voice was rich with laughter as she continued. "By the time we reached halfway the launch was being tossed in every direction. As the only female on board, I was determined not to let my gender down by being seasick. I resolutely kept my eyes fixed on the horizon. When someone started grilling bacon for breakfast, I turned a delicate shade of green. I managed to hold on to my dignity, but I was relieved to set foot on solid ground, I can tell you."

Walker's mouth quirked with humor. There was something warm and enchanting in hearing her laugh. The wind kicked at her hair, blowing it in complete disarray. She looked so alive, with pink tinged cheeks and sparkling blue eyes, which he swore had changed to a deeper hue.

The pain and wariness he had previously noticed had vanished. She looked relaxed, as if she didn't have a care in the world. Her features had softened now that her guard was down. Walker caught a spark of some indefinable emotion in her eyes. Without knowing it, she had the ability to arouse him like no other woman ever had, and despite his determination not to become involved, his body had other ideas.

As the boat sped over a rough stretch of water, their eyes briefly locked, and they shared a moment of intense physical awareness. Skye stood so close to him that he could feel the heat from her body. He closed his eyes, breaking contact. Clearing his throat, he pretended to be unaffected by what had passed between them.

"The entrance to the marina is just past the end of that breakwater." He took his hand off the helm, and pointed as he spoke. "The village is a short distance away. We can walk or can you ride a bicycle?"

"Sure, it's like sex, isn't it? Once you've learnt how, you never forget." Skye blushed as the words tumbled from her mouth. Her lips trembled with the need to smile. Finally, her sense of humor overtook her embarrassment at her unintentional word choice.

Walker threw back his head and laughed heartily. The afternoon was turning out to be full of surprises. He quickly brought the boat alongside and secured it to the quay. Together they followed the footpath towards the exit. When Walker sought her hand, Skye gave it freely.

The sun had come out, and here and white cotton candy clouds dotted the sky. They hired two ancient-looking bicycles from the chandler's store. Satisfied that Skye could indeed ride a bike without falling off after five yards, they cycled toward the village.

"Hungry?" he asked after they had gone a little way.

Now that she thought about it, Skye realized that she hadn't eaten since her scant breakfast with Debbie, many hours ago.

"Mm, coffee and a sandwich would be good."

"I think I can do better than that. How about a bowl of the best clam chowder in the Pacific Northwest?"

"That good?"

"I'll stake my reputation on it."

"And what if I disagree?" Skye asked a hint of challenge in her voice.

"Let's see…" Amusement flickered in Walker's eyes as they met hers. "I'll buy you dinner."

"And if you're right?"

A mischievous smile tipped the corners of his mouth. "If I'm right, then you agree to spend a day with me."

Skye ignored the voice inside her head that wondered why spending time with him had suddenly become so important.

"Okay, you've got a deal."

Half an hour later, Skye let out a long sigh. She mopped up the last of her clam chowder with a piece of sourdough bread.

Walker watched her obvious enjoyment of the simple meal. "Well, am I right?"

Skye licked her lips. "Okay, you win. That was the best chowder I've eaten in a long time."

"In that case, you owe me a day of your time, to spend how I choose." He reached across the table and brushed his finger against the side of her mouth in a gentle caress. "You missed a bit," he said huskily.

Skye gasped in delight. She watched as he lifted his finger to his mouth and licked it clean. Nervously, she moistened her dry lips. There was a far deeper significance to his actions than she was ready to contemplate. An invisible thread seemed to draw her closer. If she didn't do something to break it, she would be unable to stop herself from falling headlong into his arms.

Stars twinkled in the sky as they sailed back to San Juan Island. Skye hadn't realized it was quite so late as she had enjoyed herself so much. She shivered in the late spring frost, despite the heavy sweater she wore and was glad of the shelter afforded by the boat's windscreen. She wrapped her arms around her midriff, but failed to stop the odd shudder rippling through her body.

Walker's deep husky voice broke into her thoughts.

"There's a jacket under the seat. It's probably way too big, but at least it will keep the chill out. Here, take the helm." He placed her hand on the wheel and covered it with his own. "Keep your eye on the compass and hold it steady on this heading." His warm, strong hand guided hers. He raised the seat on the port side and lifted out the old waterproof jacket he kept there, and draped it around her shoulders.

Unconsciously, Skye settled back, enjoying the feel of his body against hers. He placed his right hand over hers. His left circled her waist, steadying her against the pitching of the boat. Her breath hitched, and a warm sensation flooded her body.

Walker bent his head and rested his cheek against hers. "See that light over there? Keep heading toward it. Steering a boat is like driving a car, the only difference is that the boat is slower to respond."

Skye could scarcely breathe. The touch of his lips on her cheek was a soft caress. She stiffened slightly and drew in a ragged breath.

"This is a bad idea," she said nervously. "I always get confused between my right and left hand when people give me directions. Ask anyone who knows me. Debbie and I once planned to drive to Santa Cruz and ended up in Santa Rosa."

"Relax. I'll make sure we don't wander off course."

"Really," she said, and ducked out of his arms. "I'd much prefer it if you handled the boat."

Walker released her and allowed her to slide back onto the seat next to him. "If you're sure? We've not got far to go now."

He watched Skye in the moonlight and could see she was fighting an inner battle, and wondered if it was the same battle he was fighting. There was no denying she was beautiful, just as there was no denying he wanted her. He was sure she was involved in his current investigation, but he just couldn't figure out how. He'd never used a woman in his life. It was against his code of ethics. However, he couldn't allow his business to go under. Swearing under his breath was becoming an uncontrollable habit, he thought dryly. Perhaps he ought to learn another language—it might give him a wider choice of expletives.

Skye fought to control her swirling emotions. Her feelings towards Walker were confused. When they had first met, she had hated the sight of him. Now, she found herself responding to his every touch. Was it possible? Was she really attracted to this arrogant, complex, but devastatingly handsome man?

Deep in thought, she didn't feel the fender bump the dock as the boat finally came to rest. The sudden total silence brought her out of her reverie and back to the present.

Saddened that their afternoon together had ended, she stepped ashore. Guided only by the moonlight, she was quiet and withdrawn as she strolled up the path to the cabin. She blinked away the sudden tears that appeared for no reason that she could fathom, other than a fear of overwhelming loneliness.

Stopping midway, in an attempt to prolong their remaining minutes together, she realized she no longer wanted to be on her own, but what choice did she have? She could hardly ask Walker to stay on the strength of a few moments in his arms.

A knot rose in her throat, making her voice soft and husky. "Isn't that a wonderful sight?" she said, looking up and pointing at a myriad of stars. "We have so much light pollution in London. You never get to see a star, let alone a sky full of them." She dropped her gaze as her voice trailed away to a whisper.

"I guess we're kind of lucky out here," he replied. "We tend to take nights like this for granted."

Walker kept his gaze steady as he bent his head to hers. Her eyes were filled with a curious deep longing that shattered all his resolve. His lips brushed hers. When she didn't object, he slowly deepened the kiss, his tongue tracing the soft fullness of her lips.

They looked at each other for what seemed like a long time but was probably only several minutes. Finally, Walker looked away. He took her hand and they walked up to the cabin. He wished her goodnight, then, without another word, strode down the path to his boat.

Skye felt strangely bereft as she stood in the doorway watching Walker's boat vanish into the darkness. Quietness descended, and she struggled to get her thoughts into some kind of order. When fatigue settled in her body, she let herself into the darkened cabin and shrugged off the jacket he had wrapped round her shoulders.

Moonlight filtered through the windows, bathing the lounge in a strange ethereal light. It was too late to start a fire, so she sloshed a measure of malt whisky into a glass. The amber liquid warmed her body, but did little to calm the war of emotions that raged within her.

All day long, the tension had crackled between them. Even so, she was unprepared for Walker's sudden show of emotion. His kiss had lasted for seconds, but it had seemed much longer. The gentle massage of his lips on hers had sent shivers of desire racing through her. He had awakened feelings deep inside her, feelings that she had long ago buried, and never thought would resurface.

For the first time in months, she felt truly alive and utterly feminine. Her heart swelled with a feeling that she had thought long since dead. Although tired, she felt content, and her last conscious thought before going to sleep was that tomorrow had never looked so promising.

CHAPTER NINE

Walker returned to the Lodge and found the light on his answering machine flashing. The last thing he needed was yet another problem. He switched on the coffee pot and waited for it to brew, before hitting the play button.

"Walker, if you're there pick up," McCabe's disembodied voice demanded. "I guess you're out. The Seattle police stopped a tanker truck on the freeway this afternoon for some minor traffic violation. The cop became suspicious when the driver couldn't say what was in the tank or explain why a loaded truck wasn't displaying the obligatory tags. Rather than let the driver off with a warning, the cop hauled him in. The tanker is currently in the pound north of Seattle. I thought you might want to examine the contents. Sorry this is short notice, but I only got to hear about it this evening. Give me a call when you get in."

Walker punched in McCabe's number. This was the first decent lead they had, and what was he doing? Messing around on a boat, playing Romeo to his tenant's Juliet. Talk about stupid. McCabe answered on the second ring.

"Joe, I only just got your message. When did this happen?"

"About four-thirty this afternoon. I called as soon as I could. I even tried your cell phone, but I guess you had it switched off."

"Yeah, sorry about that. I'll fly over first thing in the morning. Has anyone questioned the driver?"

"He's a contractor. Just told to connect his truck to a tank and drain the contents. Cash up front and no questions asked."

Disgusted, Walker grunted. "And he had no idea what he'd been paid to haul?"

"Nope. He'll be prosecuted for the violation of course. As a first time offender, he'll receive a fine, unless we prove he carried an illegal substance, and planned to dump it on an unauthorized site. I thought you would want to test the contents, rather than have the County lab do it. If my suspicions are correct, then maybe we could persuade the Public Prosecutor to make a deal."

"We should be thankful he hadn't dumped the load. Give me the address of the pound and I'll send one of my lab technicians over or take the samples myself in the morning." He scribbled the address McCabe gave him on a notepad by the phone. "Any news on the survey?"

"I'll check up on that when I get to the office. What time do you think you'll be here?"

"Mid-morning. There's something I have to do first."

Late, as it was, Walker considered phoning Skye to say he was unable to keep their commitment to spend the following day together. He dismissed the idea, and decided that challenging her to spend the day with him had been the dumbest move he'd made since he learned how to shave.

He settled for writing a short note and figured there were two possibilities. She would welcome the space, especially if she was as stunned as he was by the chemistry that existed between them or she would slam the door in his face. Either way, he didn't have time for romance in his schedule at present—he needed answers and he needed them fast. If Skye was innocent, and things between them took their natural course, then she would merely be an interesting diversion. If she was involved, then he would make damned sure she rotted in jail.

Shortly after six am, Walker freewheeled his truck down the track to the cabin. He stepped out from the behind the wheel and had a quick look around. There was no sign of life, but then no self-respecting tourist would be up at that hour unless they were a masochist or up to no good. He slipped his hastily written note from his pocket and pushed it under the cabin door.

Five hours later, the lead that seemed so promising, fizzled out like a dying Roman candle. As McCabe suspected, the tanker carried a lethal cocktail of chemicals, which, if the driver had succeeded in dumping, would have had repercussions on the environment for years to come.

Alternatively, he and McCabe bullied and cajoled the driver. Despite threats of being jailed for years, he steadfastly refused to say anything, other than he had been contacted by phone and offered an obscene amount of cash, which he found stuffed in his mailbox.

Walker and McCabe felt sure the site where the driver had filled his tanker had nothing to do with the production of the chemicals. The police agreed to watch the address on the chance someone turned up, but it seemed unlikely that it would be used again.

Walker was amazed that no one had been hurt. These people had no idea how many innocent lives they were putting at risk. If the tanker had been involved in a traffic accident, the resulting catastrophe could have left many injured. Walker's anger became a scalding fury. Skin irritation, liver, stomach, and fertility problems could be attributed to pesticides such as DDT and polychlorinated biphenyls or PCBs, as they were more commonly known.

In the late 1970s, the USA had banned their production, but PCBs where still found in the environment, and mankind was now paying the price for thinking that it could dispose of these chemicals without first figuring out a way to make them safe. Nothing like shitting in your own backyard, Walker thought ironically.

He and McCabe spent a long time with the District Attorney, finally persuading him to cut a deal with the driver. They agreed to drop charges in return for the police placing a tap on the driver's phone. If approached again, the police department would be able to trace the call.

The sonar survey had drawn a blank. Walker was disappointed, but realistic. He knew extending the search area was out of the question and that he was fast running out of options.

There was nothing to keep him in town, and sleeping at the office held even less appeal than crawling into the cockpit of his plane. He'd put in more flying hours in the past month than he had in the previous six. If he kept this up, he'd have enough airtime to pilot a seven-forty-seven.

Two hours later, he walked into the lodge. The house was cold, unappealing, and had a decidedly unlived-in feeling. What he needed most was a long hot shower to wash away the fatigue and strain of the day, followed by a stiff drink. He turned up the thermostat and traipsed into the bathroom.

With drops of moisture clinging to his forehead and a towel slung low over his hips, he entered the lounge. He was about to pour himself a large scotch when a devilish look came into his eyes. He replaced the stopper in the decanter and walked over to the wine rack selecting a bottle of *Woodward Canyon 1994* instead. He placed it on the table before dressing in a pair of black slacks and smoke gray shirt. With a sweater thrown casually over his shoulders, he grabbed his keys, cell phone, and the bottle off the table.

The mellow sound of a saxophone drifted from the open window of the cabin as he switched off the engine. He sat and listened to the lush sound as it floated on the evening breeze. Skye had great taste in music, and he wondered if her body would be as responsive as the instrument he could hear. Alighting from the truck, he grabbed the bottle of wine off the passenger seat. He stepped up to the cabin and knocked on the door.

"Hi. I know you weren't expecting me." He gave Skye a boyish grin. "I got free earlier than expected and thought you might like to share this with me." He held up the bottle for her inspection.

Skye paused in the doorway and offered a welcome smile in return. There was something lazily seductive in Walker's eyes, which she felt unable to resist.

"Your note said a couple of days."

Walker's gaze took in her rich auburn hair, her slim waist, and the outline of her full breasts under the bronze shirt. He took a deep breath. Her perfume was a heady oriental fragrance that echoed her very essence. His body moved up a gear as their gaze locked.

"If it's too late, I can come back another evening." He turned to leave.

"No, no, don't go. I was about to have dinner. It's nothing special, just a casserole, but you're more than welcome to join me," Skye said. She stood to one side to allow him to pass.

"Well, if you're sure it's no bother." The rich aroma of something cooking in herbs assaulted his senses. His gaze rested on Skye's slightly flushed face. He dropped a kiss on her cheek.

Instinctively, her fingertips touched the spot. She felt nervous and slightly distracted, just like a teenager on a first date. Walker's voice broke through her thoughts.

"Where do you want me to put this?" He held up the bottle. "The wine…"

"Sorry…you'd better open it and let it breathe. Dinner won't be long," she finally stammered. She handed him the corkscrew. Their fingers touched and she became conscious of his very male presence in the tiny space.

Under Walker's steady scrutiny, she found it hard to think—correction, hard to breathe. All she could think about was the way Walker made her feel. Trying hard to keep things light between them, she busied herself laying another place at the table.

"You never did tell me why you decided to take your vacation here," Walker said, pouring the wine. "A month is a long time for a vacation, especially when you're on your own. You must have a very understanding employer."

Skye was glad of the momentary diversion to bring her wayward body under control. She carried two laden plates to the table.

"I co-own a business, so I'm my own boss. My partner had no objection to me taking an extended vacation." She raised her glass and sipped the wine. She savored its intense plumy flavor. She felt relaxed and quite mellow, and combined with the smoldering looks Walker was giving her over the rim of his glass, the effect on her pulse rate was alarming. "As for being here on my own, I enjoy my own company. I guess it comes from being an only child. We get plenty of practice while growing up."

"But the San Juan's?" he pressed. "The islands aren't exactly known for good weather at this time of year. I would have thought you'd be more at home on the beaches of the Caribbean, than the rocky shores of these islands."

"Haven't you heard that too much sun is overrated? Not every woman wants to parade herself on the beach for every lothario within a twenty-mile radius to prey on her. Besides, I have my reasons for spending my vacation here."

Walker studied her face. Some sixth sense warned him that he'd put her on the defensive, and if he questioned her further, she would clam up. Her long, slender ringless fingers played with the stem of her wine glass. His eyes swept over her delicate features, to the creamy skin of her throat and he wondered how she would react if he were to kiss her there.

"What about your boyfriend? He can't be happy about you being away for so long." If he had a woman as attractive as Skye in his life, there was no way he would let her out of his sight for more than a day, let alone a month.

Skye's lashes brushed her cheek. For a brief moment, a shutter closed over her face. She pushed all the negative thoughts to the back of her mind and gazed at him. The look of concern she saw on his face melted her heart.

"There is no boyfriend." Realizing how sad that sounded, she tried inserting some humor into the conversation. "My business partner, and self-appointed big brother would have every applicant for the vacancy positively vetted given half the opportunity. As it is, work keeps me busy. What about you? How does your significant other feel about you spending all your spare time fishing?"

"Like you, there is no significant other, though that's not completely my choice. I move around too much with work. When a guy constantly calls and cancels, dates get fed up waiting around. Sometimes going fishing seems a better alternative to having the phone slammed down in your ear."

A thoughtful smile curved Skye's mouth. "I thought you said you worked out of Seattle."

Walker played with the napkin. "My office is there, but like I said, I travel quite a bit. That makes it hard to maintain a relationship. Not all women understand that a man can't always be there when they want."

Skye's eyes darkened with some unspeakable emotion. "Surely, if you met someone who really cared, it wouldn't matter to them—so long as the time you spent together was quality time. A few weeks or months apart shouldn't be that big a hurdle, not when you've got a lifetime to look forward to. Isn't that what love is all about? Surmounting the obstacles and loving someone for who they are?"

"I'm sure you're right. I've yet to meet such a woman. Some women are more demanding of their partners, wanting the best of everything—a home, a car, an endless supply of credit cards, membership of the local country club, and so on. It probably explains why there are so many single women. You Brits tend to be more stoic, or at least, you seem that way."

CHAPTER TEN

Walker enjoyed the easy conversation. When he sensed it was getting too heavy, he deftly changed the subject. He raised his glass to Skye and turned up his smile a notch.

"I thought you Brits lived off baked beans and fish and chips. I didn't realize you were such good cooks."

Skye laughed aloud. "It's a common assumption, but totally wrong. You should thank my mother for my culinary skills. She was determined I should acquire some housewifely attributes as well as a degree, so insisted I took a cookery course before I went to university. Like all students, my cash was tight. I became very adept with a can opener. You should have tasted some of the concoctions me and my friends came up with."

Walker became very aware of the woman sitting opposite him. His feelings had nothing to do with reason. He wanted her every way a man could want a woman. Until now, he'd never met a woman he couldn't walk away from. Skye was different. She was smart, sassy, and sexy, yet had no appreciation of the effect she had on men and him in particular. With his life turning from sugar to shit with every passing hour, an affair would be the dumbest move he could make.

However, the enigmatic Ms. Dunbar, damn it, had crawled under his skin, like a two-day-old itch that refused to be scratched. She was the reason he'd taken more cold showers in the last ten days than he had since tenth grade. She was also the reason his temper had been off the Richter scale all week. From their first meeting, he'd wanted to know what it would feel like to hold her in his arms. Now he knew—she felt too damned good.

That was part of his problem. His body wasn't satisfied with just holding her and tasting her honeyed kisses, it wanted more. No matter how many times he reminded himself he was a grown man and not a hormonally charged teenager, he still wanted her.

On the drive over to the cabin, he had convinced himself that he could do whatever it took to save his company. If that meant seducing his sexy auburn-haired tenant, then he would do so with no regrets. Having felt Skye's lithe body against his, he knew that he couldn't go through with it. While he wasn't sure what his feelings for the seemingly fragile woman he'd cradled in his arms were, he knew he wouldn't be able to live with himself, or the accompanying guilt if he used her. If they had sex, it was because she wanted it too. Otherwise, he would walk away and spend the next month chewing out anyone who came within a twenty-mile radius of him. That, or move to the northernmost end of Alaska.

He finished the last of his wine and mentally ticked off all her knew about her. She worked in London. So did a third of the population of England, or so he'd read. She had a degree, and was a partner in a business. She was obviously intelligent, but what subject did she hold her degree in? What did her company specialize in?

For all he knew, she could be a designer as her clothes weren't from the local chain store. It was what she *hadn't* told him that intrigued him. He couldn't help pondering about her business and her partner. Something didn't add up.

Skye's soft voice broke into his thoughts. "I don't have any brandy, but I do have a good malt whisky if you'd like one to go with your coffee." She placed the tray on the table next to the couch.

"That sounds great," Walker said and threw another log on the fire.

For an instant, there was a burning, faraway look in his eyes, as if he was wrestling a problem. By the time, she handed him the glass, the fleeting expression that lingered momentarily, had vanished.

Walker placed his glass on top of the fireplace. His right hand captured hers, his thumb stroking the soft skin below her wrist. His left hand slid down her arm and tightened around her waist, molding her soft curves to the contours of his hard, lean body. He lowered his head and kissed her.

Standing on tiptoe, Skye's arms wound round his neck, her fingers burying in his thick black hair. His mouth moved slowly over hers, savoring it, until Skye moaned softly and parted her lips. Walker deepened the kiss, giving her what she wordlessly sought. He meant to take it slow and gentle, just as a man should when he kisses a woman for the second time, but Skye's response broke his resolve. Hungrily, he took all she gave and more, his tongue exploring the soft recesses of her mouth. He lifted his lips from hers, his pulse hammering in his ears.

Skye rested her cheek on his chest with a sigh of pleasure, her breathing almost ragged as his. He could feel her heart beating and the answering thud of his own. He watched her taste his kiss and remembered to breathe— just. Gently, he stroked her hair and kissed her again, before lifting her into his arms and carrying her to the couch. One kiss was not enough; he had an aching need for more, and to hell with the consequences.

His eyes locked with hers. Huskily, he said her name. "Skye?"

Skye's emotions whirled and skidded. Walker's kiss roused her passion. She knew she ought to resist, that this wasn't a good idea, but her desire for him overrode everything else. She ran her tongue over her warm, moist lips unaware of the sensual picture she made.

She didn't need to hear Walker's unspoken question; her body already knew the answer. His intense blue eyes never left hers as his mouth sought hers once more. When he released her, and eased her down onto the thick cushions, she didn't object.

His gaze slid from her face to her breasts, his hand gently outlining a firm globe through the silk of her blouse. His touch was soft, yet teasing. Skye's nipple hardened instantly, her body hungry for his touch. She moaned softly as the hardness of his arousal pressed into the soft flesh of her thigh.

She heard Walker suck in a ragged breath. He kissed the pulsing hollow at the base of her throat, the gentle massage sending currents of desire though her.

"Skye...honey, look at me."

Walker's voice seemed to come from a long way off. Skye opened her eyes. There was an invitation in his eyes as they gazed into hers.

"Mm..." She trailed her fingers up and down his back and across the expanse of his shoulders, exploring every contour, committing them to memory. Unable to disguise his reaction to her soft caress, she felt his body stiffen with need.

Walker raised himself on one elbow. "Honey, unless you tell me to stop, I'm going to make love to you."

Skye's voice was silky and full of passion. "Walker—"

"Tell me, sweetheart, tell me what you want. I can't make this decision for both of us."

Skye's heart hammered in her ears. She swallowed hard. With a delicate finger, she traced the outline of the scars on his eyebrow and chin before moving to his firm sensual lips. Without warning, his mouth captured her finger, gently sucking it. She couldn't deny her feelings for him any longer. She wanted him with every part of her being. His raw sensuousness took her higher and higher, until all she could think about was having him fill her body with his. She inhaled sharply.

"I...want...I want you."

"Honey, that's what I hoped you would say." There was a faint tremor in his voice as though some deep emotion had touched him.

He threw the cushions onto the rug in front of the fire. He knelt in front of her and kissed the soft skin at the base of her neck. With unsteady fingers, he reached for the buttons of her blouse, slowly undoing one button and then another, before slipping it off her shoulders and down her arms.

The soft light from the fire cast a warm glow on her creamy skin. Walker inhaled sharply, drinking in her subtle perfume. His lips trailed soft kisses down her neck and shoulders. He outlined her full breasts through the lace of her bra then brushed his fingertips over her hardening nipples. Hurriedly, dealing with the buttons of his shirt, he shrugged it off.

Her fingers wove into the crisp dark curls on his chest, and he luxuriated in the wealth of sensations flooding his body. His hands moved down the length of her back, to the zip on her skirt, while his tongue lightly traced a path from her ear to the pulse at the base of her throat.

Walker sucked in a breath as his body responded to the vision of Skye in nothing but her underwear. God, she was beautiful, and it took every ounce of his control not to rip the scraps of lace off her and bury himself in her soft, moist folds. Dragging in air, he tried desperately to slow the pace. His hands slid across her silken belly, making her tremble with desire.

Quickly, he discarded the rest of his clothes. He eased her down onto the cushions, one muscular leg slipping between hers. With passion-darkened eyes, his hands sought the fastening on her bra. Heat surged in his groin as the lace fell away and his eyes drank in the fullness of her breasts and her swollen nipples. He fondled one firm globe then the other, and then lowered his head, his tongue seeking, and finding the taut dusky pink nipples.

Pleasure rippled though Skye's body and found its center in her groin. Her skin burned where Walker's lips and fingertips touched. Her hands dug into his hair, pulling him closer, as the hard shell that she had so carefully built around her shattered into a million pieces. When his tongue circled her nipples, teasing and sucking the hard nubs, her body ached for the sweet release that she knew only he could give. In response, she stroked his hard, silky erection.

"Honey—"

"Don't you like that?"

He liked it too much, that was the problem. Waves of pleasure throbbed through him, his body trembling with liquid fire.

"Honey, look at me."

Skye's eyes told him everything he needed to know about how she felt. He rolled her onto her back and entered her. Just when he thought he couldn't get any deeper, he felt her relax, welcoming him further into her body. His body picked up the rhythm that was as old as time. He moved slowly at first, not wishing to hurt her, but desire and passion overwhelmed them as they sought release.

He felt her tremble as the first waves of her orgasm washed over her. Her body arched in final surrender to his, and he claimed her for his own. The hot tide of her passion tipped him over the edge, and his own powerful orgasm exploded in a million fiery sensations.

It was a long time before either of them moved. Walker felt Skye's tears on his chest and swore to himself. He'd given her the chance to say no, but she hadn't pushed him away or told him to stop. So why the tears?

He rolled her just enough so they were side by side. He kissed the top of her head and gently raised her face to his. What he saw there almost tore his heart in two. Her deep blue eyes were full of longing as she looked at him, yet he could sense she was dealing with some inner turmoil. His arm tightened around her shoulders. With a single finger, he traced the line of wetness on her cheek.

"Tears?" he said in a gentle tone.

"They're tears of happiness, not sadness. No one has made me feel this way in a long, long time." For a year, she had convinced herself that she could never trust another man sufficiently to let him get close to her, let alone give him the gift of her body. Yet, this strong, self-opinionated man had crept under her skin and into her heart.

"They should have. You're beautiful and you deserve to be loved. Hell, every woman is beautiful in her own way. Some men just don't know how to make a woman feel special."

Skye lowered her gaze, savoring the moment. This wasn't the time to open a bitter wound.

CHAPTER ELEVEN

Alone with his thoughts in the darkness, Walker reconsidered his assessment of the woman sleeping so trustfully in his arms. Skye lay with her back to his chest, her body snugly fitting against his. His right arm curved over her waist, holding her breast.

Why was he so suspicious of her? Many people took vacations early in the year, and he had no reason to suspect Skye was any different or that she had an ulterior motive. Her sudden appearance was purely coincidental. What if their paths had crossed more than once during the first few days of her visit? There was nothing prohibiting his tenants from walking in the woods. They were one of its attractions, along with the uninterrupted sea views and magnificent scenery.

Skye wasn't willing to talk about herself. So what? Why should she tell him everything about herself, from the color of her toothbrush to the size of her bra? A quick smile crossed his face. At least, he knew the answer to that question. He gently caressed the warm globe in his hand—more than enough to drive a man wild. As for the toothbrush, he would find out what color it was in the morning.

Skye wasn't the type to use her body for material gain, she was far too naïve to be playing that sort of game. No, he decided, she was just who she appeared to be, a single woman on an extended vacation. His mouth curved into an unconscious smile as he remembered the first time they had met and how antagonistic they'd been toward each other. He'd been a fool to take his anger out on her. In his defense, he could only offer the feeble excuse of lack of sleep—that, and the fact he'd found more evidence of illegal dumping only that morning. Give Skye her due, she returned his hostility with her own brand of hot temper. He would never forget the sight of her small frame bristling with indignation as she stood up to him. Now that they had stopping fighting, they had connected in a way he hadn't expected.

He shifted the arm he was resting on into a more comfortable position. Skye yawned, and burrowed deeper, seeking the warmth of his body. Her skin was even softer than he had imagined. His body responded, making him long to make love with her all over again.

The dying embers of a log glowed in the grate. The air in the cabin felt distinctly chilly. He brushed a kiss across the shoulder nearest his mouth.

"Skye, sweetheart, wake up. It's cold and you don't want to catch hypothermia. Come on, it's time I took you to bed."

Skye's eyes blinked open. The scent of Walker's body and their lovemaking filled her senses. Slowly, she became more alert as he rubbed her arm. He was right; she felt chilled to the bone. His lips brushed the back of her neck and he eased her body away from his. He stood and looked down at her slender form, then stretched out a hand to her.

"Come on love, let's go to bed."

She didn't hesitate. She took Walker's hand and allowed him to lead her into the bedroom.

In the early hours of the morning, while the moon was still high in the sky, Skye listened to Walker's rhythmic breathing. The sheet barely covered his hips and her fingers longed to touch, to explore.

Slowly, she traced the line of his jaw and his lower lip. Her hand followed the line of his collarbone, luxuriating in the feel of the coarse hair on his chest. No longer able to stop her exploration, she traced a sensual circle around his nipples. They hardened instantly, drawing a moan from his lips. Her hair brushed his face and chest as she touched her lips to his.

Suddenly, Walker opened his eyes and looked deeply into hers. His arms wrapped around her waist. She lowered her mouth, her tongue continuing the journey her fingers had begun.

Walker lay still, allowing her to touch and taste him. When he could take no more, he rolled onto his back. Their coupling was hot, demanding, and as satisfying as it had been earlier. Skye rested her head on his chest and fell asleep listening to the drumming of his heart.

Someone in Skye's dream was whistling, and off key at that. Only it wasn't a dream, she really could hear someone whistling. Something else too—she could smell toast. No wait, burnt toast. She opened one eye and closed it again. The bedroom was bathed in brilliant sunlight. The brightness drove shards of pain into her fuzzy brain. She sat up and tipped her head away from the light before opening her eyes, and snatching her robe off the foot of the bed.

"I wondered when you'd surface," Walker said, as she entered the kitchen.

Skye opened her mouth to speak and thought the better of it. Silently, she padded over to the sink, poured herself a large glass of water, and drank it down in one gulp. The icy coldness lifted the fog from the gray cells in what passed for her brain.

Walker's eyebrows rose inquiringly. "Bad head?"

Her gaze took in the fact that he was wearing the clothes he'd worn the night before and now he really needed a shave.

She glared at him. "I don't have a hangover if that's what you're inferring."

He held up his hands defensively. "Hey, I was just checking." He watched her and wondered if this she was about to tell him to get the hell out of her kitchen, her life, and how much she regretted last night.

"Okay, concern accepted," she replied. "Before you ask, I remember everything about last night. It's just... well, I didn't expect to find you still here, that's all." She pushed a hand through her tousled hair and blushed delicately at the memory of their lovemaking.

Walker let out a relieved chuckle. That's what was eating her, finding him in her kitchen. He struggled hard to bring his features under control.

"I get it. Your lovers usually disappear into the night, do they? Wham, bam, thank you ma'am. Is that what you expected? That's not my style. I happen to think the first kiss of the day is the most rewarding." He clasped her body to his and proved his point.

When he released her, Skye was breathless. Her bones had turned to jelly, and most of her brain to mush, but her one functioning brain cell had to agree with him.

"See what I mean?"

"Mm." Skye blinked and focused her gaze on Walker's strong features.

"Nope, you're definitely not a morning person are you, honey?" Amusement flickered in his eyes as they met hers.

Skye shook her muddled head.

"That's all right. I'm wide-awake for both of us. Why don't you take your sweet ass off to the shower? By the time you get back, breakfast will be on the table."

Walker swatted her derrière and pushed her in the general direction of the bathroom. He turned back to the stove, tied an apron around his waist, and deftly set about preparing the eggs.

Skye clamped her jaw shut and tilted her head to one side, glancing at him from under her lashes. She shook her head and wondered why some woman hadn't dragged him up the aisle.

Stepping into the shower, she allowed the hot water to stream over her. It had been a long time since she'd had sex and she hadn't expected to feel so attuned to Walker's wants and desires. She felt shaken by the strength of their passion and her feelings for the tall dark-haired man with the ice blue eyes, now cooking breakfast in her kitchen.

Yesterday morning, she had been a levelheaded businesswoman with only bitter memories. Today, she had given her body, her heart and probably her soul, to a tall, ruggedly handsome man with an irresistible smile.

"Two minutes," Walker called from the bedroom doorway.

Skye turned off the faucet, and toweled herself dry. By the time she had dressed and entered the kitchen, Walker was turning a fluffy omelet onto a plate.

"You lied."

"What do you mean, I lied?" Walker's face was grim. He turned away from the stove and sought to remember what he'd said to make her think that way.

"You said two minutes. It's been more like seven."

"Why you ungrateful—" The words died on his lips as he saw the teasing laughter in her eyes. "I see the shower woke you up."

"Sure did, sunshine. Is that omelet for me or am I going to have to start gnawing on your leg?"

"That hungry, huh?" He placed a plate on the table in front of her, and then turned back to the stove and poured some more of the egg mixture into the skillet.

Skye's face was devoid of expression. "I seem to have quite an appetite this morning. It must be something to do with the workout I had last night."

The skillet clattered down on the stove. Walker laughed. A two year old couldn't look as innocent, even if they'd had their hand in the cookie jar. "Workout?" He tried hard to appear hurt, but a smile played at the corners of his mouth.

"I worked up a sweat, and at times, I felt as if I'd run a marathon. Does that count?"

"Yeah, that counts." His mood switched from amusement to seriousness. He wanted to know what Skye really thought. He knew he could make her respond, but he'd made other women respond too. Skye was different. She had fire, passion, and something else.

Suddenly, he wanted more with her than just great sex. He wanted to wake up to find her by his side for as many mornings as she was willing to give. The question was did this auburn-haired angel want the same. Had he crept under her skin, as she had his? Only she knew the answer, and he would be damned if he felt he had the right to ask.

He kept his voice calm as his eyes anxiously searched her face. "Is that how you think of last night?"

Her elbows resting on the table, Skye studied his face. Just how much should she tell the virile man standing at her stove and wearing an apron? Was he was ready to hear the message her heart was sending her brain, when she wasn't one hundred per cent certain she wanted to hear it either? A slow smile trembled over her lips. One thing was certain, if Walker's expression was any indicator, he wasn't finding her teasing much fun.

If discretion was indeed the better part of valor, then she ought to tell him the truth, or as much of the truth as she knew, otherwise he might be tempted to tip his omelet over her head.

A blush covered her cheeks. Their eyes locked. Sapphire blue met ice, but ice that held a savage inner fire. In a voice that was little more than a whisper, she found the words and the strength to reply.

"Last night was wonderful. And if I never have another memory to make, I will always hold it in my heart." She couldn't look at him anymore, so turned away, brushing away the tears that threatened to spill over her cheeks.

Walker was unprepared for her blatant honesty. Her body language told him she meant every word. All thoughts of eating forgotten, he knelt next to her chair. He cupped her chin in his hand, his eyes full of concern.

"Sweetheart, you've more memories to make, I'm sure of it. There's no need to feel sad."

Skye tried to swallow the lump in her throat. "I'm not in the least bit sad or angry nor do I have any regrets. As I said, last night was so special. You made me feel so wanted, so desirable, and for that I can never thank you enough."

The underlying sensuality of her words captivated him. He tucked a stray strand of hair behind her ear then took her hands in his.

"Sweetheart, I got more pleasure out of last night than I've ever had. I just want to be sure you did too."

The heavy lashes that shadowed Skye's cheeks fluttered up in surprise. Walker's tender expression bit to her very core. She could no longer deny that he had captured her heart. Unable to find words to express her feelings for this unpredictable man, she brushed her lips against his in a kiss as soft as a downy feather.

"I did."

"Then that's okay." He studied her thoughtfully. He was full of questions, but intuitively knew now wasn't the time to pry. Obviously, some bastard had hurt her—he sincerely hoped he wasn't about to become the next.

CHAPTER TWELVE

Skye agreed to Walker's suggestion that he stay at the cabin for the remainder of her vacation. Consequently, joy bubbled in her laughter and she smiled more often in the following days than she had in months. Finally, the sadness of the previous twelve months was behind her and her life was back on track. Not even the unpredictable weather dampened her spirits.

As if by some tacit agreement, neither spoke of their lives at home should they remind themselves that the clock was ticking the hours away to when they knew Skye would have to leave.

Skye found Walker a knowledgeable and amusing guide. When they visited the historical site at the north of the island, he told her how the English and the Americans had gone to war over a pig. At first, she thought he was making it up, and it was only when she read the free handout that she believed him.

When the rain clouds cleared in the afternoon as they often did, Walker took her sailing. They dropped anchor in one of the many coves, had lunch and a bottle of wine or sailed round to Lime Kiln Lighthouse, where he told her about the pods of Orcas, pointing out individuals by name.

They spent the evenings talking, listening to music, and enjoying each other's company. If the weather was fine, they strolled along the beach, stopping every now and again to kiss under the stars, or sat on the deck and watched the clouds cast shadows on the moon. Later, when they turned out the lights, they lay in a hot tangle of sheets, the raw passion of their lovemaking lifting them both higher and higher until their bodies were spent.

Then Walker's cell phone rang and shattered the dream.

Skye was loading the dishwasher when the first call came through. Walker went into the bedroom, half closing the door behind him to take it. After that initial call, he made several of his own. Although she tried hard not to listen, Skye heard him bark out instructions to a nameless individual on the other end of the line. Her face clouded with uneasiness, she turned and stared out of the window. Moments later, Walker slipped his arms around her waist and held her tight.

"Skye, honey," he said softly.

Skye kept her back to him, not wanting him to see the tears that threatened to fall. She bit down hard on her lip and regained control of her emotions, then turned to face him. When she lifted her face to his, the pain still flickered there.

He looked tired and the anxious, and she wondered why she had never noticed the dark shadows beneath his eyes before. The phone call obviously worried him. She touched a fingertip to his lips as if to silence him before he said the words she knew in her heart he was about to say.

"I know you have to go. It's okay, really it is." But it wasn't in the least. Instead, she wanted to scream and tell him a dozen reasons why he should stay. Her faint smile held a touch of sadness. "I understand, really, I do." The old sensation of distrust had returned, and suddenly her life was taking on an all too familiar pattern.

Walker looked down at her pale face and felt guilty for causing her pain. Talk about bad timing. He didn't want to leave her, but he knew he had to. If the phone call had been about an environmental disaster in some far-flung corner of the world he would have sent someone else, but he had no choice, this was something he had to deal with himself.

"I'm sorry, but I have to go to Seattle. It shouldn't take too long, and I'll be back before you know it. Then we can pick up where we left off. In the meantime, keep smiling for me. He rested his cheek against hers. Her hair smelled faintly of apples, reminding him of the shower they had shared that morning. He gently stroked her cheek, his own expression grim.

Skye managed a small tentative smile and nodded, unsure how to respond. The wound that had taken so long to heal was sliced open again. She didn't want Walker to see how badly she was affected by his imminent departure and tried hard to keep her feelings under tight restraint.

Crushing her to him, he pressed his mouth to hers. "I'll phone you from the office." Then he was gone. The door of the cabin closed behind him with a soft thud. A car door slammed. An engine roared away.

She covered her face with her hands; it was only then that her tears began to fall. She told herself she was being stupid feeling this way. Walker hadn't made any promises and she hadn't asked for any. She knuckled away her tears. All she could think about was how she would feel when the time came for her return home. But she already knew—the same as now, only ten times worse, bereft, empty, and desolate—and a hundred and one other adjectives in between. By then, Walker might say he loved her, but past experience taught her that they were just words men said in the heat of the moment. They carried no weight, had no meaning.

Michael had taught her that.

Michael, who had said he loved her, but who had hurt her so badly that she believed she would never love again. Now, when she was beginning to think that love was something that didn't only exist in fairy stories, history was repeating itself. Another man had captured her heart, the only distinction being, Walker had walked out the door without saying goodbye, not her.

Apart from a log crackling in the grate, the room was oddly quiet. Skye stared out of the window into early the evening gloom. Deep in thought, she watched the wind whip the waves into a white frothed frenzy. Her mind was in overdrive finding reasons and excuses for Walker's sudden departure. None of the answers satisfied her and, too late she realized, he'd left without giving her the number for his cell phone.

Wretched and frustrated, she could only wait. Patience, the one virtue she needed the most and the one she possessed very little of. Her vacation wasn't over yet. Walker surely would return before she left for home.

***

Walker ignored the island's speed limit, his truck bouncing over every rut and pothole in the road. Pain jarred his spine, reminding him how stupid he'd been. His temper rose with every passing mile. More than once, his fist pounded on the dashboard in frustration. He blamed himself for becoming distracted. He should have concentrated on the investigation rather than spending time with Skye. He was so sure there was a link between her and the attacks on his company that getting to know her had seemed like a good idea.

She was everything he wanted in a woman and more besides. Intelligent, funny, and so passionate, that a man could drown in her. However, his timing stank. He should have trusted his instincts rather than becoming involved with a sassy auburn-haired beauty from across the pond. The blame for this fiasco rested squarely at his door. His cell phone rang again. He snatched it from his shirt pocket and hissed out a gruff 'hello.'

"Mr. Walker?"

"Yeah. Who's this?"

"Sam Richards. I'm the night security guard from your building."

"What can I do for you, Sam?"

"I was finishing my round when I found the door to your offices ajar. I thought I'd take a look around just to make sure, you know. There are papers everywhere, desks overturned. The place is in a right mess. It looks as if there's been a break-in. I've called the cops, but I thought you ought to know."

Walker's temper flared from simmering to white-hot anger. What else could go wrong? He raked his hand through his hair and wondered which God he had angered this time to be thrown yet another curve ball.

"Thanks for letting me know. I'm on my way back to Seattle. I'll arrange for someone to meet the police and make a preliminary assessment of what's missing."

The truck skidded to a halt outside the lodge. Walker let himself in, hit the light switch, and picked up the phone on his way to the study. Punching a pre-stored number, he paced the floor while he waited for the call to connect. He'd been totally irresponsible, there was no other explanation for it. He wouldn't blame McCabe if he hung his ass out to dry. He had done the one thing he always promised himself he would never do; relax on the assumption that the illegal dumping and attacks on his company had stopped.

His lips thinned into a hard line as he wondered why no one was answering the phone. He disconnected the call in disgust and punched in the number for the laboratory instead. Someone answered immediately.

"Have the cops arrived yet?" he ground out between his teeth. "Is there much damage?"

"Yeah. The cops are crawling all over the place like a rash. As for damage, someone made a thorough job of trashing the place, that's for sure."

Walker ran a hand through his hair. "What about the equipment, the microscopes and the slide drawer, are they intact?"

"The 'scopes were thrown off the benches. The slides are everywhere underfoot, and the chemical cupboard is completely empty. I keep on yelling at the cops to watch where they walk, but those guys take no notice of me. Until we get the worst of the mess cleared up and check the records, assuming the computers still work, we'll never know."

Walker sighed. "We still keep a paper record of the contents of the slide drawer though, don't we?"

"Until tonight we did—depends if it's still here under all this mess."

"Do what you can. I'm arranging for extra security. When they arrive, go home. There'll be enough to sort out in the morning."

Walker leaned back in the large leather chair and stared out of the study window. Both his Seattle office and the laboratory to the south of the city had been broken into that evening. Luckily, no one had been hurt. Instinct told him his company had been specifically targeted, but by whom? He had no doubts as to why.

Not only was someone out to ruin him, but he'd also left the one woman who stirred him in ways he hadn't thought possible. The sadness in Skye's eyes had cut him to the core. He hadn't given her a reason for his departure other than to say that it was business. How many men used that excuse when they walked out the door never to return? He felt like a first class jerk.

His hand hovered over the telephone on his desk. Was it too late to call or would it simply make matters worse? There would be time for explanations later, he decided. He had enough to worry about and his love life wasn't top of his list of priorities.

The grandfather clock in the corner of his study struck the hour. He'd spent far longer at the lodge than he'd planned. He doubted that he would achieve anything by flying to Seattle, but he decided to make the journey anyway.

Two hours later, he walked into the shambles that was his office. The security guard hadn't lied. The cops were trawling over the debris, checking for fingerprints as they went. It would take days to shift through the chaos and assess what was missing.

Filing cabinets lay on their sides, their contents strewn across the floor. Computers were smashed to pieces. Equipment was easy to replace, but the data they contained had taken years to collect, and the information was invaluable. Walker Environmental Research had built a record of every business in the USA and some in other parts of the world that disposed of toxic waste by illegal means. Thankfully, the majority of the reports he'd prepared over the years were a matter of public record, and the data could be reassembled from those. However, he had a hunch that all the information from this current investigation would be missing.

CHAPTER THIRTEEN

Skye tossed the book she was reading onto the floor and hurriedly snatched the phone off the table.

"Skye?"

"Oh, Debbie, it's you." Crestfallen, Skye's smile quickly faded.

"You sound disappointed."

"Sorry, I was expecting another call."

"I only rang to see how you are. If you're waiting to hear from someone else, I can ring back later."

"No, it's all right. He's probably not going to call."

"Who, John? I thought you weren't going to give him this number, or are you waiting for a more interesting member of the male species to call?"

"I haven't changed my mind and given John this number." Skye remarked pleased at how nonchalant she sounded.

"Oh, come on, Skye. This is like pulling teeth. Who are we talking about here?"

"I'm expecting Walker to call."

"Walker! Well, I'll be damned. You mean to tell me, you two have been spending time together. I thought you couldn't stand the sight of each other."

"We can't. I mean we couldn't. Oh, it's entirely your fault!"

"What makes you think that?"

"If you hadn't forced me to spend the afternoon with him, I would be out enjoying myself instead of...instead of—"

"Sitting around, waiting for him?" Debbie chuckled. "You've been telling me for several months that 'no' is the only word in your vocabulary. Why didn't you exercise your right to use it?"

"Debbie, this is not funny. If you hadn't backed me into a corner, we wouldn't be having this ridiculous conversation."

"Maybe not. Stop moaning and accept things for what they are—a change for the better."

Skye sighed. "I guess you're right."

"You know I am. So come on, spill. I want all the drippy, gooey, romantic details."

"We spent the afternoon together. A few days later, he called round with a bottle of wine, and we had dinner together."

"And? There has to be more to it than that, otherwise you wouldn't be sitting by the phone waiting for it to ring."

"I'm not."

"Yes, you are. Don't deny it."

"It's no big deal. Anyway, he's gone away on business."

"And that's all? I don't believe you. There's something you're not telling me."

Skye let out a long, audible breath. "No, there isn't."

"You're hiding something major. You've slept with him, haven't you?"

Skye's relationship with Walker was too new to share with anyone, especially her best friend. Finally, she settled for half-truths. "It was late when we finished dinner, so he spent the night here."

"Oh yeah? Next, you'll tell me there are mermaids in the cove and you're one in training. I suppose he was a perfect gentleman and slept on the couch fully clothed. I'm not buying it, Skye. Walker's one red blooded American male and anyone can see he's attracted to you. Come on this is *me*, remember? I can tell when you're holding something back."

"So, we slept together! I'm told it's all the rage between consenting adults."

"At last. You know it's taken me ten minutes to drag that out of you." Debbie's tone softened. "What came over you? You keep men at arm length and look at them as if they've got two heads. What's so special about Walker that made you change your mind? Was this just a one-night stand or are you two a couple? You weren't a little tipsy, were you?"

"I was not drunk. I guess we got off on the wrong foot. Now, we've stopped arguing, we actually get on quite well."

"You get on well together, huh? I get on with my next-door neighbor, but I wouldn't sleep with him. I prefer someone who's a good kisser and makes me tingle from head to toe. Do you find Walker attractive?"

"Now you're being stupid."

"Not as stupid as you for letting it take this long. I can't see what all the fuss is about. The guy's had to go off on business, so what?"

"He said he'd call when he got to the office. He's been gone two days, and I've heard nothing."

"So, be a big girl and call him."

"I don't know the number."

"A small thing like that shouldn't stop you. There is such a thing as a telephone directory. And you know his office is in Seattle, he told you that, right?"

"Yes, he did. Even if I knew the name of his company, I can't call him. I have to wait, and then I'll know."

"Know what?"

"Know that he's telling me the truth."

"Skye, Walker's not like Michael. I'd bet my life on it. If he said he'd call, I imagine he will. Maybe things just got out of hand, and he's not able to get to a phone, right now. You of all people know that things aren't always as straightforward as they seem. Give the man a chance."

"That's what I am doing. But I have this nagging feeling that history is repeating itself."

"I can't answer that as you've never told me the full Michael story. Maybe it's time you did. Who knows, I might understand why you think like this. You don't want what happened with Michael to control your life forever, do you?"

In spite of her reluctance to reveal the extent of Michael's transgressions, a hint of despondency crept into Skye's voice. "I wish it was that simple. Besides, you're at work."

"You're right, now's not the time. I'll call when I get home. If you feel up to telling me then, fine. If not, we'll talk about something mundane, like the weather. Cut Walker a little slack, okay?"

"Okay."

"I'm sure he'll call as soon as he can. When he does, you can forget we ever had this conversation. I'll call you tonight. Bye."

Skye replaced the phone and leaned back into the cushions. Debbie was right. She was being over-anxious and expected too much of Walker. However, she felt trapped by her memories and the emotion they stirred within her. Even now, she could remember every detail of that fateful Thursday and the appalling events that followed.

As the image focused in her memory, she fought waves of fear and nausea. She ran to the bathroom. Her hands shook as she splashed cold water onto her face. When the worst of the gut wrenching spasms passed, she raised her head and looked in the mirror above the basin. The face she saw there was hardly recognizable as her own. Deathly pale and drawn, her bright blue eyes were dark with fear. She tore herself away with a choking cry. Blackness enveloped her and she crumpled to the floor.

When she woke up, she was lying on the floor shuddering. She crawled across the room, too exhausted to stand, and rested her back against the bath. God knows she had tried hard to move on—to forget that terrible day.

Skye sat motionless, her heart thudding, her life a bitter battle. Darkness pressed in threatening to engulf her once more.

Why, why couldn't she just forget, instead of living her life in fear and pain?

After more than a year, she was no nearer to finding an answer. It had taken all her willpower to make this trip in an attempt to put those weeks behind her. It seemed as though her efforts had been wasted as the past had resolutely followed her and was bent on destroying her carefully constructed cocoon.

The phone rang, but she made no effort to answer it. Whoever it was could wait, and that included Walker. He was the last person she wanted to talk to. What would her friends think when they finally learnt the truth? And what would John think of her when he discovered that she'd allowed herself to be manipulated by someone as shallow and callous as Michael?

Misery hung like a steel weight around her neck. A sob rose in her throat. Such was her despair, she considered ending her life. It wasn't as if she would be missed. Life would go on. In time, Debbie and John would forgive her. With more time, they would forget her, but then Michael would have won. No matter how humiliating telling Debbie would be, there was no way Skye could to allow him to do that.

Exhaustion overcame her, and she fell asleep curled up on the cold bathroom floor.

CHAPTER FOURTEEN

Debbie phoned the cabin, but failed to get an answer. After her conversation with Skye that afternoon and her unexpected news, she wasn't surprised that Skye needed some space. What a turnaround! What if she had helped fate to bring Skye and Walker together, it had worked, hadn't it?

Walker was just what Skye needed to get over Michael and move on. Debbie searched her brief memory of the man. There was something unfathomable about him. He asked questions, yet rarely divulged any information about himself. In that respect, he was rather like Skye. They say opposites attract, but Debbie knew those who are alike spark much greater fire.

Michael was different. The mere thought of mentioning him and Walker in the same breath, made Debbie shudder. She'd never met the man, and was glad she never would. During the time he and Skye corresponded, Michael sent Skye numerous photographs from exotic locations in far-flung corners of the world. Skye in turn, had shared them with her. Debbie could tell Michael had a love affair with the camera, and his fake cold smile made her stomach tighten and skin crawl.

Despite her warnings, Michael had wormed his way into her friend's affections with his overtly romantic letters and Skye had fallen for the sickly sweet bait. It was unlikely that Skye was the first woman Michael had seduced with his smooth ways and glib tongue.

While she couldn't imagine what Michael had done to Skye during her visit last May, she could never forgive him for transforming her friend from a happy, self-assured young woman into someone who jumped at the slightest noise. The man was a grade 'A' son-of-a-bitch.

Disgusted by her thoughts, Debbie glanced at her watch. She pressed redial, but there was still no answer from the cabin. She looked at the photo of her and Skye on her desk. She tried to ignore the nagging voice in her head, which told her something was wrong.

She wondered whether to buzz John, but dismissed it as a bad idea. After all, what could he do from six thousand miles away? No more than her, that was certain. She'd try phoning one more time before going to bed. If there were still no answer, she would assume Walker had turned up unexpectedly and whisked Skye off for a romantic dinner, and would ring in the morning.

***

Skye stretched her cramped body and winced with pain as the blood flowed into her stiff limbs. Shivering, she rubbed life back into her cramped leg muscles. She placed a hand on the washbasin to steady herself then slowly got to her feet. Every movement was an effort, and if she turned her head too quickly, the room spun. She felt physically sick and her teeth chattered from the cold.

Instinct told her she needed to get warm. She ran a hot bath and started to undress, but her fingers were so numb, that she found it impossible to undo the buttons of her shirt. With a moan, she yanked it over her head. She peeled off the rest of her clothes then stepped into the steaming tub. Submerging herself in the hot water, she closed her eyes and tried to relax as the warmth seeped back into her chilled and aching bones. The shuddering slowed, and then ceased.

Some twenty minutes later, wrapped in her bathrobe, she padded into the kitchen to make a hot drink. Although she felt warmer, less seismic, and reasonably human, her head throbbed horribly, but the feeling of nausea had passed. It was dark outside, and in her confused state, she assumed it was early evening. When she switched on the radio on top of the microwave to listen to the news channel, she was astonished to hear that it was three-twenty a.m. She'd been out cold for the best part of twelve hours.

Leaning against the worktop, she sipped her scalding tea. Her mind was a total blank and the more she tried to force the memory, the more frustrated she became. She rubbed her aching temples. She had a vague recollection of talking to Debbie, but the details of their conversation remained a mystery. She remembered waiting for Walker to call, but nothing else until she had woken up on the bathroom floor. Perhaps when her headache had gone, her memory would return.

Turning off the lights as she went, Skye stumbled towards the bedroom. Completely drained and exhausted, she swallowed two painkillers then slipped under the soft quilt. As soon as her head touched the pillow, she fell into a deep, dreamless sleep.

**

Over on the mainland, Walker felt under pressure. His reputation as a hard hitter in the world of environmental issues was fast going down the toilet. Until he replaced the damaged equipment, his company was effectively out of business. When he wasn't fending off phone calls from prospective clients, he was over at the labs trying to sort out the chaos.

The break-ins weren't the only thing on his mind. He'd failed to contact Skye, but had no choice other than to put his personal life on hold. Ironically, there was nothing new in that. In the past, his date either accepted his sudden departure or moved on. Either way, he wouldn't have been too concerned. This time he was.

Whatever happened, he needed to return to Friday Harbor before Skye's vacation ended. He couldn't allow her to fly out of the country and out of his life without so much as a simple 'goodbye.' It would serve him right if she slammed the door in his face. He deserved it for being a complete and utter fool.

In a rare moment of solitude, he thought about ways to apologize. Perhaps he should send her flowers, or he could make a reservation for dinner at the *Duck Soup Inn*. She would surely enjoy its old world charm. Alternatively, he could fly her over to Seattle, and they could drive to one of the lodges at Snoqualmie Falls in the foothills of the Cascade Mountains. The scenery would be spectacular at this time of year. Yeah, that's what he'd do. He'd reserve a suite at the *Salish Lodge*, and hope that dramatic mountain scenery, stunning waterfall, and the romantic and elegant lodge would get their relationship back on track.

His decision made, he turned his attention back to his problems. Thankfully, there were no more reports of dead fish washing up on the island beaches. Yesterday, he had assigned two members of staff to catalogue all the undamaged slides, a task that would take them the best part of a week. Only then, he would know if the evidence he had collected had been stolen.

Not content with breaking-in, the thieves had trawled through the computer system, opening and closing files until they located the information they wanted. Rather than deleting every file, they had infected the system with a malicious virus, which slowly ate its way through the tattered network.

He met with one of the University of Washington's top IT experts hoping to salvage something from the hard drives. Half an hour into the meeting, he knew he was wasting his time. Cyber crime, the bespectacled geek informed him, was a huge problem, targeting not only conventional businesses, but also the newer E-commerce or dot.com businesses too. Walker listened to a detailed explanation of the issues involved and knew that finding a solution was going to be difficult. When terms such as 'viruses,' 'worms,' and 'Trojan horses' were mentioned Walker frowned. As far as he was concerned, a virus was something he caught, and worms lived in soil.

Before any software could be developed to eradicate a virus it first had to be identified, then an understanding of how it spread from one program to another or from file-to-file had to be gained. When the geek started discussing 'exploits,' 'script kiddies,' and 'spoofs', Walker's eyes rolled back in his head. One thing he did understand was that the Internet was a perfect hiding place for anyone with malicious intent.

As he reached the door, Walker turned and asked one last question. "By any chance have you of heard of a software developer called Ridge? I don't know his first name."

"The name is familiar; let me think." The computer expert adjusted his glasses, and tapped his temple. "I remember now, I attended a seminar last year. The guest speaker was James or John Ridge. Arrogant and outspoken... that's him. He made all sorts of claims about his abilities and the software he was developing, whether he can back them up, remains to be seen. Sounded like a load of hogwash to me."

Walker felt as if all his Christmases had come at once. "That's great. Do you know how I can contact him?"

"Sorry, no. These software developers are all the same. They keep very much to themselves. He's English on top of it all, and they're against sharing information at the best of times—no team spirit. I suppose you could try the organizer of the seminar, but I don't recall who that was, I'm afraid."

Frustrated, Walker felt as if everyone was conspiring against him. Other than the out of date article in the magazine, he'd found little information about Ridge. What was it with the guy? Why couldn't he be listed in the phone book like normal people? But then, if he about to make millions of dollars from writing software that could potentially put an end to computer crime, he wouldn't want to be listed in the phone book either. Come to think of it, he'd hire a bodyguard because if Ridge's name weren't on a hit list already it sure would be when the software became available.

Back in his office, Walker paced the floor. Walker Environmental Research would re-open for business in two days and about time too. It would entail a major public relations campaign and a lot of effort on his part to restore faith in his abilities.

There was no real reason for him to remain in Seattle, but he decided against returning to the lodge that evening.

He would check in with McCabe in the morning to make sure there were no new developments, and then fly back to Friday Harbor in the afternoon. Then he would call Skye.

CHAPTER FIFTEEN

When Debbie reached her office the following morning, she phoned Skye. As she listened to the phone ring out, the nagging fear in the back of her mind refused to be stilled.

"Damn it, Skye. Pick up the damned phone!"

This was so out of character, even for Skye. A cold shiver ran down Debbie's spine. What if Skye had gone for a walk and fallen, or suddenly taken ill? She could be lying somewhere for days before anyone found her.

She nursed a cold latte and thought about what to do next. Abruptly the phone on her desk rang. She snatched it up.

"Skye, is that you?"

"Sorry to disappoint you Debbie, but it's me, John."

"Oh John, hi. How are you? It must be the early hours of the morning in London. What are you doing up this late?"

"I'm okay. Over-worked, under paid—you know how it is when a work colleague goes off on an extended vacation. What's this about Skye?"

"I'm glad you've called. I'm worried about Skye and was thinking about emailing you. I haven't been able to reach her since yesterday afternoon. I don't know if she's had an accident, she's sick or what. Did you know the cabin she's rented is way out in the boonies and her nearest neighbor is miles away?"

"Hey, stop worrying. She probably went out for the evening and forgot about your arrangement. I'm sure nothing is wrong."

"John, I called every hour up to midnight and then again this morning. There's still no reply. Don't you think that's odd?"

"It's not like her to say one thing and do another. I still don't think it's a reason to call out the National Guard. Have you two argued, by any chance?"

"We did have a misunderstanding, but we've made up since then. In fact, we had a long chat yesterday about… about men and stuff. She finally agreed to talk about what happened with Michael. But now that I can't reach her, I'm seriously scared."

"I'm sure there's a simple explanation. Give her some space. You know how uptight she gets when you mention Michael's name. If there's one thing I've learned over the last twelve months it's not to push her on this. If you do, she'll close up tighter than a duck's arse. She'll talk when she's good and ready and not before. Stop panicking."

"I hope you're right. I have a strange feeling that everything is not as it should be. Do you think she could have gone to Bremerton?"

"What, back to that naval base? There is no way she would go there. Besides, Michael will have been redeployed by now. I'm sure she said something about him waiting for orders before she flew out last year."

"You're right, it's a stupid thought. I'll wait another twenty-four hours, but if I haven't heard from her by then, I'm flying up there." Then she realized that John must have his own reason for calling. "So what's with the call? Don't tell me you're reneging on our long-overdue date yet again."

John laughed heartily. "You've rumbled me." Ever since her first visit to England, Debbie had tried to persuade him to have dinner with her. So far, he'd managed to wriggle out of it. "Actually, I was ringing to ask you for the number of the cabin as Skye's not replied to my email. There is a problem with our latest project, and I need her to check something for me."

"You don't expect her to work while on vacation, surely. I'm scared to death for the girl, but you realize she'll hang me out to dry if I give you the number, don't you?"

"Under the circumstances, I don't think she'll object. And it means we can both try phoning."

"You're right, as usual. Okay, here it is, but you have to do me a favor."

"Sure—"

"If you speak to her before me, be a sweetie and tell her you used your considerable charm to persuade me to hand it over. That way, she can take her temper out on you rather than me."

"Thanks at lot." John laughed. "I'll be sure to tell her."

John replaced the handset on its cradle. He leaned back in his chair and put his feet up on the desk. Now that he thought about it, Skye had been in an odd mood of late. He'd just begun to believe she'd got Michael out of her system when she announced she was flying to Seattle. As if that wasn't bad enough, she'd chosen to take a vacation at the precise moment their project was about to go live.

It would have made more sense if she had chosen another destination. However, she was adamant she wanted to visit the San Juan Islands. He didn't buy the lame excuse that she couldn't put the past behind her until she'd been back to the Pacific Northwest. That was total bullshit. He should have persuaded her to stay at home, rather than agreeing to her traveling halfway round the world on a whim. At least he could have kept an eye on her.

It was almost a year since she had phoned from Heathrow and asked him to pick her up. He would never forget the sight that greeted him that chilly May morning. Sat on her suitcase outside the terminal building, Skye was waiting for him as he pulled up at the curb. He was shocked by her appearance, for the happy, smiling young woman he'd left there a mere three weeks earlier had vanished, to be replaced by a gaunt, disheveled woman with dark circles under her eyes. Wild eye and quivering, she looked awful, John recalled, and when he placed his arm around her shoulders, she had shrunk away from his touch.

Skye had sat hunched in the passenger seat and not said a word. It was as if her mind had shut out everything, except the basic instinct of survival. When he parked outside his house rather than hers, she made no comment. He'd half-carried her into the kitchen and made her a pot of tea, while she sat slumped in the chair, staring at the wall. Later, when he suggested she go and rest, she had not argued, but like a small child, had allowed him to lead her to the spare room, undress her and put her to bed.

Skye stayed in her room for two days, and ate nothing more than toast. When he arrived home from work on the third day she had gone. He drove like a lunatic to her house, where he found her in the garden acting as if nothing was wrong. It was as if her vacation had never taken place, for she never mentioned it. Not once.

A muscle quivered at his jaw. Could Debbie be right? Could Skye have gone to Bremerton?

He would phone the cabin and keep doing so until Skye answered. He didn't care whether she was happy to hear his voice or not. Her safety and wellbeing were all that mattered to him.

***

Oblivious to the commotion she had stirred up on both sides of the Atlantic, Skye ate a late breakfast. Although tired, her headache had eased to a dull ache, and a couple of painkillers would finish it off. The cabin felt stuffy and claustrophobic, but she lacked the energy for a long walk. As it was warm and sunny, she carried her book and the rug from the couch, and threw open the French windows leading to the deck. She sat down in a wicker chair, placed the rug over her knees, and settled down to read.

The woods were alive with chattering birds, their song mingling with the sound of the waves gently washing upon the shore. It wasn't long before she felt drowsy. Her book slipped out of her hands and onto her knee as she fell asleep.

A small fishing boat chugged into the cove and dropped anchor. The men on board were paid well for their work. Their only concern was disposing of their cargo. They had chosen the cove because the water under the hull of their vessel was deep enough for their purpose, not that it mattered to them.

But it should have done.

A simple miscalculation in navigation meant that they were dumping their deadly cargo in far shallower water than intended. Already the contents of the first container were seeping into the sea. If they had kept watch on the cabin, they would have noticed a woman taking a keen interest in their activities.

Skye jolted upright in her chair and watched two men roll something off the deck. She was too far away to see exactly what splashed into the water, or the name of the vessel painted on the bow. Abruptly, the engine pitch changed as the vessel pulled anchor and sailed out of the cove. She dismissed the incident as nothing important, but made a mental note to mention it to Walker if, and when, he called.

She picked up her book and started reading. She reached the end of the chapter, just as the phone rang. Positive it would be Walker, she hurried inside to answer it.

"Hello."

"Hi there, Sweet Pea. Enjoying your vacation?"

"John! How did you get this number? Why are you calling? Is everything okay?" she asked, breathless.

John thought carefully before replying. He had no wish to frighten her. "I should be asking you those questions. Do you know how worried Debbie and I have been? We've been trying to reach you for the last thirty-six hours. Are you okay?"

"Sorry. I had a bad migraine and crashed out. I can't have heard the phone. I'll call Debbie later and put her mind at rest."

"Well, make sure you do. She's all set to call out the Washington State Militia if there is one or worse, fly up there to check on you personally."

Skye groaned. "I'll ring her as soon as we finish talking, promise. Why are you ringing?"

"I wouldn't bother you unless it was important. I asked Debbie for this number, as you weren't picking up your email. So don't chew her out, it's not her fault."

"All right, but that doesn't answer my question."

"There's a problem with the software. It worked fine for a while then failed. There's no problem with the hardware. I've checked for viruses and the like, and we're clean. There must be a bug in the code, but I can't find anything wrong. Would you look to see if I have missed anything obvious? And don't tell me you can't because I know you have your laptop with you."

"I'll do it, but you'll owe me."

"I knew there'd be a catch."

"If I locate the problem, I'll add two days to my vacation for every day it takes me. Otherwise, my laptop stays in its case and you'll have to wait till I get back."

"Just remember, we're scheduled to give the presentation three weeks after you arrive home. It doesn't leave us much leeway to sort out the gremlins, and complete the testing."

"I haven't forgotten. Oh, and as I'm going to be working you can call Debbie and tell her that under no circumstances is she to fly up here and disturb me."

John groaned. "You drive a hard bargain. Do I have to call Debbie? You know she only wants me for my body."

Skye laughed. "Yes you do."

"Okay, I'll call her."

"Email me the details and I'll contact you as soon as I find anything. Talk to you soon, bye."

Damn it! The last thing she wanted was Debbie mounting a search and rescue party. Well, Debbie would have to wait—she would phone her once she and John had sorted out their technical problems.

CHAPTER SIXTEEN

Skye set up her high-spec laptop, and then put the kettle on to boil. Guilt gnawed at her for not keeping in touch with John. After all, they had a lot riding on this project, and not only in terms of financial reward. If successful, their company would rank amongst the top twenty software development houses, and that was something they'd been aiming for.

Walker still hadn't phoned. In spite of everything she felt for him, in the end he was no different from any other man, for whom picking up a phone to call a woman friend presented a major challenge. Why should she put herself out? Her days of waiting around were over. She had more important things on her mind now. Finding a reason for Walker's continued absence wasn't one of them.

Setting her coffee mug down next to her notebook and pen, she downloaded her email. Sure enough, there was an encrypted message from John. Very early on in their careers, they realized that sending information openly over the Internet was risky, and one of the first programs they developed encrypted data. By hitting a specific key on her laptop the contents of the email unscrambled in seconds.

Armed with only John's vague estimation of where the problem lay, Skye inserted the first of five CD-ROMs into her laptop and opened an obscurely named file. Examining each string of code was time-consuming work, and by midnight, she had found no errors. Briefly, she considered working through the night, but the dull ache in her temples threatened to develop into another migraine, she shut down her laptop. She locked the doors, then turned out the lights and went to bed.

By mid morning, Skye still hadn't found the problem. Perhaps the cool sea breeze and a stroll along the beach would clear her mind. She pulled on her Aran sweater and locked the door. The sun had come out, and she stood for a moment, feeling its warmth on her face. A gull's cry startled her, and she watched the bird drift out to sea on a current of air. In the distance, Lopez Island and the mountains beyond glittered in the sunlight. Turning, she half expected to see Walker emerging from the woods as he had done on that first day, but the only movement came from the trees as they swayed gently in the breeze.

She sauntered along the beach and wrinkled her nose in disgust. The air was full of a strange odor. It was as if something had crawled out of the sea and died. She gagged and coughed, and tried to clear her head of the awful stench.

Picking her way over the pebbles, she paused to examine a large tangled mass of seaweed. Kicking it with the toe of her boot, she jumped back in disgust when she found several fish in among the fronds, their bodies bloated out of all proportion.

Her stomach heaved in revulsion. She spun round and ran back to the cabin, and drank a glass of water in an attempt to remove foul smell from her senses. She leaned against the sink and thought hard. What had caused the fish to die and why had they washed up now? She would have to report this, but to whom? The Parks Department? Or maybe the Coast Guard? Their business was ships and people lost at sea, not dead fish rotting on a beach.

The US Government had a department for every conceivable contingency, and it was just a case of picking the right one. She studied the phone book for several minutes until she came across a listing for the Department of Wildlife and Fisheries and dialed the number.

Half a dozen transfers later, a helpful man took down the details and assured her that he would send someone to collect the fish. In the meantime, could she remove at least one of the carcasses to a safer position to prevent the sea carrying it out on the next tide? Her stomach swirled at the thought, but said she would try.

Armed with the largest bucket she could find, a broom, a pair of rubber gloves, and a clothes peg for her nose, she stomped down the beach. If anyone could see her now, they would think she'd gone over the far edge of the deep end. As she approached the offending fish, she yanked on the gloves and put the peg on her nose. She struggled to get her bucket under one of the fish, but couldn't scoop in the smelly, slimy carcass. Five attempts later, she swept the head and part of the body into the bucket only to see it slide out again when she lifted it.

Dab, Dab, Dab! She swore, the clothes peg hobbling her consonants. She needed a net or a boat hook, but as she had neither, she would have to improvise. She tramped back to the cabin. After a thorough search, she was about to give up. This wasn't her problem. She was only the tenant for goodness sake. Let whoever the State Department sent deal with it. Then she spotted the coat hanger on the back of the door.

She cut a length of string off the reel she found in a drawer. By tying the coat hanger to the head of the broom, she managed to fashion a hook of sorts, although it looked like something Heath Robinson would have dreamed up. If she could insert the hook into the gills of the fish, then she would be able to drag it up the beach onto the grass.

Twenty minutes later, sweating from the effort and with her arms aching from the strain of dragging a fish that weighed at least fifteen pounds, she maneuvered it onto the grass. It stank, even with the peg on her nose. She tried not to look too closely at the staring eyes and grossly bloated body as she covered it with a piece of sacking she'd found in the garage earlier.

After scrubbing her hands in the hottest water she could bear, she went back to work. She had scrutinized this particular string of code for over three hours, and not found any errors. Such were the jumble of letters and symbols, that it appeared as if some eight-legged creature had walked over the keyboard randomly striking the keys, but to Skye it all made perfect sense. Her intuition told her the fault lie somewhere in this section of nonsensical appearing code.

She rubbed her tired eyes and wandered around the cabin to ease the stiffness in her limbs. She needed a sugar fix. She opened the refrigerator door, peered inside, and took out the butter, and cheese. A few minutes later, she carried her sandwich and mug of coffee back to the table. If she hadn't found the error by the time she finished lunch, she'd re-write each command line by line and see if that solved the problem.

Her sandwich half eaten and her coffee solidifying in the mug, Skye's concentration was so intense that the sound of a vehicle pulling into the driveway made her jump. Careful to ensure that the screen of her laptop wasn't visible, she opened the door. A burly young man stood in the doorway and parked behind him on the driveway, was a green truck with the Department of Wildlife and Fisheries insignia on the door.

"I'm guessing you're here for the fish."

"That's right." He flashed his ID badge at her to prove it.

"It's down on the grass under a sack. I dragged it above the high water mark as your colleague requested, but there are more fish down on the beach."

"That's okay, I'll retrieve them. You didn't touch it with your bare hands, did you?"

"No, I wore gloves. And I haven't checked the rest of the cove, so there may be others."

"I'll scout around once I've bagged the ones you found."

Skye cringed at the thought of another stench-filled excursion. "Do you want me to come with you?"

"There's no need. I can mange."

"Good, because it smells to high heaven down there. I'll leave you to it then."

She watched him walk to the end of the dock and look around before retrieving a pair of waders and a net from the back of his pickup. It was amazing, she thought, how he could withstand the odor that had nearly made her vomit. A short time later, he dragged half a dozen fish from under the dock and proceeded to bag and label them. He then carried them up the beach and placed them with the others in his truck.

Moments later the official knocked at her door.

"Sorry to trouble you again, ma'am, but I've a few questions."

"You'd better come in." Skye stepped aside to let him enter.

"Has anything like this happened before?"

"I wouldn't know. I'm only renting the cabin. Is this a common occurrence?"

"Not really. Most salmon die of natural causes. We occasionally find some that are contaminated. Have you seen anyone acting suspiciously? Have there been any strange vessels in the cove or vehicles using the track?"

Skye thought of Walker, who had been in the cove when she first arrived. While the man could be infuriating, he was far too knowledgeable about the island and its wildlife to want to destroy it.

"No, I haven't, but then I'm often out."

"Okay, just thought I'd ask. If you find any more fish, call the office and we'll send someone over. Here's my card."

"I will." Skye examined the card. There was no name, just the departmental information, and a number.

Skye closed the door and sat down at the table. Resting her head in her left hand, she thought about Walker. Could he really be involved in anything illegal, she wondered.

He'd certainly had a habit of disappearing and re-appearing without warning. Smuggling was rife in this part of the States, or so she'd read. Perhaps Walker was involved in a smuggling racket and used the cove to bring his illegal haul ashore. He'd been quick to suggest he move into the cabin as their relationship became more intimate. Was that so he could keep an eye on her?

She bent her head and studied her hands. It was a stupid idea. Like most people, Walker had to earn a living. He drove a relatively new truck and had an expensive looking cruiser. There was nothing unusual about that. Most of the inhabitants on the island owned both a car and a boat, so why should Walker be any different.

It was none of her business, and besides, she had better things to do than sit there all day allowing her imagination run riot.

By ten that night, her concentration had evaporated. When she looked at the screen, the code merged into a single blurry mass. She pressed save and rubbed her eyes, and then shut down her laptop.

CHAPTER SEVENTEEN

Walker grabbed his bag from the apartment and drove out to Elliot Bay where he kept his seaplane. It had been a grueling week. Now that his company was running at full speed, he could give all his attention to the investigation. This time, there were no delays in take off and soon he was on final approach to Friday Harbor.

He rubbed his hand across the stubble on his chin and decided to shower and shave before making his apologies to Skye. However, it was one conversation he wasn't looking forward to.

McCabe's call came through as he drove out of town.

"Say again, Joe. You're breaking up. There's too much static."

Joe's voice crackled over the line. "Fish… washed up… island… cabin… north of… Harbor… off… road."

"Joe, can hear me? I can't make out what you're saying. Hold on while I pull over." Walker stopped his truck on the side of the road. "Okay, run that by me again."

"The department took a couple of calls from home owners on the island. Both found dead fish, either washed up on the shore or floating in the water. The local office sent a guy out. He bagged and tagged the carcasses and took them away for analysis."

Walker groaned and ran a hand through his hair. "Where are they now?"

"At the University Laboratories. One of their marine biologists is doing the autopsies. Can you go take a look?"

"Sure. I assume they have all the details."

"Yeah, it's all waiting for you. How soon do you think you can be there?"

"About twenty minutes, I was just on my way to the lodge."

"Let me know what you find."

"I'll be in touch."

These days he felt like a badly operated puppet, string tangling into string. He turned his truck around and drove back to town. Twenty-five minutes later, he showed his ID to the security guard on the gate and drove into the Laboratory Campus of the University of Washington.

The campus covered a four hundred and eighty-four acre tract of land overlooking one of the many bays on San Juan Island. It was a marine biologist's dream. There were ten research and teaching labs, all equipped to an exceptionally high standard. The University also owned a number of biological preserves around the island, where scientists undertook research in controlled environments.

He parked next to the cafeteria and followed the path down to a group of low buildings housing the main laboratories. The short, balding biologist was in the process of peeling off his gloves when Walker entered the lab. From the look on his face, what he'd found wasn't good news.

"Mr. Walker?"

"Yeah, that's me."

"Mr. McCabe said to expect you. I've completed the autopsies on the fish that came in yesterday. The two from Rocky Bay appear to have died from natural causes, although I can't be certain until I have the results of the biopsies. However, the ones from the location off Roche Harbor Road were definitely contaminated—"

"—with a high concentration of PCBs?" said Walker.

"That's right. How did you know?"

"Call it an educated guess. Can you let me have a detailed analysis of the chemicals involved? I want to make a comparison with the fish I discovered earlier to see if they're identical."

"Sure. My secretary is typing up my report now."

"Thanks. Just one more thing—do you have the exact location where the fish were found?"

"It's all in my report. You can collect a copy on your way out."

"Thanks."

Walker sat in his truck and opened the brown folder the secretary had given him. While he couldn't be sure until he checked his notes, he had a feeling that the composition of the chemicals was the same as those in the fish he'd found. He shoved the papers back in the envelope. He would read the rest of the report once back at the lodge and then visit the two sites, before contacting McCabe and telling him the news.

An hour or so later, his suspicions were confirmed. Crossing his study to a bookcase on the far wall, he selected a map of San Juan Island and studied it carefully. Any chemicals dumped at sea would be dispersed by the action of the waves and tide, and affect fish in a wide area.

The islands of the San Juan archipelago were rocky and rimmed by precipitous shores, with the occasional deeply cut fjord-like inlet. Therefore, whoever was dumping the chemicals not only had access to a small vessel, such as a fishing boat, but also knew the waters around the islands.

Walker shuffled through the papers on his desk searching for the report. Halfway down the first page he found the address of the homeowner in Rocky Bay, and on the second, the address of the property off Roche Harbor Road. The color drained from his face.

The second address was that of his cabin.

He grabbed his coat off the stand in the hall and dashed out the door.

***

Skye had been up since five breaking down the strings of computer code into single commands and was now a third of the way through the program. So far, it registered every piece of legitimate information sent and received over the Internet from her laptop. She needed to test the software against unauthorized access from a hostile computer and for that she required John's help.

She divided the screen into two separate windows and connected to the Internet. She sat back and waited. If the software John was using in London infiltrated her laptop, a warning message would pop up on her screen giving the IP address of the rogue computer. Nothing happened. At last, she had found the error. Now all she had to do was re-write the section of code, integrate it back into the program, and test it. Another couple of days, then she could enjoy what remained of her vacation.

The front door of the cabin burst open and Walker crossed the floor in a few quick strides. He yanked Skye to her feet.

"Are you okay?"

Skye's heart pounded in her chest. Anger shot through her. "Haven't you heard of knocking? You scared the living daylights out of me."

His voice was rough with anxiety. "I'm serious. Are you okay?"

"Why shouldn't I be? What the hell's the matter with you, Walker?"

He took a steadying breath and released her. "I heard about the incident with the fish and was worried about you."

"And that was enough for you to nearly take the door off its hinge? It was only a few fish. They stank to high heaven. I didn't even touch them."

He attempted to play down his overreaction. "It can't have been a pleasant experience."

"It wasn't. But it doesn't explain why you came storming in here as if your tail was on fire."

He faked boyish grin. "Aren't you pleased to see me?"

"A phone call would have been appreciated. Or don't you have phones in Seattle?"

He rubbed the back of his neck. "If you offer me a cup of coffee, I'll explain. You can hate me if you like."

Skye looked at him suspiciously before returning his smile with a shake of her head. "A cup of coffee? And I'm allowed to hate you as well? Seems fair. I'll put the kettle on."

Before she could move, Walker pulled her into his arms and kissed her long and hard. All her anger shattered into a million pieces and she returned his kiss. When he turned her loose her heart hammered in her ears. She cleared her throat and tried to regain control of her wayward emotions.

"Coffee... right... hatred..."

She escaped to the safety of the kitchen. The man was downright dangerous, what with his devastating grin and lethal kisses.

"Apart from finding a pile of rotting fish on the beach, what else have you been up to while I've been away?"

"Nothing very exciting. Reading, walking, and watching the tide come in and go out."

"What's this?" He picked up the notepad from next to her laptop and scanned the page.

Skye handed him a cup, then snatched the pad from his hand. "Just something I've been working on. Nothing that would interest you."

"Thanks." He took the cup from her hand. "What makes you think I wouldn't be interested?" He nudged the mouse next to her laptop. The computer screen sprang to life, and he stared at the jumble of symbols and letters. He glared at Skye.

"Skye, I may not be a computer geek, but I can recognize computer code. You're involved aren't you?" He slammed his cup down on the table, spilling some of the contents, and caught hold of her arm.

"Involved?" Skye gasped. "Involved in what? It's what I do for a living, I'm a software developer."

"Oh yeah, and I fell off the proverbial turnip truck yesterday! I knew your turning up here was more than a coincidence. Your big blue eyes don't fool me anymore, honey." He squeezed Skye's wrist. There was a bitter edge of cynicism in his voice. "I'll get the truth out of you sooner or later, so you might as well admit it."

"Admit what?" Struggling free, she seethed with mounting rage. "I have no idea what you're talking about. I'm on vacation, you know that."

"Do I? You've told me very little about yourself. My gut tells me you're involved up to your sweet little neck."

Skye shook her head and nervously moistened her dry lips. "You disappear for days, and then storm in here without so much as a word of warning. Now you're accusing me of—just what are you accusing me of?" Skye demanded in a shrill voice.

"You've been hacking into my company's computer system, destroying files in an attempt to discredit me and my business."

Skye would have laughed aloud if she weren't so angry. The steely glint in Walker's eyes, warned her that he was serious. She turned her back on him and went to stand by the fireplace while she gathered her thoughts.

"You're being cruel, presumptive and preposterous! I don't even know what you do."

"I'm an environmental and marine biologist." He crossed the room and stopped inches from her.

Acutely conscious of his tall frame looming over her, Skye tilted her head and stared into his eyes. "Why would I want to hack into your computer?"

"To find out how close I am to discovering who's responsible for dumping chemicals offshore."

She threw up her hands in disgust. "What? You're being ludicrous. And you're forgetting one important detail—I don't live in America!"

"No, but you can hack into a computer from anywhere in the world."

"True, but that's not the issue here."

"What is?"

"The truth and… trust? This is my first visit to the San Juan Islands. I don't know anyone here apart from you, so how could I be involved in anything illegal?"

"You might not be directly involved," Walker countered, "but someone could have hired you and sent you over here. You're a beautiful woman. They probably reckoned you would attract my attention and that sooner or later you would find your way into my bed."

The lascivious glint in Walker's eyes sickened her. Her hand shot out and she slapped his face.

"How dare you!" she said, shaking with anger. "How dare you think such a thing of me?"

Walker's face stung from the blow. "Oh, I dare, especially when my business and reputation are at stake." He clamped both her arms to her sides in case she tried to hit him again.

"I don't know anything about any chemicals or illegal dumping. Besides, I can prove what I say is true."

Walker's lips twisted into a cynical smile. "Yeah? And just how do you propose to do that?"

"My business partner will confirm everything I've said."

He relaxed his hold on her arms. Skye stepped back, putting a little distance between them.

Walker shook his head. "He's probably in on it too. Why should I believe him anymore than I believe you?"

Skye's body sagged in defeat. Although John could confirm everything she had said, there was no reason why Walker should accept it as the truth.

"You obviously won't listen to reason, so just get the hell out of my sight."

"Sorry, but I'm staying here twenty-four/seven until you tell me the truth or your friends with the nasty habits turn up."

"Now look here," Skye yelled. "You can't just waltz in here and accuse me of some hideous crime and ride roughshod over me. I have rights!" She glanced at the phone and weighed up her chances of reaching it. "If you'd be reasonable and listen to what I say, I'm sure we could clear this up," she continued. She softened her tone in the hope that he wouldn't notice she was edging her way towards the phone.

Walker ran a hand through his hair. Skye was a world-class liar; he'd give her that. She may be beautiful, even passionate in bed, but the woman standing in front of him was five foot five inches of seething anger and he didn't trust her at all.

"Call the realtor. She will have checked my credentials before I rented the cabin. Perhaps she can convince you that I'm an honest, law-abiding citizen."

If she could just distract Walker, she might be able to make a lunge for the phone. She tried to remain calm, but under her anger, all the old feelings of betrayal were flooding back. Fear glittered in her eyes. Walker didn't care about her. Her trust had sadly been misplaced, but this time she wasn't about to be used against her will.

Walker frowned, his eyes level under drawn brows. "The only thing the realtor is interested in is whether your credit card was good. Any more suggestions?"

"You stayed here for three days and three nights. If I'm involved, don't you think I would have pumped you for information?"

"Too obvious. Although I have to say the innocent act you put on, had me fooled for a while. Remember, that once you let the passion genie out of the bottle, it gets real hard to play the naïve lover. It's just a pity I left when I did, otherwise I might have got to enjoy your full repertoire."

"You bastard! Do you really think I'm the type of woman who uses her body to get something?" Skye spluttered, bristling with indignation.

"It's been my experience that some do," he replied.

"That says a lot for the type of person you are and the company you keep," Skye retorted. "I've never slept with a man just because I wanted something." She was through with trading insults, and wished with all her soul she were somewhere else.

"So you say." Deep down, he knew she was telling the truth, but wasn't about to apologize for his crassness. The look she gave him would curdle milk and rather than face her icy stare, he looked away.

Skye made a grab for the phone, but Walker had the reflexes of a boxer. Before she could punch in nine-one-one, a strong hand circled her wrist and removed the instrument from her hand.

"That was a real stupid move, Skye."

"Let go of me." She shook with rage and fear.

"So you can call your buddies? No chance."

"I wasn't calling 'my buddies' as you put it. I was calling the police. Let them sort this out. I promise to leave as soon as they've been. You can even put me on the plane to London yourself."

"I'm staying right here, whether you like it or not. Flashing your big blue eyes won't work. Either, tell me who's behind this, or shut up!"

"How many more times do I have to say it? I'm working on a project that's due to be presented to the Gov... to clients in a few weeks' time." If only she was in a position to reveal who her client was then he might believe her. "At least let me switch off my laptop."

Walker's voice hardened. "Okay, but then give it to me."

"Since you're determined to impose your presence on me, I'll fetch some blankets and a pillow. You can sleep on the couch."

"No need. I'll share your bed." He looked at her with a sardonic expression that sent her temper soaring.

"Now wait a minute. If you think—"

Walker frowned in exasperation. "I've had about as much as I can take, Skye. My patience is wearing thin. The subject is not open for discussion. If you know what's good for you, you'll—"

"I'll what? Behave like the whore you obviously think I am, no way. I'd rather sleep on the floor than share a bed with a bastard like you!"

"Whatever. It doesn't change a thing. Unless you want me to toss your laptop into the sea, why don't you shut it down and hand it over?"

Skye looked away swiftly. She could feel his sharp eyes boring into her as she saved her work, and switched off her laptop. It was futile trying to reason with him. For the time being at least, she had little choice but to accept his presence in the cabin. She could only hope that she could find a way to prove her innocence or someone came looking for her. Then she would be free of this frightening sham of a relationship.

CHAPTER EIGHTEEN

Skye stared out of the window at the ever-darkening sky and mulled over the events of the evening. Deep down, she seethed with anger. How Walker could believe she was involved in anything as abhorrent as illegal dumping, was beyond her comprehension. The only plausible explanation she could come up with was the man must be temporarily insane.

Two deep lines of worry creased her brow. Logic must prevail. It was what she was known for. She could understand how he might assume she was guilty of hacking into his computer, but how had he reached the conclusion that there was a connection between her and the dumping of chemical waste?

He was being downright pig-headed and insufferable, not to mention stubborn, mean, and judgmental. If only she could penetrate the deliberate blankness present in his eyes, then she would offer to secure his computer system.

As it was, he could toast evenly over a spit in hell before she would lift a finger to help him.

A wave of apprehension swept through her. He was much stronger than she was and there was no telling what he might do while he was in this black mood. It was vital she remain calm and avoid riling him. She had to find away to reach him, to make him listen, and then convince him she was innocent.

Walker sat in the armchair next to the fireplace reading a book. Skye stole a glace at his face. His emotions didn't turn on a dime; they turned on pennies, nickels and quarters, as well. One moment, he was hot and accusing, the next he was just sitting! He should be out there trying to catch whoever was responsible rather than blaming her for this environmental disaster.

Her eyes darted round the room in frustration. She flopped down onto the couch, picked up a magazine, and flicked through the pages, only to put it down again when it failed to catch her interest. She tried reading her book, but the words on the page distorted before her eyes. She was in no mood to watch television.

She walked over to the window. The scenery hadn't changed. Walker's stony silence was getting to her. She felt hemmed in and wasn't sure how much more she could take before panic and hysteria set in. Too restless to sit and do nothing, she needed a vent for her nervousness and all her pent up feelings.

"Skye, sit down," Walker growled. "You're getting on my nerves wandering around the room all the time."

"I can't. You've got me caged up like... like some circus animal."

Walker's eyes darkened dangerously. "For God's sake! Do you think I'm enjoying this any more than you are?"

Skye glared at him, the tension between them increasing with frightening intensity.

"You're the one keeping me here against my will. You've already acted as judge and jury and found me guilty of some hideous crime. Well, let me tell you this, Mr. High and Mighty Walker, you're wrong. When the police come looking for me, you're the one who's going to have some explaining to do, not me."

Walker held her gaze. He didn't like what he saw there anymore than he liked the tone of her voice.

"I'll be real pleased to see the cops. I'll even watch while they haul you away. Computer hacking is a federal crime in this country, and we don't look too kindly on people who dump chemical waste either. You'd better get used to being locked up, because you'll be spending time in a place a great deal smaller and less attractive than this cabin."

"You're impossible! You know, I give up. Arguing is getting us nowhere. I'm going to have a bath. And I don't need a chaperone!"

Walker crossed the room with two quick strides and stood face to face with Skye. He tipped her chin with a finger and looked down into her eyes.

"Oh, darlin', and here's me thinking you were issuing an invitation."

Skye clamped her jaw shut and slapped him hard across the face for the second time that day. Turning on her heels, she stormed into the bedroom, slamming the door so hard that the windows rattled.

She climbed into the hot water and tried to relax. Her only chance of escaping lay with John. He would want to know whether she had solved the problem with the software, and ring her. When he made contact, she would scream bloody blue murder until Walker listened to him. If she failed to answer the phone, then perhaps John would contact the authorities and let them know something was wrong.

When the police or CIA or whoever knocked at the door, Walker would have no choice but to listen. With luck, he would be arrested. When that happened, she would sit back and enjoy every minute of his embarrassment.

How could she have been so stupid to relax her guard, when all her instincts told her not trust a man, especially one she had only just met? She had believed Walker to be honorable. That he wasn't the type of man to use a woman, and that he actually cared about her. How wrong she'd been.

One thing was certain—there was no way she was going to allow him to bully or blackmail her into doing something against her will, and vowed to fight him until he admitted he was wrong. Then she would walk away without a backward glance and with her head held high.

As she pulled on her dressing gown and brushed her teeth at the washbasin, she thought about her options. Walker couldn't watch her twenty-four hours a day. He had to sleep at some point, and that would be her chance to use the phone. The only other option was to try to make a run for it. It certainly wouldn't be easy, not when he guarded her like the Kohinoor diamond. She still had the keys to her rental car, something he had overlooked. However, he would hear the engine start, and was bound to come after her in his truck. He was taller than she was, so hitting him over the head with a heavy object was out of the question, although it might knock some sense into him.

Walker heard the water drain from the bath. He sat down and picked up his book, but paid no attention to the words on the page. For such a small thing, Skye had one hell of a temper. What if he was wrong and she was telling the truth? She had maintained her story throughout his questioning. If she really was a software developer, then he was going to look damned foolish, but it was a risk he would have to take.

Skye strolled into the room. Her cheeks flushed from her bath. She'd pinned her damp hair to the top of her head, exposing the alabaster expanse of her neck. Something primitive stirred deep within him. He didn't trust her, but he still wanted her, he realized. He tried to ignore the rush of emotion, but failed.

Barely glancing in Walker's direction, Skye slapped butter on two slices of bread and layered it with cheese. His voice cut through the air like a switchblade.

"If that's supper you're making, make enough for two. I haven't eaten all day."

"I am not your servant. If you're hungry you know where the refrigerator is, you can make your own damn sandwich."

Skye carried her plate and a glass of milk, and settled down on the couch as far away from Walker as possible. She took a bite of her sandwich. Although it was like chewing cardboard, she would choke rather than admit it. She picked up her glass, took a long swallow, and wondered what the prison sentence for murder would be, because if Walker didn't cut her some slack, she was sure to find out.

Walker watched her with frank amusement. She was madder than a rooster locked out of the henhouse. He wouldn't be surprised if she weren't thinking about ways to stick a knife in his back.

"Want some mayo on that?" Walker asked. "It might make it easier to chew."

Skye ignored him and took another bite. He suppressed a laugh. No wonder she was still single, he thought. It would take a strong man to handle her.

"You're going to regret this."

"You've said nothing to convince me you're not involved in this sorry mess. Unless you've got something new to tell me—"

"Such as?"

"Such as the name of your contact and who's responsible for dumping the chemicals."

Her faced paled with anger. "I don't know why I'm repeating myself, but I'm going to. I don't know what you're talking about."

"In that case, shut up and eat your supper."

"Bastard."

A satanic smile spread across his face. "I already know how you think of me."

"You make me sick."

"You can be as rude as you like. It won't make any difference. Now, I finish your milk like a good little girl and go to bed. I'll be along shortly to tuck you in."

"There is no way I'm sleeping in the same bed as you," Skye sputtered and slammed her plate and glass down in the sink.

"There's no need to yell, I'm not deaf."

Skye stopped midway to the bedroom. "No, just dumb."

She stared at the quilt covering the bed. Walker's lovemaking had been so tender that she could hardly believe he was the same hard stranger sitting in the next room. She dragged a blanket and a pillow from the top of the wardrobe.

"The bed's big enough for both of us."

Skye jumped. She spun round and glared at him with impassive coldness. "I'm not going to—"

"You've made your feelings abundantly clear, as have I."

Close to tears, she pressed both hands over her eyes. Weariness and despair engulfed her body. Arguing with the man who had gone from stranger to lover to stranger again was futile.

"How can I trust you, when you won't believe me?"

The sadness in her voice made Walker feel as if he'd been hit in the guts. The unwelcome tension between them stretched ever tighter until finally he let out a long, audible breath.

"Despite what you might think, I'm an honorable man. I give you my word. Now please, just get into bed."

Skye thought his attitude towards her was softening, but then he shattered the illusion.

"It's a pity you can't be as honest with me." He shrugged his shoulders, sat down on the side of the bed, and pulled off his shoes and socks.

Unable to tear her gaze from his profile, she watched him unbutton his shirt. When his hands went to the zipper on his jeans, she felt the blood rush to her face. His nearness evoked too many memories, and she suddenly felt weak and vulnerable in the face of his anger. She climbed into bed and buried her face in the pillow in case he saw the confusion in her eyes.

CHAPTER NINETEEN

Walker became aware of the sensuous woman sleeping in his arms. Nothing prepared him for the intimate picture they presented and for several minutes, he remained perfectly still, listening to the birds' early morning chorus.

He lay on his back, the crumpled sheet riding low on his hips. Skye's head rested on his shoulder. Her rich auburn hair fanned out on his chest like a silken veil. His left hand held the soft fullness of her breast through the thin fabric of her nightshirt, and her right leg rested intimately between his.

He tried to ignore the heat building inside him. How ironic, he thought, that their bodies gravitated towards each other as if it they were born to be lovers. Reluctantly, he lifted his hand from her breast and climbed out of bed. She moaned softly, but didn't stir. As he dressed, he listened to her rhythmic breathing, and wished his life hadn't completely collapsed in the space of day.

Skye woke some time later and found herself alone in the large bed. For a brief moment, she wondered if Walker had relented and returned to wherever he lived. She was congratulating herself on her newfound freedom, when she heard the sounds of his whistling outside the window.

Crestfallen, she sat on the bed and rested her head in her hands. At least he had kept his promise. She should be thankful for that, but the prospect of another day holed up in the cabin filled her with apprehension and dread.

Twenty minutes later, showered and dressed, and feeling less confident than she looked, Skye went in search of breakfast. She carried her mug of coffee and a muffin onto the deck.

Walker's rich voice cut through the air. "I see you finally managed to drag yourself out of bed. You've missed the best part of the morning."

Skye screwed her eyes up against the glare of the sun and shot him a twisted smile. "I think that depends on your point of view. The less time I spend in your company the better."

"So that's the way the wind blows."

"Surely, you don't expect me to play happily families."

"I was hoping we could be civil towards each other."

Skye looked at her coffee mug and considered the satisfaction she would get from throwing it at him. "Go to hell."

"In due time I probably will, but not before I see you and your nasty friends put behind bars."

Skye didn't even dignify his statement with a reply. Instead, she ate her breakfast and thought about getting through the day without committing murder. One thing was certain; if Walker continued his incessant tirade, she was going to need a lawyer and a damn good one.

"If you release your stranglehold on that mug, I'll get you a refill."

What a pity its not your neck, she thought. She handed him the empty mug. Their fingers touched briefly. Her anger dissolved into desire at the realization, that despite his harsh treatment, she still loved him. She snatched her hand away.

Lost in thought, she didn't hear him return until he gave a slight cough. She blinked, then focused her gaze and accepted the mug he offered.

"There's not much food. We ought to go into town to stock up."

Walker snorted, not rising to the bait. "Make a list. I'll phone it through to the store and get them to deliver the order."

"Okay." Skye said, giving him a grudging nod.

At the very least, he expected her to argue, and wondered what had brought about the change in her demeanor. While he could live with a temporary truce, he would keep his wits about him all the same.

The hours passed. Just after supper, there was a knock at the door.

"Expecting someone?" Walker asked.

"No. Are you?"

Walker shrugged his shoulders in response and went to the door. He lifted a heavy walking stick from the stand, and then drew back the bolt. It never paid to be careless this late in a game. He opened the door a few inches and glared at the stranger standing on the step. The guy looked about forty and was dressed in designer jeans, turtle neck sweater and an expertly cut leather jacket. He was roughly the same height as Walker although a few pounds heavier. Walker relaxed; the man's hands were in plain sight, and empty.

"I'm sorry to disturb you. I'm looking for 8971 Roche Harbor Road and think I may be—"

"You've found it," Walker interrupted.

"Then who are you?"

Walker's eyes narrowed. "I think that should be my question."

The stranger stood his ground and returned Walker's scrutiny with a hard stare of his own.

Skye ignored the conversation then realized one voice held a familiar ring.

"John? John, is that you?" She dropped her book and ran to the open doorway.

"Sweet Pea?"

Walker's brows slanted in a frown. Was the guy talking about Skye? Sweet Pea couldn't be the same woman who would sooner scratch his eyes out than offer him a cup of coffee. This guy looked more like a college professor than a criminal, but then appearances could be deceptive. His grip on the walking stick tightened. He turned to Skye.

"Do you know this guy?"

"He's my business partner, you overgrown moron! Are you going to keep him standing there all night, or are you going to let him in so that we can clear up this mess?"

Walker stepped aside and allowed the stranger to enter.

"I've been wondering when you'd show up. Take a seat on the couch where I can see you, while we wait for the cops to arrive." He made sure the man saw the hefty walking stick.

Skye threw herself into John's arms and hugged him with desperation. He held her at arm's length and looked her up and down. She looked bad—exhausted, and there were dark circles under her eyes.

"Are you all right? This, this ape hasn't hurt you has he?"

Skye was close to tears. "I'm fine, just a little tired. What are you doing here? Shouldn't you be in the office testing?"

"I decided I was being unfair asking you to work during your vacation. When you failed to contact me, I became worried. Debbie gave me the address. I caught the first available flight to Seattle. I had to wait for the connection to Friday Harbor, but I managed to get a seat on the last plane in."

"Whatever your reasons are, I am relieved to see you."

Walker cleared his throat. "Well isn't this cozy? Skye, introduce me to your friend. Then we can discuss why you and your associate hacked into my computer." He nodded his head in John's direction. "And despite who she tells me you are, I want to see some identification."

John kept a protective arm around Skye. "I don't know who you are, but if you've laid so much as a finger on Skye, I'll personally see that you walk with a limp for the rest of your life."

"John, meet Mr. Walker. He thinks I'm involved in the illegal dumping of chemicals."

John looked at Skye and then at Walker, and roared with laughter. "I've never heard anything so preposterous in my life. Are you serious?"

Skye said nothing. He could see that she was.

Skye fixed her icy blue eyes on Walker. "Walker, meet Dr. John Ridge, co-owner of Dunbar and Ridge Computer Consultants."

Walker was stunned. John Ridge, well, well. He was the last person he expected to see. He turned to Ridge.

"I presume you've got some identification to prove that."

John reached inside his jacket and removed his passport. He handed it to Walker.

"Is that good enough for you, or do you want to call passport control in Seattle and have it verified?"

"I'm certainly going to get it checked out. I don't trust one word that comes from Skye's sweet mouth." He picked up the phone, dialed McCabe's number, and quickly reeled off the details. McCabe promised to get back to him within the hour.

"If you're telling the truth, why would Skye hack into my computer?"

Skye stiffened at Walker's accusation. John placed a restraining hand on her arm.

"Skye has never hacked into a computer. While she's more than capable of doing so, her talents lie in other directions."

Skye groaned inwardly at John's admission, but she listened as he qualified his statement.

"When it comes to innovative design, she is one of the best. Many of the software products on the market contain code we developed."

Walker eyed the two of them skeptically.

"If you don't believe me, ask your buddy to check with the British Embassy. I am sure someone there will verify who we are."

Walker's grin was derisive. "That sure of yourselves, huh?"

John's expression was one of pained tolerance. "We are. *Your* government will take a dim view of your actions. Now, before this situation gets out of hand, I suggest one of you explains exactly what is going on here."

Skye interrupted Walker before could do more than take a breath. She spent the next five minutes explaining how she had met Walker, leaving out the intimate details of their relationship. By the time she had finished, John was stern faced, and angry.

"Why didn't you tell me you were in trouble? How long has this idiot been holding you against your will?"

"Since yesterday afternoon, when he found me using my laptop. He decided I was both a hacker and an environmental terrorist. I pleaded with him to let me call you or the police, but he's convinced I'm involved—" her voice faltered.

John gave her hand a reassuring squeeze and cast a murderous glance in Walker's direction. "Take your time."

She took a deep breath then continued, "Walker is convinced I'm involved. He insisted on staying here to see who showed up."

"Is this correct?" John asked.

Walker shrugged his shoulders. "Yeah, give or take one or two minor details." Like the fact we're lovers, he added silently.

The phone rang, and Walker snatched it up. He listened intently. He replaced the handset and gave Ridge an embarrassed, conciliatory smile.

"Seems your identification checked out."

"What a surprise. And?"

"And you've done work for both the British and American Governments," he admitted. "Skye I owe you an apology—"

John bristled. "You owe her more than an apology, but you can tell it to the cops. Skye, go and pack, we're leaving."

"Wait," Walker interrupted. "Let me explain."

Skye kept her gaze firmly fixed on John.

John frowned. "You have five minutes then we're leaving."

Walker leaned forward in his chair. "For a number of months, someone has been dumping chemicals in the waters around the San Juan Islands. So far, only marine life has been involved. At the same time, someone hacked into my company's computer system. Then a few days ago, someone ransacked my headquarters and laboratories in Seattle. I think someone is trying to find out how close I am to discovering whoever's responsible for this environmental atrocity."

Skye looked directly at Walker. "Is your virus software up-to-date? Have you tried to trace the hackers?"

A half smile crossed Walker's face. "I've done both. McCabe, my contact in the Department of Wildlife and Fisheries, suggested I contact a British guy. Someone named Robert J. Ridge. I assume that's you."

"Possibly," John replied. "It's a common enough name."

"Well, you're damned hard to track down," Walker said. "I found an email address for you in a journal and wrote to it, but as of three days ago there was still no response."

Skye turned to John. "Did you receive an email from Walker?"

"Did you use a web-based email address? They are the address of choice for would-be hackers and spammers. I don't read them. Most people who need to contact me use the phone."

"Yeah, well we try not to ask the British for help very often."

"No, because you think you have all the answers," Skye mumbled under her breath.

For a moment, there was silence. Eventually, Walker turned to Skye, a silent pleading in his eyes.

"I'm sorry. I've behaved reprehensibly. I've got no right to ask this of either of you, but would you help?"

Skye remained silent. John's face was immobile. They looked at each other, an unspoken question passing between them. John was the first to speak.

"What makes you think we can?"

"McCabe told me that you're about to present some new software to the British Government."

"We develop new software all the time. What makes you believe it has anything to do with tracing hackers?" Skye asked.

Walker shrugged his shoulders. "Maybe McCabe's information is wrong." He ran a hand through his hair. "I don't know about you two, but I could do with a drink."

He went to the kitchen and poured a measure of scotch into three tumblers. When Skye realized who was at the door, she had fallen headlong into Ridge's arms. Were they more than business partners, he wondered? Ridge was certainly hostile towards him, but then what did he expect? A primeval emotion coursed through his veins. For the first time in his life, he felt jealous.

Skye and John each took a glass of whisky from the tray.

"I understand your reluctance to acknowledge such software exists. These people don't know what they're messing with. Eventually someone will die. I'm sure the two incidents are linked. If I can find out who is accessing my company's computer files, then I may be able to find those responsible for dumping the chemicals. Don't give me your answer now; think about it overnight. I'll come back in the morning and you can give me your answer then."

John stroked his chin. "You make a compelling case, Mr. Walker, but you've got a bloody nerve asking for our help after the way you've treated Skye. If it were up to me, I'd have you arrested. However, this is Skye's decision. I suggest you leave before I forget I'm a gentleman and tell you what I really think of you."

"Okay. I need to speak to a few people, anyway. Just one thing before I go—"

Walker downed the contents of his glass in one swallow and placed it on the table. He stepped forward and dragged Skye to her feet. His arms circled her waist, his lips covering hers. For the third time in as many days, her hand lashed out and hit him a stinging blow across his cheek. He tightened his hold on her waist and drew her closer until her face was only inches from his.

"That's the last time you touch me in anger, Skye. Next time, it will be because you want me."

"Don't be to sure about that," she spat.

Walker let her go and strode to the door, slamming it shut behind him.

CHAPTER TWENTY

Walker's kiss caught Skye completely off guard. It wasn't anger that made her body shake, but a far more primitive emotion. A soft gasp escaped her lips as her knees buckled and she collapsed onto the couch. Her beautiful face was pale, but there was a slight flush to her cheeks and her eyes sparkled.

"I can't believe the nerve of the man. He keeps you here then has the audacity to kiss you. He hasn't touched you in any other way has he? Because if he has—"

"John, don't go there!"

"He should be locked up for the way he's treated you. I hope you're going to report him to the police."

"John, forget it. No harm's been done," Skye exclaimed in irritation and jumped to her feet.

"But—"

"I said forget it."

For a moment, the silence between them hung heavily in the air. They stared at one another. Skye couldn't bear his fury and looked away.

"You're attracted to him, aren't you? Once the reality of the situation kicks in, you'll see that he means nothing to you."

"Whatever happened, it's between Walker and me. And no matter how much you try to persuade me, I will not be reporting the matter to the police."

"If that's the way you want to play it."

"It is. We have more important things to discuss—"

"Such as?"

"Such as when did you last eat?"

"I ate in Seattle. Stop trying to change the subject."

"John, the matter is closed." Skye placed a hand on his arm. "I've had enough for tonight. I'm shattered."

A smile crossed his face. "I'm not surprised."

"And you're still on London time. We'll talk about this in the morning. The second bedroom is this way, and there are towels in the bathroom."

"Eight hours sleep wouldn't do either of us any harm," John said, and followed her into the hallway.

***

A subdued Walker arrived at the cabin at noon the next day. He knocked at the door and was surprised when Skye opened it. Despite the tension of the previous few days, she looked as if she had slept well, which was more than he could say for himself.

Unsmiling, she stepped aside to allow to him enter. "Would you like a coffee or should we get down to business?"

"Coffee would be good, but don't go to any trouble just for me."

Moments later, Skye thrust a steaming cup into his hand. Ridge crossed the room and rested his thigh on the arm of her chair. He put his arm about her shoulder. His message to Walker was loud and clear. *Hands off!*

"Are you willing to help?" asked Walker.

"Assuming this software exists, give us three reasons why we should," Ridge answered.

Walker took a sip from his mug and gathered his thoughts. "People who dump chemicals illegally not only risk their own lives, but those of others. As I told you last night, luck has been on our side, and no one has gotten sick. However, it's only a matter of time. Do you know what a high concentration of PCBs—?"

Skye interrupted. "PCBs? Could you put that into plain English for the benefit of us computer geeks?"

"PCBs or polychlorinated biphenyls are a family of chemicals for which there are no natural sources. We no longer commercially produce them here in the US, but they are still out there. They don't degrade readily, and once released into the environment, they can enter the food chain. They tend to accumulate in the fatty tissues of animals because they are stable in nature. These accumulations increase as the animal moves through the food chain."

Ridge concentrated hard and did his best to absorb the information. "Let me get this straight," he said. "If a seal eats fish that's been polluted, then it becomes contaminated too. The more fish it digests, the higher the concentration of these chemicals in its body."

"Basically, that's correct."

"And what effect do they have on the human population."

Walker inclined his head toward Skye. "I'm glad you asked that question. PCBs are highly toxic. They can cause tissue irritation, liver damage, and damage to the nervous system. They also may cause reproductive problems and cancers. This is one group of chemicals you don't want to mess with. The majority of companies behave responsibly when disposing of them. However, there are those who are less conscientious and who are not averse to disposing of them illegally. I think you use the term 'fly tipping' in the UK."

"I've read about that," remarked John. "It doesn't explain why you want our help."

"My first task, when asked to head up this investigation was to carry out autopsies on the fish. From the chemicals I found in their systems, I was able to narrow the list of companies handling them down to seventeen. One of them, a consortium based in the U.S., I had dealings with before. I was responsible for shutting down its South American operation for eighteen months while working practices and disposal methods were improved. The company was heavily fined, and on the brink of bankruptcy. As a result, I'm not very popular with the board of directors or shareholders. Recently, they've—"

"How do you know the same company is involved?" Skye asked.

The lines of concentration deepened along Walker's brow. "I don't. Not for sure. Ten months ago, the directors applied for a permit to build a new plant in Anacortes. The application was refused on the grounds of previous poor management and disposal methods."

"That isn't proof they're responsible," Skye insisted.

"It's a pretty strong coincidence. Shortly after permission was refused, contaminated fish started washing up on the mainland and here on the islands. There's no doubt the chemicals are being dumped at sea, but despite an extensive search, I've been unable to establish exactly where."

"Something like that wouldn't go unnoticed," John said.

"Thousands of vessels sail though Puget Sound each day. It's a huge area to cover and the Coast Guard is stretched as it is."

Skye's thoughts drifted back to the afternoon of John's telephone call and the boat she had seen in the cove. An icy chill crawled down her spine.

"What sort of vessel would they use?"

Walker thought for a moment or two. "Nothing that would look out of the ordinary. Possibly a fishing boat or a small inter-island cargo boat."

A shadow of alarm touched her face. "I saw a boat in the cove. It was a little way offshore. I assumed the crew were putting out some form of fishing equipment."

Walker barely managed to conceal his annoyance. "This is private property, and that extends to the fishing. Was this before or after you found the fish on the beach?"

"Before. It was too far away for me to see clearly, but the men on board struggled to put something overboard."

"For Christ's sake! Why didn't you tell me?"

Skye lowered her eyes and studied her hands. "You didn't give me a chance to say anything. I thought they were just fishing."

"You do realize that if you'd told me about this sooner that we might have been able to trace the vessel? Of all the stupid, irresponsible—"

"Let's not get into a slanging match," John interrupted. "If you're right and the chemicals are being dumped at sea, then it's a matter for the Coast Guard and the Navy to sort out. You need don't need our help."

Walker leaned forward and rested his elbows on his knees. "I believe whoever is dumping the chemicals is also hacking into my computer, which is why I'd like your help."

Skye and John exchanged glances. "Computers get infected with viruses all the time, mainly from attachments contained in email. They could be the reason your computer crashed," said John.

"The system is protected by anti-virus software and a firewall. And it doesn't explain why my offices were broken into."

"Supposing this consortium you mentioned is responsible, why don't you inspect the plant and check its records?"

"We have a duty to notify them of an impending inspection. By the time the paperwork is issued, they would have cleaned up their act," Walker told them.

Skye thought back to something Walker had said earlier. "The consortium can't be the only company you've investigated."

A muscle flicked angrily at Walker's jaw. "There are a number of companies around the world that have me at the top of their hate list. The consortium is the only one in Washington State licensed to dispose of PCBs. You're welcome to review the evidence. But time isn't on our side, I need your help today, not next week."

Walker stood and thrust his hands deep into his pockets. It was obvious that Skye and her partner were going to refuse to help. Yet he couldn't give up, he had to find a way to persuade them. As the minutes ticked by, the tension in the room stretched ever tighter. He turned to Skye.

"I owe you an apology," he began awkwardly. "You turned up at the cabin as things took a turn for the worse. I saw the computer code on your laptop, and I'm afraid I put two and two together and didn't come up with four. I'm sorry, but you must understand I felt I had no other choice. Can you forgive me?"

An apology was the last thing Skye expected, and from the expression on Walker's face, he was sincere. She leaned back in her chair and looked at John questioningly. On a professional note, helping Walker was the right decision. It could prevent an environmental disaster, and would be good publicity for their business. However, she wasn't sure she could put her personal issues with him to one side.

Before she had chance to respond, John's slow handclap broke the silence.

"Well, that was a pretty speech, but words come cheap."

Walker glared angrily at Ridge. "Butt out! This has nothing to do with you." He focused his attention on Skye. "When this is over, I promise I will do everything in my power to put things right between us."

"Do you really think Skye will hang around for your grand gestures?" John tightened his grip on her shoulder.

Walker ignored Ridge and looked directly at Skye once more. "Skye?"

Skye dropped her eyes before his steady gaze, torn by conflicting emotions. Should she walk away and let Walker solve his own problems, she wondered, or should she stay and help the man she loved?

Walker was halfway to the door, before she reached a decision.

"We'll help, but only if you agree to our terms."

Walker stopped in midstride and turned to listen.

"Firstly, your company agrees to pay for our time and expertise, and I should warn you we don't come cheap. Secondly, I want a written undertaking that you will not reveal any details about the software. Finally, there will be no further contact between us once the hacker is located. Do we have a deal?"

Walker glared at her. "I'll agree to the first two, but I'll be damned if I'll agree to the third!"

Skye lifted her chin and met his gaze. "Well, good luck. I hope you can find someone with the necessary expertise to help you. Close the door on your way out."

Walker's expression darkened. He retraced his steps and jerked her to her feet. "*Sweet Pea*, this is one conversation you and I are having in private." He gripped Skye's elbow, ushered her out the door and down the path to the shore, impervious to her objections and those of Ridge.

"What the hell did you mean back there?" he demanded. "Don't look to Ridge for support. I have had as much of his interference as I can take. If he moves so much as a muscle in this direction, I'll take the greatest pleasure in putting him flat on his back."

Skye flattened her palms against Walker's chest. Over his shoulder, she could see John standing in the doorway of the cabin. She shook her head indicating that he should stay put.

"I meant exactly what I said. Once this is over, there will be no further contact between us."

Walker searched her face for a trace of emotion and found none. "Do you mean to tell me that what we shared meant nothing to you?"

The anger Skye felt welled to the surface. She wanted to lash out and hurt him as much as he'd hurt her.

"What exactly did we share? Three days of mediocre sex. Sorry to disappoint you, but it meant nothing." She struggled to free herself from his arms.

Walker tightened his grip on her waist. "You're lying. It wasn't *mediocre sex,* and you know it. It was fantastic, and if I kissed you now you'd want me as much as I want you."

Skye found her body responding to his. Fear and anger overcame desire, giving her the strength to push him away.

"Don't flatter yourself. This isn't the dark ages. Women are just as capable of having meaningless affairs as men are. We don't have to fall in love with every man who takes us to bed." She could see from his eyes that her arrow had hit its mark. "Now, are you going accept my terms or not?"

Walker felt wounded beyond comprehension. He took a deep breath. If he had to abide by her rules, then so be it. Releasing his grip on her waist, he stepped back.

"You've got a deal. When this is over, I'll prove what we shared is real. Don't say you haven't had fair warning. Without waiting to hear her answer, he spun on his heel and strode back up the path to the cabin.

Skye gazed at Walker's retreating figure and pressed both hands over her eyes in despair. Weariness enveloped her, but she knew she had to concentrate. There was no doubt in her mind that he would carry out his threat. She pushed aside her worries and walked back to the cabin.

John had set up her laptop next to his and was examining the new code she had written. Skye sat down next to him and said nothing.

Walker paced up and down in front of the fireplace. He watched Skye and Ridge, their heads bent in concentration as they gazed from one screen to the other. Jealousy coursed through his veins. He needed to get Skye alone, but that wouldn't be easy with Ridge hovering over her all the time like the proverbial British bulldog.

Skye's silken voice broke into his thoughts. "We'll need access to your company's mainframe and server in Seattle."

"No problem."

"Do you have any information that might be of interest to our cyber thieves… something that would tempt them to hack into your system again?"

Walker gave a brief nod. "I'll ask Joe, my friend in the State Department to prepare a press release to the effect that a prosecution is imminent. That ought to grab their attention. Want me to make the call?"

Skye looked at John.

"As far as I can tell without thorough testing, the code looks all right. Make the call. While you're on the phone, book three seats on the next available flight to Seattle. I absolutely detest boats."

"No need, I'll fly us over. Do you have an aversion to small planes?" Walker asked.

"I don't," said Skye, then she looked at John for signs of objection. "What about you?"

"I'll cope," replied John. "Now can we get on with this before you two start discussing such niceties as in-flight service?"

Two hours later, they walked into Walker's Seattle office.

"I've seen bigger coffins than that plane," said John.

Skye laughed. "You should see your face—it's green."

"If you'd seen the way the wing almost hit the sea as we took off, you might not be laughing!"

Twenty minutes later, the virus program Skye ran finished checking Walker's computer for signs of infection. The tracking program had been loaded into the mainframe.

"We're all set," John said. "Are you sure that press release will stand up to close scrutiny?"

"McCabe doesn't make mistakes," Walker replied.

"Then let's hope someone takes the bait and hacks into the system."

"Do you have any idea how they're gaining access?" Walker asked.

"There are a number of methods they could use," replied John. "The simplest would be to have someone working on the inside. Someone who has access to all your files—say a secretary or a lab technician. If that's not feasible, then they'd have to gain access via the back door."

Walker shook his head. "No one gets employed here without criminal, reference, and credit checks."

"Ever heard of false IDs?" asked John.

Walker ignored the question. Instead, he turned to Skye.

"The back door? As in climbing up the fire escape and breaking in?"

Skye laughed. "Most operating systems have vulnerabilities and hackers take advantage of these 'back doors' to gain access. Or they could send an email with a small, self-executing file." Skye's face became animated as she warmed to her subject. "A few extra lines added to a screen saver, a picture file or hidden in a virus, is all it takes. They're known as a Trojan horse."

Thoroughly bewildered by the jargon, Walker raised an eyebrow questioningly.

"A Trojan horse?"

Skye sighed. "A Trojan horse is simply a computer program that claims to be one thing, such as a game, but is something else entirely. When activated, it causes damage such as erasing data on your hard disk. Once downloaded, a Trojan horse can lurk undetected in your operating system until something triggers it. It can be set to search for certain key words, such as *pollution* or *fish*. When you open a document containing those words, the information is sent to the hacker. A hacker's second goal is to get root access—"

"Root access? Isn't that something you have done at the dentist?"

Skye giggled, enjoying the gentle sparring against her better judgment. "Root access is every dedicated hacker's ultimate goal. It gives them unrestricted access to the inner working of your system, and the ability to copy, delete or even change files, authorize new users, and install a back door to allow regular access."

Walker ran a hand through his hair. "And I wouldn't be aware that they had this power over my system?"

"That's correct. Most companies only realize they have a problem when money goes missing from a bank account, or as in your case, documents are destroyed. Most hacking is relatively innocent and carried out by bored teenagers, but even that can prove annoying and costly. Hackers tend to start writing viruses, and progress to more destructive software such as worms and Trojan horses. When that ceases to give them a satisfactory high they turn their talents to criminal activities."

Walker held up his hands in defeat. "You obviously know your subject. Why do you think my system was attacked?"

"You head the investigation, and therefore are of paramount interest to them. As to how they gained access, John, what do you think? Internal access or back door?"

"Back door, almost certainly. Didn't you say this system was protected by a firewall?"

"Yes it is," Walker replied.

"It's not very effective," John replied. "Look at this, Skye. Does this string of code look as if it's part of this program? Could it be how they gained access?"

Skye crossed the room and leaned on John's shoulder. She studied the lines of code. "I don't think its part of the program. Well spotted."

"Yeah, well if you hadn't been so busy talking you might have noticed it yourself."

The tension in the room was almost palpable. Skye squeezed John's shoulder.

"Does it matter which of us found it? At least we know how they gained access and can prevent them returning." She swiveled round to face Walker. "Could you ask your friend to send out the press release?"

Walker did as Skye requested and gave up asking questions. He turned his attention to the pile of paperwork on his desk. He sifted papers from one stack to another, pausing now and then to glance at the odd letter. Ridge had given up glowering at him and now sat at a secretary's desk monitoring two laptops and the secretary's computer for signs of anything untoward.

Skye took advantage of the temporary truce and stood by the window, apparently lost in thought. She rested her head against the cool glass and gazed down on the lights of the city far below. Despite the memories it held for her, she never tired of Seattle's skyline. Odd how life had a way of turning in circles, she thought. Twelve months ago, she had run away from Michael. When this was all over, she would be leaving again, only this time, it would be from the man she loved.

One of the laptops pinged.

"We've got a hit," John shouted over his shoulder. "Let's just hope the guy hasn't spoofed his IP address."

Baffled, Walker turned to Skye for an explanation.

"Spoofing is the term used when someone hides their Internet Protocol address. If our hacker has spoofed his address, then he might bounce his communications through many intermediate computers scattered around the world. We have to find all the bounce points before we can locate him."

Walker pushed his chair away from his desk and crossed the room to stand by her side.

"How long will that take?" he asked.

Skye looked thoughtful. "It depends. It's not as straightforward as it sounds. If he's using computers in third world countries to hide his location, as many hackers do, then it might take a while."

Walker glanced over his shoulder at Ridge, who concentrated on the three computer screens to take any notice of Walker's proximity to Skye. Finally, he could talk to her without Ridge running interference.

"The view is fantastic, isn't it?"

"It's better than the view from the Space Needle, but I've never been up there at night. How far can you see in daylight?"

"As far as Bainbridge Island and Bremerton, and if the weather is really clear you can see the Olympic Mountains. Sometimes, when the clouds are low, and only the tops of the other buildings are visible, it's like looking down on cotton candy."

He came closer, looking down at her with eyes full of tenderness. "I'm sorry for my behavior. When this is over, will you have dinner with me? I'd like us to spend some time together before you return to London."

"I don't know. I've spent so much—"

Before Skye had chance to finish, Ridge shouted.

"Found him! He's here in the city. A few more minutes, and I should be able to tell you the name of his Internet Service Provider."

Walker stared at Skye's back as she ran across the room and hugged Ridge.

"It works! We've done what everyone said was impossible and written a program that will be the curse of every hacker!"

Walker couldn't hear Ridge's response, but the sight of him returning Skye's hug and kissing her was enough to blacken his mood. Anger and jealousy tore into him. His first opportunity to talk to Skye and Ridge had ruined the moment. The man was a positive menace. Somehow, he had to find a way to keep her in the States until the investigation was over.

CHAPTER TWENTY-ONE

Things moved quickly. The hacker's IP address turned out to belong to the waste management company on the south side of Seattle. By ten thirty the following morning, Walker and McCabe were on their way to the plant. They decided Walker would ask most of the questions and McCabe would lend the weight of the State Department should the manager be reluctant to co-operate.

As they drove though the security gates, they could see the plant was run down and poorly maintained. Walker felt his skin crawl. No attempt had been made to hide leaking pipes or steaming vents. Oily puddles covered almost every inch of tarmac. The air was heavy with an obnoxious smell, which he felt sure was covered by a piece of legislature preventing whatever it was from being released into the atmosphere.

None of employees wore protective clothing. Not even simple facemasks or specialist gloves and footwear. Walker wondered what the staff sick rate was and how many of the illnesses were attributable to the chemicals and products the employees handled.

Walker spent ten minutes outlining the investigation, after which the manager categorically denied the company was involved. Walker didn't believe a word the slimy toad said, and judging by the look on McCabe's face, neither did he. No amount of persuasion succeeded in obtaining the manager's agreement to making the company records available for inspection on a voluntary basis.

Walker stared out of the grubby window, while McCabe threatened to close the plant down until he and the State Department were satisfied that everything was above board.

He listened to the heavy rumble of a plane's engines as it passed overhead, and in a blind moment of panic wondered whether Ridge had carried out his threat to take Skye back to England.

He pushed his personal problems aside and turned his attention to a truck parked next to a pipeline. From his vantage point on the second floor of the administration building, he watched it being loaded with oil barrels. He dragged his attention back to the conversation and gave McCabe their pre-arranged signal. They concluded the meeting, promising to return later that day with a court order.

They left the building and ran toward McCabe's four-wheel drive, and climbed inside. A few moments later, the fully laden truck pulled away from the pipeline and headed toward the exit.

"Quick," Walker said. "Follow it and see where it goes."

McCabe lost no time. He slammed the four-wheel drive into gear and pressed down hard on the accelerator, and settled in behind the truck. From the plant just south of Seattle, the truck made its way onto Interstate 5 and continued steadily north.

McCabe broke the silence. "I think we ought call the cops and have this guy stopped."

Walker shook his head decisively. "There's not much point in contacting the cops just yet. Look what happened last time—it got us nowhere. Let's just wait and see where that truck is heading. If my suspicions are correct and those barrels are destined to be dumped at sea, then the driver is not going to do it from the deck of a State ferry. He'll stop somewhere and load those barrels onto a smaller vessel."

"Then what?"

Walker laughed. "You know, McCabe, sometimes you can be real slow on the uptake. Then we wait some more. If my hunch is correct, the driver will wait for either nightfall or high tide or both. That will give me a chance to take a closer look at those barrels. Then you can call the cops."

"I'll hold you to that. Just remember, I'm only a pen pusher, not some action hero. My wife will beat me to death with the microwave if I get caught up in something nasty."

"I wouldn't worry about your wife killing you. If my suspicions about the contents of those barrels is correct, it will do the job before she's had chance to pick up her rolling pin."

On the outskirts of Anacortes, the truck followed the road signs for the port. As Walker predicted, the driver ignored the queue for the late afternoon ferry to Friday Harbor, and continued for a short distance before turning into one of the wharfs.

McCabe parked in front of the shipping office.

"You were right." The truck had pulled up next to a vessel moored at the end of the wharf. "I'll contact the local gendarmes now, and they can take it from here."

Walker placed a restraining hand on his friend's arm. "Not yet. I want to see what's inside those barrels first."

"And just how do you plan to do that?"

"Like this," Walker said, and opened his door.

"Hey, now wait a minute. You didn't say anything about taking a look in broad daylight."

Walker was already out of the car and walking towards the shipping office. He hadn't lied when he said he wanted to inspect the barrels, but he also wanted to check the vessel's sailing schedule. He pushed open the door to the office. Lady luck was on his side; the only person present was a blonde woman in her mid twenties. He walked up to the desk, turned up his smile a few notches, and thought fast.

"Hi, there… Cindy," he said, reading the name badge she wore.

Cindy looked up from the paperwork on her desk. "Hello."

"I wonder if you could help me," Walker asked and offered her another dazzling smile.

"Sure, sugar," Cindy, drawled in a Texan accent. "What can I do for you?"

Cindy's sexy looks did nothing for him. He'd met her type before—a fashion victim looking for a brain.

"The small inter-island transport moored at the quay, is it due to sail tonight?"

"You mean the *Rosario Queen*? Why do you want to know?" Cindy pouted her lips.

"I'm expecting a delivery and I need to make sure there's a truck waiting when it docks," Walker lied. He took a long look at Cindy's ample cleavage and then held her gaze with a smile.

Cindy's ego went into overdrive. For the first time, since she had taken this lousy job a halfway decent looking guy had walked into the office and noticed her. This was a welcome relief from the married union slobs who pined after her all day.

"Well, now, sugar. How about you buy me a drink when I finish here and I'll tell you then?"

Walker had other plans, and they didn't include Cindy or any of her ilk, but he wasn't about to tell her that.

"Tell me now, and I'll buy you dinner."

Cindy leaned forward and stared at Walker's zipper, leaving him in no doubt as to what she expected to be on the menu for desert.

"Okay, sugar. Seeing as you're offerin' to be so generous an' all, I'll tell you. She's due to sail at nine tonight. What time are we gonna meet then?"

Walker suppressed a shudder. He disliked women who openly came on to a man.

"How about eight at the Ship Inn, we'll have a few drinks first."

"Sure, sugar, anything you say."

Walker strode to the door and grinned. He had no intention of turning up for dinner, and while Cindy would be mad, he somehow doubted that she would be on her own for very long.

He got back into the car just as quietly as he'd left. "There's no point us both hanging around. Until they start to unload the truck or it gets dark, there's not much we can do but watch and wait. How about you get us some coffee? You can bring back a couple of sandwiches too. "

McCabe looked skeptical. Once he was out of sight, Walker would be sniffing around those barrels like a hound after a rabbit. From the corner of his eye he watched Walker settle into his seat, and then got out of the car. He walked to the coffee shop at the entrance to the wharf. While he waited for his order to be filled, he contacted his office.

Just as dusk was falling, he slipped back into the car. He handed Walker a Styrofoam cup. He lifted the lid off his own and took a mouthful of the gray liquid. With a nod of his head, he indicated the truck where a forklift was now busily removing the barrels.

"It looks as if they're getting ready to load them onboard," McCabe said.

"Yeah, the stevedores appeared a few minutes ago. If they load those barrels into the hold, I'm in trouble. I don't like the idea of climbing aboard that ship in the dark. Let's hope they break for coffee soon, otherwise we'll have to think of something to get everyone away long enough for me to take a look." Walker raised his cup to his mouth and swallowed. "Christ, what is this stuff?"

"Coffee?" replied McCabe somewhat optimistically.

"You could have fooled me. It looks and tastes more like dishwater."

"Wouldn't know, never tried it. You'd never make a cop."

"Why's that?"

"You'd never survive a stakeout."

Walker laughed. McCabe was right. Apart from preferring his food to be recognizable as such, he hated being cooped up in an office.

"Cheese sandwich," McCabe offered before Walker had chance to ask.

Walker eyed the contents of his sandwich with mild suspicion. "Are you sure of that? It looks more like a strip of cardboard to me."

"For crying out loud, quit complaining. Either eat it or feed it to the birds."

The stevedores working alongside the truck disappeared. This was Walker's opportunity to examine the barrels. He swallowed the contents of his cup and got out of the car. He leaned in through the open window and plucked his jacket off the back seat.

"If I'm not back in twenty minutes call nine-one-one."

Straightening, he pulled on his jacket and shoved his hands into the pockets. He pulled out a pair of heavy leather gloves, along with a couple of glass sample bottles and a length of twine.

After a quick look over his shoulder to make sure there was no one in sight, he ran towards the *Rosario Queen*. He kept to the shadows and close to the warehouses lining the wharf. For the last twenty yards, he was in plain sight of anyone who happened to look towards the vessel. He took one final look around and sprinted across the wharf to the side of the truck. He skirted the back of the vehicle to where some of the containers were stacked in a cargo net ready for the ship's crane to lift them aboard.

The first five he examined were all tightly sealed. Cursing, he checked the remainder, always conscious of the fact that the stevedores could return at any moment. Among a group of three, he found one that was leaking. He bent down and ran his gloved hand over the seal. It was covered in a thick black liquid. When his glove didn't disintegrate, he let out a sigh of relief. At least the contents weren't acidic. He raised his glove to his nose and sniffed cautiously. The substance smelt noxious, but he couldn't identify any particular chemical. He loosened the small seal on top of the barrel and removed it then lowered a sample bottle on a length of twine into the contents.

"Hey, you! What are you doing?"

Walker peered at the figure running towards him. In his haste to get away, he dropped the cap to the bottle. He bent down to retrieve it and his world went black.

CHAPTER TWENTY-TWO

Skye ignored the 'Do not disturb' sign hanging on the knob and rapped firmly on the door. A muttered curse came from within as the occupant struggled with the bolt.

"For God's sake, can't you people read?" The door sprung open. "Skye! What do you want?" John growled. "What's the matter? Is the hotel on fire or something?"

"I'm sorry, I know you're tired. It's just that... I want to fly home... now, today!"

"Be reasonable. I'd just fallen asleep for the second time in seventy-two hours. Can't I have one night's sleep in a comfortable bed before I spend twelve hours cramped in a metal tube?"

Skye faltered, all her well-rehearsed words vanished. She was tired too, both physically and emotionally, and John's grumpiness was more than she could bear. The tears that had threatened to fall suddenly found their way down her cheeks.

John leant against the doorframe and ran a hand through his sleep-tousled hair.

"Oh, hell! I didn't mean to bite your head off. You know how irritable I get when I'm suffering from sleep deprivation. I guess whatever it is you have to tell me shouldn't be discussed in a hotel corridor." He opened the door to let her pass. "You'd better come in."

Skye stepped inside and sat down in the solitary chair. The drapes were closed, and the only light came from a lamp on the bedside table.

John regarded her quizzically. He'd never seen her in such a state and wondered if all her pent up anger towards Walker had somehow transmuted into anguish and despair.

"Give me five minutes to shower and dress, then we'll talk."

Overwhelmed, Skye yielded to the compulsive sobs that shook her body.

The shower turned off, and John emerged, fully dressed from the bathroom, and thrust a box of tissues in her lap.

"Blow your nose and stop crying." He pushed aside the quilt and sat down on the end of the bed opposite her. "I had the impression you wanted to finish your vacation. What made you change your mind?"

Skye lost control of her emotions and sobbed again. "I want to go home. Isn't that reason enough?"

"Sure it is, and I can understand why you might want to leave. We have to be practical about this. My body clock is so screwed I'm not sure whether it's night or day. In the last seventy-two hours, I've flown across an ocean and a continent, and traced a computer hacker on less than six hours sleep. You're not much better. Delaying our departure by a couple of days won't make much difference. Besides, your luggage is still at the cabin. You can't just leave it there."

Skye sniffed. "I'll ask the realty company to send it on."

"I suppose they might agree, but what if they forget something? It's not as if it's a five-minute car journey to come back and collect anything. What about your rental car, you can't just leave that at the cabin. It would be far better to return to the island, pack up your things, return the car, and fly home a few days' time, don't you agree?"

"John, I've had enough. I can't cope anymore. Everything has become so sickeningly familiar, I just want—"

"Hold it right there. What do you mean *everything is so familiar*?"

Skye flung her arms out in despair. "I mean this whole situation. The ruined vacation…Walker… everything!" she cried.

"I know I'm not at my sharpest, but you're not making any sense. You've never stayed on the San Juan Islands before, and you'd not met Walker before, had you?"

"No, but—"

"Then I don't understand. I think you had better explain exactly what you mean. Before you do, I'm going to call room service and order some coffee. Want some?"

Skye nodded, not trusting herself to speak. Perhaps something to drink would help calm her down. She bit down hard on her bottom lip in an attempt to stop her renewed waterfall of tears. Her head was pounding. A couple of painkillers and a night under a duvet was a comforting thought, but she would forego both if it meant getting away as soon as possible.

"Here, drink this." John held out a glass of amber liquid.

Skye looked at him questioningly.

"It's brandy, from the mini bar. As Walker is paying the bill, I don't see why you shouldn't have some. It might help."

The mere sound of Walker's name was enough to make her weep again. She took several deep breaths before she managed to stem the flood long enough to lift the glass to her lips. The brandy was liquid fire coursing through her body. Little by little, warmth crept back into her weary limbs.

"Feeling better?"

"Y-yes."

"Now take your time. Start at the beginning and tell me what's made you so desperate to go home that you can't wait forty-eight hours."

A glazed look of despair spread over Skye's face. For over a year, she'd kept her own counsel, but had no option but to tell him the truth. Ashamed and humiliated by what she was about to reveal, she found it impossible to look John in the eye. In a voice that was barely audible, she started to tell him why she wanted to leave.

"You assumed I cut my vacation short last year because Michael had been recalled to his ship."

"I never made any assumptions. I figured that whatever had happened between you two was best left alone. I thought it unwise to ask questions, and that you'd tell me in your own good time."

"Michael wasn't the person I thought he was. At first, he was attentive and loving, but then things changed. We would go to dinner and he would rush back to the ship without warning, leaving me to pay the check." She paused to catch her breath and closed her eyes as she recalled the memory. "One morning, he was recalled to his ship, so I caught the ferry to Seattle. It's always busy with commuters, and that morning was no different. When I got back to the hotel later that afternoon, he was waiting for me. He was in a strange mood."

"Don't tell me he'd been drinking or taking drugs?"

"I don't know for sure. But he seemed, at odds with himself, if you know what I mean."

John shook his head. He didn't know what she meant, and felt that he was going to like what she was about to say even less.

"Before I could say anything, he grabbed hold of my arm and asked me how my boyfriend was. I didn't know what he was talking about and he accused me of being a liar. Then he said something about the guy I had coffee with, and I remembered that I'd shared a window table with one of the early morning commuters."

"But I thought you said Michael had been recalled to his ship?"

"It turned out that he'd finished early. The dockyard is near the ferry terminal. He must have seen me waiting for the ferry and followed me. He saw me sharing a table and decided that I was two-timing him. When I told him he was being unreasonable, he became aggressive." She covered her eyes and began to shake as the fearful images built in her mind.

John took her icy hands in his and rubbed them. "He can't hurt you now. Just take your time."

Skye wiped her eyes. Her mouth felt dry. "He wouldn't let go of my arm, he just held it tighter and tighter until his fingers dug into me." She rubbed her arm as if the bruises were still there and she was trying to ease the pain. "I tried to calm the situation down, but he wouldn't believe anything I said. He insisted I was cheating on him and lying. I told him he was the one with the problem not me—that he was being too possessive. We just went round in circles, until I noticed he was holding something in his hand."

Skye clenched her hand until her nails dug into her palm. She had known John long enough to realize he was exercising supreme control over his temper. How much more could she tell him before it boiled over and he vented it on her, she wondered. A chill black silence enveloped the room, while she struggled to find the courage to continue.

"He'd been through my luggage and found my diary—"

"I thought you kept everything on your laptop."

"I carry a small dairy for making notes and keeping odd papers in."

"What did he find?"

Skye gazed at John in despair. "He found the photograph of Laura."

John knelt down, took Skye in his arms, and hugged her. He rocked her gently back and forth.

"Shush, it's okay. Come on now, stop crying."

Skye buried her face against his shoulder.

"I never told him about Laura, you see? I've only myself to blame for what happened next. But I never meant to deceive him."

"So he threw you out?"

"I offered to leave, but he wouldn't hear of it. Instead he forced me… he forced me to—"

"Christ almighty Skye, the bastard didn't rape you?"

Skye swallowed the sob that rose in her throat. "He found another way to punish me."

John swore heartily, no longer able to hide his anger. "Go on."

"He blackmailed me. He said that if I didn't do this thing for him, he'd make sure that no one, no Government or company, would employ us. He'd make sure that they knew we couldn't deliver, that our work was third rate, and… and until I agreed, he kept me locked up in the hotel room."

"So what did he want?"

"He didn't only want money. We were bidding for that big contract, and I was so frightened that he would carry out his threat to make our company bankrupt. I had no choice but to do as he asked. You do understand that, don't you?"

The only outward sign of John's irritation was the tightening of his jaw muscles. "No wonder you've been afraid of your own shadow for the past year. If only you had told me this a year ago, I would have made damn sure the little shit was kicked out of the Navy. How much did you give him?"

"Ten thousand, but it didn't come from the company account, I swear! I couldn't do that to you. I used the money from the trust fund my parents set up for me."

This time John didn't hide his shock and rage. "Why didn't you call the cops, for God's sake?"

"I couldn't. He never left me alone. He unplugged the phone. When room service delivered our meals, he locked me in the bathroom until they left. I had no chance to call for help."

John's eyes darkened dangerously. "You said he asked for more than money. What else did he want?"

Skye flinched as she spat out the words. "He said that if I didn't write a piece of software for him, he'd invite some of the guys off the ship to—"

"He said what?"

"Please, don't make me say it." Skye cradled her head in trembling hands. "I… I can still see him leaning over me…"

"I get the picture, for goodness sake! So you agreed to help him."

Skye nodded woodenly.

"And this software you wrote for him, what did it do?"

"It automatically emailed copies of military documents that he—"

John leapt up as if propelled by an explosive force. "What in God's name were you thinking? How could you take such a risk? Never mind what it would have done for our reputation, didn't you realize you could be locked away for years?"

"It's not as bad as it sounds."

"Really? This ought to be good. Surprise me."

"John, I may have been desperate, but my brains hadn't totally deserted me. I had plenty of time to think while I worked on the software. It struck me that Michael was selling military documents for one reason only—money."

"The bastard was short of cash, so what?"

Skye took a deep breath and moistened her dry lips. "If money was his objective, he wasn't interested in the finer details of how the software worked. Besides, he was strictly an end user. I wrote the software and showed him how to use it, but omitted to tell him one thing."

John raised an eyebrow. "And this one thing was?"

Skye smiled through her tears, but didn't answer.

"What did you do, write a string of code that deleted the email rather than sending it?"

"Not quite. I added a string of code that ensured that every email sent from Michael's computer was copied to the Judge Advocate General's Office."

"And who or what is the Judge Advocate General?"

"He's only the most senior attorney in the US Navy."

Despite the emotional tension in the room, John laughed heartily. "You played the little shit at his own game. If he kept you locked up, how did you get away?"

"He became careless. He came back to the hotel one night very drunk, or high or both. He kept saying something about a big pay off. He passed out. I managed to get the keys off him and sneak out of the room. I hailed a cab and asked the driver to take me to a hotel, any hotel in Seattle. He dropped me off at the most run down, seedy motel imaginable. I remember bolting the door and collapsing on the bed, and then the rest is a blank. I woke up two days later and booked myself on the first plane back to London. The rest you know."

John was disappointed that she had been so unsure of his reaction, that she carried this burden alone for over a year. "I'm glad you've told me, but you didn't have to bear this alone."

Skye smiled. "I know, but you helped me once before. I thought if I told you, you'd hate me, be so disappointed in me that you'd never forgive me."

"Dry your eyes." He offered her another tissue from the box. "No matter what happens to you, no matter what you've done, I'm always here for you. I could never hate you, don't you know that?"

Tears still trembled on Skye's eyelids. She couldn't trust herself to speak and merely nodded her head.

"What happened to Michael, do you know?"

"When I returned to London, I contacted the Judge Advocate General and his commanding officer, and made a complaint. I made it abundantly clear that not only had I been coerced into writing the software against my will, but also made sure they knew I was responsible for ensuring that any information he passed on via email was copied to them."

"And?"

"I went to the American Embassy and made a formal statement which was used at his trial. The Navy charged Michael with stealing military documents. He's been dishonorably discharged, and has lost all rights to his pension and is currently languishing in a military prison."

"Thank God for small mercies. But what about you?"

"If you're asking whether I'm going to be charged with stealing restricted information, the answer is no."

John offered up a silent prayer of thanks. "I understand about Michael, but what has this to do with Walker?"

"Don't you see? It's as though everything has come full circle. Michael… Walker, they're the same. They both used me in their own way."

"But you agreed to help Walker when you could have said 'no,' walked away, and left him to fight his own battle. Why? And why the rush to fly home?"

"Because… because I love him!" Skye blurted out.

"Ah!"

"Is that *all* you're going to say?"

"What else can I say? I assume that being in love with Walker doesn't exactly make you happy?"

Skye sighed. "He lied to me. He doesn't trust me, and he certainly has no feelings for me. The man's cold—cold as the fish he studies. The only reason I agreed to help him was because I don't want to see innocent people hurt."

"I see. And that's why you want to go home?"

"Yes."

John considered her predicament. He wasn't convinced she was in love with Walker, although he did believe that Michael and Walker were cut from the same cloth.

"I dare say I can fold my body into an airline seat once more. I'll see if there are any seats available on this evening's flight to London. In the meantime, phone the realtor and ask if they can help you with your things. Don't forget to ask them about returning your rental car too."

Skye rose to her feet, her tear stained face eager and alive with affection. She hugged John, kissed him on the cheek, and rushed from the room.

CHAPTER TWENTY-THREE

Walker opened his eyes, closed them, and opened them again. It took him a few moments to orientate himself to his surroundings such was the pulsating in his head. He ignored the searing pain, and tried to shift into a more comfortable position only to discover his hands and feet were tied.

In the yellow glow cast by a single bulb on the bulkhead, he noticed a vertical steel access ladder rising up to a watertight access hatch about twenty-five feet above his head. The unmistakable throb of a diesel generator came from below deck. He was in the cargo hold of the *Rosario Queen.* The vessel rose up and down with the gentle swell, and he assumed that it was still moored to the quayside.

In one corner secured by ropes, stood some crates and the barrels he'd seen on the quay. The smell of rotten fish and heavy diesel oil filled his nostrils making want to vomit. He swallowed hard, forced the acid back into his stomach, and tried to concentrate.

Breathing through his mouth, he made a quick assessment of his situation. He didn't like what he found. His boots were missing, but he was still wearing his socks and jacket. With a great deal of effort, he sat up. His head ached abominably, but he no longer felt nauseous.

The bulkhead door groaned as it opened. Voices approached out of the half-light. Walker closed his eyes and slumped forward feigning unconsciousness. Heavy boots crossed the deck, stopping inches away from him. A hand shook him roughly. He opened his eyes and groaned for effect. Two men stood over him. Both were heavy set, weighed a good two hundred pounds, and sported broken noses. The words Dumb and Dumber sprung to mind. Dumb was the first to speak, and wasn't as stupid as he looked.

"So you're awake. What's your name? And what were you doing on the dock?"

"The name's Walker."

"You, *pal*," Dumb said, jabbing a finger at him, "were sticking your nose in where it had no right to be."

"I've told you the name's Walker—not *pal*."

"Look, *pal*," Dumber repeated, "we saw you sniffing around our cargo like a dog after a bitch on heat. What did you find that was so interesting?"

Walker watched the two men. They irritated him, but antagonizing these goons would not be a wise move. He'd seen a few bar room brawls in his time to know that even if he was able to take these two on without a weapon, his chances of surviving were slim.

"There's been a misunderstanding. I went to the office to inquire about some cargo I was expecting. I came out and decided to walk along the quay, noticed my bootlace was undone, and bent down to tie it. Next thing I know, I wake up in this stinking hold, with my hands and feet bound, and you two are standing over me. No hard feelings, guys. Untie me and let me out of here. I won't cause any trouble."

"Yeah, and I'm the fairy on the Christmas tree. No way, pal. Cindy told us about the little chat you had with her. We're not carrying anything for the islands, so why all the interest in the *Rosario Queen*?"

Walker's mind raced. *Cindy?* The woman he'd conned out of information a few hours earlier. The same woman who was itching to get into his pants? Nah. Impossible.

"I told you I was expecting a delivery."

"Maybe you are expecting a delivery, but not from this ship. You were paying too much attention to our cargo for someone just out for a walk. Seeing as you're so interested, you're coming with us." Dumber gave Walker a shove. He fell sideways to the deck. "We'll decide what to do with you later. In the meantime, enjoy the ride."

The door to the hold slammed shut with a resounding thud. Walker listened as the footsteps retreated, then shuffled across the deck on his backside. Breathing hard, beads of sweat popped on his forehead. Using one of the crates as a backrest, he tried to break the ropes binding his wrists, but they refused to budge. The deck beneath him shuddered. Deep within the freighter the engine cranked up—they were getting underway.

On the quayside, McCabe waited impatiently. He checked his watch for the third time in as many minutes. There was still no sign of Walker. He watched the *Rosario Queen* through his binoculars. The small freighter bristled with activity. Then suddenly, the rusting hulk nudged away from the quayside and steamed out of harbor. McCabe swore heartily and picked up his cell phone. He punched in nine-one-one and requested the Coast Guard, identifying himself to the young rating on the line. He explained the situation, and requested they intercept the *Rosario Queen* escort the vessel back to port.

The rating was most apologetic. "Sorry, sir. The Coast Guard cutter is off station dealing with a major incident. It will be a couple of hours before it's free and able to comply with your request. As soon as things quieten down, I'll send the cutter to investigate."

"Yeah, by that time the *Rosario Queen* will be miles away."

"Provided she's switched on her radar, which is a Federal requirement, then—"

"*Switched on her radar?* Which palm tree did you climb down from, sailor? Do you really think a freighter involved in illegal activities is going to use ships' radar for Christ's sake?"

"Well, I—"

"Put me through to your commanding officer—now!"

***

Walker listened to the steady throb of the engine. He had no idea what time it was and could only guess how long they had been at sea. A newly commissioned vessel of a similar size would make no more than ten knots. This rusting hulk had a lot of hard sea time under her keel and he estimated was making six to seven knots at best. The Coast Guard cutter should have no problem catching up.

The freighter's captain would run without navigation lights and without radar too, to avoid his ship being identified, even if it meant risking a collision with another vessel. That meant one thing – whoever was in command of the *Rosario Queen* was familiar with the waters of Puget Sound.

Walker closed his eyes. Everyone knew that fish stocks were diminishing and there were too many boats. It was a worldwide problem. Illegal dumping in the ocean would be easy cash to a less-than-scrupulous skipper. That left two possibilities, either the owners of the *Rosario Queen* were in deep financial shit, or the ship was owned and worked by one of the many migrant crews who had moved into Anacortes from mother Russia. They cared little for the environment and often exploited every regulation in order to maximize their catch. They probably weren't averse to a little illegal dumping either, provided the price was right.

He wriggled his toes to bring the circulation back into his numb feet. He felt certain that when the time came, the barrels wouldn't be the only things being dumped overboard.

The freighter pitched to port and then to starboard as it rolled with the current. In the eerie shadows, Walker thought he saw the glint of something metallic on the deck. He shuffled over, his shoulders burning with the effort, until his fingers closed around a sharp object.

Whether he held metal or glass, he didn't care. Gripping the object, he twisted it in his fingers until he could rub it against the rope. The technique always worked in the movies, and he hoped it would work for him. More than once, he felt it slice into his skin. Despite the pain and the blood trickling down his wrists, he continued to saw away at his bonds. After a while, he tested the ropes. They were as tight as ever.

He leaned back against the bulkhead. He'd been in tricky situations before, but always managed to find a way out. This time, he was in way over his head. Unless the Coast Guard arrived soon, or an opportunity arose for him to escape, there was little he could do other than conserve his energy. He closed his eyes and tried to sleep.

Up in the wheelhouse, the captain cut the engines and dropped anchor. Silently, the crew went about their business. Using only hand signals, they released the well-oiled bolts on the access hatch, and maneuvered the small deck crane into position.

CHAPTER TWENTY-FOUR

"The Coast Guard cutter is on her way, sir, and the Navy's has scrambled a helo—a helicopter from Whidbey Naval Station. It should be with you shortly. It's a big area to cover, but a freighter that size can't have gotten far."

McCabe rubbed his chin. "Sailor, I don't need you to remind me how big the search area is! Get off this damned phone and locate that freighter before we have a major environmental catastrophe on our hands."

McCabe broke the connection as he heard the whoop-whoop of a helicopter overhead. It touched down on the quayside, and he climbed aboard. Someone thrust a helmet and headset into his hands as the large machine lifted off, and headed out into the onyx night.

The helicopter searched an area to the north and west of the cutter, using its powerful searchlight to identify any vessel it came across. Through his headset, McCabe listened to the Coast Guard cutter as its crew interrogated the captain of a fishing vessel. With its identity confirmed, the cutter moved on to the next radar target and repeated the procedure until they accounted for every vessel in the area.

McCabe's brow was damp with sweat. Time was fast running out for Walker, if it hadn't already done so. These people were ruthless; and would eliminate anyone who got in their way. He tried not to think about what fate might await his friend—he just hoped he would be in time to prevent Walker from ending up on a slab in the morgue.

He anxiously scanned the straits through a pair of night vision goggles. There was nothing in sight, just miles of open water. That damned freighter had to be out there somewhere, if only they could get a fix on it.

He paid little attention to the incessant chatter of the fishing fleet, but suddenly honed in on a conversation between the captain of a tanker and the first mate of a seine netter who was complaining bitterly about the near collision it had with another vessel, which had been running without navigation lights.

"That has to be it! Someone get on the radio and get the location of that tanker."

"Whidbey's already on it sir," the co-pilot shouted. The helicopter banked to the left. "We're receiving GPS coordinates now. It's approximately ten minutes flying time away."

"Hold on, Walker, hold on," McCabe prayed. The pilot dropped the nose of the helicopter. Skimming the tops of the waves, it gained speed with each passing second.

***

Cold, stark fear ran down Walker's spine as the watertight hatch above his head opened. This was it. This was how his life was going to end. They would toss him overboard along with the toxic chemicals whose safe disposal he had tried hard to ensure. He knew his chance of survival in the icy waters of Puget Sound was non-existent. At best, he would last half an hour before hypothermia set in.

Steel-toed boots clanked on the deck above. First, one man, then another, swung his legs over the side and climbed down the ladder into the hold. Walker felt a rush of adrenaline as panic welled in his stomach. The two rough-looking seamen dragged him to his feet. A flash of humor crossed his face. The *Rosario Queen's* crew all came from the same school of charm and etiquette—the two men could easily be cousins to Dumb and Dumber.

Whatever they planned, he wasn't about to make their task easy. He struggled violently as they hauled him towards the bulkhead door. He twisted left, then right, trying to loosen their grip on his arms. A fist slammed into his face, and his world went black. A hand grabbed a fist full of his hair, forcing his head up to meet a pair of weasel-like eyes.

"We can either do this the easy way or we can do it the hard way. Are you going to co-operate or does my friend here have to give you more of the same?"

Walker nodded.

"Okay, let's get movin'. The boss wants you on deck."

They half-pushed and half-dragged him along the corridor until they reached the companionway. Either one of them had to carry Walker's dead weight up the narrow staircase, or they must untie his feet. Walker watched as the question passed silently between his two guards. Walker saw a flash of steel as the shorter of the two men withdrew a gutting knife from his belt and bent down to cut the rope around his ankles.

As soon as the rope slackened, Walker kicked the guard standing behind him. At the same time, he head-butted the other guard in the stomach. Before either could react, he regained his balance and ducked around the stairwell, and ran along the corridor. He'd hardly covered five yards, when he was tackled from behind and brought down. A pair of heavy sea boots connected with his ribs in a vicious kick, forcing the air from his lungs with a whoosh. He lay on the deck, curled up in the fetal position, gasping for breath.

"That was a real stupid move." The tip of the gutting knife pressed against his throat. "One more stunt like that, and I'll have no hesitation in using this. Understand?"

Incapable of talking, Walker blinked rapidly.

"Good. Then, let's do as the captain ordered and go on deck."

Gulping air into his oxygen-starved lungs, Walker struggled to his knees. If he breathed deeply, the pain in his ribs was incandescent. Two pairs of strong arms hauled him to his feet. The cold steel at his throat never wavered.

Breathing shallowly through his teeth, he shuffled along to the companionway. His guards shoved him up the narrow stairway. Once on deck, they kept hold of his arms. All he could do was shudder in pain and await his fate.

The *Rosario Queen* rolled in the gentle swell. He guessed that it was slack-tide—that time when the sea is often at its calmest—perfect for dumping the barrels over the side into the black depths of Puget Sound. In the glare of the deck lights, he noticed that the small deck crane had lifted some of the barrels from the hold. The crew released them from the cargo net and rolled them off to one side. The crane swung into action again, disappearing into the depths of the hold for another load.

Walker glanced out to sea, but the deck lights ruined his night vision. The wheelhouse door opened, and three figures stormed their way towards him. The first he took to be the captain of the freighter, the second he recognized as the manager of the waste management plant. There was no doubting his involvement now. But who was the third guy, he wondered. Was he the brains behind the operation or just another monkey?

All three picked their way over the deck, avoiding trailing ropes and deck cleats until they stopped inches from him and his guards.

"We meet again, Mr. Walker. Although, this time, I have the upper hand."

"I wouldn't be too sure of that. It's only a matter of time before the Coast Guard locates this freighter."

"Ah, yes, your associate, McCabe. The Coast Guard is unable to intervene. Before we sailed there was a major incident, I won't bore you with the details. The cutter is miles away and not likely to turn up before we've finished our business, isn't that right, captain?"

"Yes, sir. She won't be with us anytime soon."

"As you can see, we're about ready to conclude our nights' work. But before we do—"

"Why?" Why dispose of these chemicals illegally?" asked Walker.

"Because your actions nearly ruined me. You weren't satisfied with closing down my South American operation. You made sure the authorities refused my company's application to build a new plant in Anacortes. I needed that plant to recoup my losses."

"Your planning application was turned down for one simple reason, his bad management." Walker indicated the plant manager with a jerk of his head.

"That's a matter of opinion. There's something else, something far more personal. I've waited a long time for this. You don't recognize me, do you?"

Walker shook his head. "Should I?"

"We've met before, under far different circumstances."

"If I knew you, I'm sure I'd remember."

"I doubt it, although most people remember my sister. And you do remember my sister, don't you?"

"Hey what's this, an inquisition? I meet many people in my job. Scientists, secretaries, and even dumb-asses like you! If you're going to kill me, just get on with it."

"Tut, tut, Mr. Walker. Where are your manners? Allow me to refresh your memory. She has blonde hair, stunning blue eyes and a figure most women envy. She captivated your attention. You even implied you loved her, although you didn't use those words. Sound familiar?"

"If you've something to tell me, come out and say it."

"You dated my sister, or more precisely my half-sister. She loved you, but you made her look a fool."

"I don't know who you're talking about—"

"It's too late to play the innocent, its payback time."

"I've always made it clear that my work makes it difficult to be involved with someone. I have to be free to travel and if your sister—half sister—couldn't accept that then I'm sorry, but it's not my fault she got hurt."

"Arlene. Her name is Arlene. Ah, I see by your face you remember."

"Arlene Allensbury. Oh, yes, I remember Arlene. We had dinner a few times when I was in town. That's all I intended it to be. Your sister started turning up unexpectedly at my office, at my apartment, when I entertained clients. She was stalking me, for Christ's sake! She told everyone that she was my fiancée. I took her to dinner to explain how I felt, but she didn't get it and started screaming. I tried to calm her down, but she just lost it, so I left. She went to my apartment, and wormed her way past the doorman. Your darling sister trashed my home. I called the cops and they took her away in plastic cuffs, frothing at the mouth. The psychiatrist who treated her at the hospital said she was psychotic."

"She was not! She loved you so much that she couldn't imagine life without you. Do you know what she did?"

"No, tell me."

"She tried to kill herself. My beautiful sister took an overdose because of you. All because of *you*!"

"Look, Allensbury, I'm sorry, but your—"

"You're sorry? It's too late to be sorry. My beautiful sister doesn't even recognize me when I visit her. She sits in a chair and drools like a baby! Can you imagine what that feels like?"

"No, I can't. I suspect your sister was sick long before I met her. My involvement with her had nothing to do with her illness. Killing me won't make your sister sane again, Allensbury. You're putting lives at risk by dumping these chemicals. Is that what you want on your conscience—the deaths of innocent people? Tell the captain to turn his vessel around and head back to port. I'm sure if you turn yourself in, we can cut a deal with the DA."

"Do you really think I'm that stupid? No, Mr. Walker you are going to pay."

"Be sensible about this. What use will you be to your sister, languishing in the state penitentiary?"

"I do not intend getting caught. Your body will never be found or at least nothing that will be recognizable. The ocean will see to that. We've talked long enough. Captain, you know how to deal with Mr. Walker."

The two guards dragged Walker to the side of the ship. A deckhand removed the bolts from a section of handrails and lifted them out of the plugs that secured them. He watched helplessly as one barrel and then another entered the water, bubbles rising from the seals as they sank.

A rough hand pushed him in the back, and suddenly he was flying through the air. There was a feeling of pressure and a bubbling sound in his ears as the water rushed past and he started sinking. A thousand icy daggers stabbed his body. He ignored the searing agony in his ribs and kicked hard for the surface.

Suddenly, he felt the breeze on his face. He coughed and gagged, trying to clear his lungs of the salt water he'd ingested. No matter how cold he felt or how much pain he was in, he had to stay afloat for as long as possible. He watched the *Rosario Queen* steam away, leaving him with only the stars for company.

CHAPTER TWENTY-FIVE

McCabe willed the helicopter to go faster. How long did it take to cover thirty nautical miles? Was his friend even alive, he wondered? His concern showed in the lines on his drawn and haggard face. Every nerve in his body tingled. A burst of static erupted from his headphones as a voice came over the radio.

"The target is changing course to the north-east." A stream of GPS coordinates followed. The helicopter pilot didn't miss a beat of the rotors, changing course before the transmission had ended.

"She's dumped her cargo!" McCabe slammed his fist into the fuselage. "We're too late."

"With respect sir, you don't know that. She could have picked up another vessel on her radar and decided to high-tail it out of there."

"No way! The captain of the *Rosario Queen* hasn't switched on his radar, nor will he. Not even if he were about to hit an iceberg and join the Titanic on the ocean floor. I'm telling you, she's dumped her fucking cargo."

"We can check that out or we intercept the vessel. It's your call, sir," the co-pilot said.

"Can't we do both? Can't we fly over the ships' original position before intercepting her? If those barrels are still floating on the surface, they represent a major shipping hazard."

"We're getting low on fuel and have forty minutes of flying time left. That gives us one shot at this. If your description of those barrels is accurate, they won't remain afloat for very long. Under the circumstances, I suggest we go after the *Rosario Queen* and stay with her until the Coast Guard cutter arrives on station. Then, we can peel off, refuel, and come back to see if there are any barrels remaining on the surface, and if necessary, drop a buoy. In the meantime, we can put an exclusion zone around her last position to alert shipping of the hazard."

McCabe thought hard. He was sure the crew wouldn't let Walker go. Chances were they would throw him overboard and leave him to the mercy of the sea. He keyed the send button on his radio mike.

"Check out that ship's last position. Go in low. I want to see the skids of this bird kissing the tops of the waves. I want to be one hundred per cent certain there is nothing floating on the surface. And get the boys at Whidbey to keep tracking that damned ship so we know exactly where she is at any given time."

"Yes, sir!"

The helicopter banked hard left throwing McCabe against the cold wall of the aft cabin. He hoped and prayed he'd called it right.

***

Walker estimated he'd been in the icy water for five minutes, but already his body temperature was dropping. Against the ever-darkening sky, he could just make out the silhouette of the *Rosario Queen* as she steamed steadily north. His initial panic had gone and he felt surprisingly calm. It took a supreme effort to keep his chin above the waves. More often than not, he found himself holding his breath whenever a particularly large wave washed over him.

He tried changing position to float on his back, but with his arms still tied, it was impossible. The ache in his shoulders was unbearable, and the ropes binding his wrists rubbed his skin raw. With immense effort, he brought his body into an upright position. While it allowed him to tread water, it also sapped his energy. Every seventh wave seemed more powerful than the six before it, driving him under, further diluting his strength, and forcing him to use what little he had left to kick hard for the surface.

Moonlight filtered through a web of clouds, and there was little breeze. A few barrels remained half submerged on the surface, a stream of bubbles rising from the seals as the contents spilled into the sea. Walker tried to stay away from them, as he had no way of knowing whether their deadly cargo was sinking or floating on the surface.

He weighed up his situation and decided it was hopeless. All he could think about was the bone-numbing coldness of the ocean. Despite the pain in his ribs and shoulders, all he wanted to do was sleep. He drifted off, only to jerk awake, coughing and spluttering. He had to stay awake—he just had to!

He couldn't die like this, but if help didn't arrive soon he knew he'd be done for. His reserves of energy would soon be depleted, and he would slip into the inky blackness without the strength or the will to kick for the surface.

Everything in his life had taken a downward spiral since he'd accepted this assignment. Turning his face skyward, he thought about Skye. He'd dragged her into this unholy mess. Too late, he realized he loved her, but his stupidity and mistrust had made her turn away from him. He wouldn't blame her if she'd high-tailed it back to London. When he closed his eyes, he could see her, as she had been that day on his boat, the wind whipping at her hair, a radiant smile on her face. Although he had not shown it, she made his life whole.

Yet in truth he knew he had lost her.

Among the stars, he spotted the twinkling navigation lights of a plane as it flew north toward Alaska. Drifting with the current, his mind wandered. He tossed his head to clear the salt water from his eyes and looked around, desperately seeking signs of a ship. There was a light in the distance, but when he looked a second time, it had vanished. Damn it! His exhausted mind was playing tricks.

His chin fell onto his chest in utter despair. He dozed for a while. When he woke, the light he had seen off to his right appeared to be getting closer. As he watched, it detached itself from the horizon and climbed into the sky. A plane! What's more, it was heading in his direction, sweeping the sea as if searching for something or someone.

"McCabe!" He shouted through salt cracked lips.

McCabe had come looking for him. Thank God. Everything was going to be all right. Over the lapping of the waves, he could hear the distinct sound of a helicopter.

"Come on, come on, baby! That's it, this way."

To his dismay, the machine changed course. He screamed in desperation, his hopes dashed. It was pointless. He may as well accept his fate and give up. The strong currents of Puget Sound dragged him along with the changing tide. The wave strength increased and he found it increasingly difficult to keep his head above water. Caught in a sudden cross current, the sea became a white churning cauldron, tossing him in one direction and then another. He kicked hard, but despite all his efforts, the sea dragged him under.

His lungs were bursting with the effort of holding his breath. He was on the point of blacking out when a semi-submerged tree trunk slammed into the back of his head. It was a long time before his unconscious body emerged on the surface, the sea once more calm as the wave rolled on towards the islands. He floated face down in the water, an invisible form in a black sea.

CHAPTER TWENTY-SIX

Skye chewed her bottom lip as the taxi carrying her and John to SeaTac airport threaded its way through the early evening traffic. John leaned back in his seat and watched her from under hooded eyes. He wondered whether to say something or to leave her alone with her thoughts. Ever since she had knocked on his hotel room door earlier that morning, he'd wanted to wrap her in his arms and tell her everything would be all right.

They had known each other since university. She had mistakenly assumed he was the professor rather than a lowly post-graduate. Since that day, he had been more than a little in love with her. However, their acquaintance never moved beyond the realms of friendship, and he'd accepted that Skye would only ever see him as a friend.

He'd always been there for her, and always would be, no matter who or what came between them. When her parents died, or something unexpected happened, he'd been there with a box of tissues and if occasion demanded,

249

his couch for the night. He reached out and laced his fingers with hers.

"We're nearly there. Are you sure, you want to go through with this? You look worn out. We could stay in the airport hotel and fly back tomorrow."

Skye shook her head. "I'd rather fly tonight."

The taxi came to a halt outside the main terminal building. John released her hand and got out. He paid the driver then helped her out of the car. He wrapped one arm around her shoulders and picked up his overnight bag with the other.

Like all airports, SeaTac was crowded with people and humming with noise. He paid scant attention to the bustling crowds as he hustled Skye through the melee towards the check-in desk.

"I know we don't normally fly first-class. However, I thought you would appreciate the peace of the upper deck rather than sitting with the rabble downstairs. Besides, I don't think my long bones could stand being cooped up in economy. Before you complain about the extravagance, I think the business can afford it now that we know the software works."

Skye focused her pain-filled eyes on him and managed a weak smile. Once again, he had come to her rescue. She really didn't deserve him as a friend, but she was so glad he was. Thoughtful, and always attuned to her needs, she just wished she could return his feelings for her, but sadly, she couldn't. That burning, all-consuming spark of passion was missing. However, her experience of passion had taught her that it was an over-rated commodity and the pleasure was short lived, while the pain it brought, lingered. Maybe she should settle for a more staid relationship, one built on trust and mutual respect.

But not yet.

First, she had to get her life back on track.

Their meager amount of luggage checked, they passed through the interminable security checks and into the departure lounge.

"We've a couple of hours to wait before our flight departs. Let's have something to eat and drink. Then you can phone Debbie and let her know you're flying home," John said.

Skye halted midstride. She clapped a hand to her cheek. Debbie would be out of her mind with worry, and yet Skye knew she couldn't face Debbie's endless probing questions. She felt a wave of momentary panic and fought hard to hold on to her fragile control.

"I can't talk to her, not now. Would you phone her? Tell her we have a problem with the business, anything but the truth. I couldn't bear that. I'll speak to her in a few days. I need ... I need some time to clear my thoughts."

John studied Skye's pale face. Her blue eyes brimmed with tears, her pain clearly visible. Against his better judgment and all the promises he had made himself over the years, he pulled her into his arms and held her tight, savoring the feel of her body against his. His lips brushed her forehead.

"Hey, no tears, remember? Don't worry. I'll take care of everything. I'll call Debbie, tell her not to worry and make some excuse to keep her off the phone until you feel like talking." When Skye relaxed, he reluctantly loosened his hold on her, letting her go when he was sure she had her emotions under control.

"If my memory serves me right, there's a restaurant along here, or if you prefer we can grab a coffee and a burger."

John grimaced. "Oh Lord, you want me to eat a hamburger? Do you know what they put in those things? Please, I'd prefer to keep my cholesterol levels as they are."

Through her sadness, Skye laughed. "Oh, John, you're such a snob. Come on, the restaurant it is."

Under his watchful gaze, Skye picked at her food, but managed to eat enough of her entree to satisfy him. She declined a sweet from the trolley. Over coffee, he brought up the subject of Walker.

"Do you think Walker caught those responsible?"

Skye's eyes widened in alarm. "I hope so. I hate to think of all those chemicals contaminating the sea. We did all we could, it's up to the authorities now."

"I suppose you're right. What about Walker?"

"I want nothing more to do with him."

John's eyes searched her face, probing her thoughts. "The man obviously loves you. The least you could do is call and tell him you're leaving."

Skye looked away, her mind a gamut of emotions. Part of her hated Walker because of how he'd treated her, but the other part cared. No, cared wasn't the right word—loved. She loved him, but he'd hurt her and right now she wanted as much distance between them as possible.

"The only thing he deserves from me is a hefty bill for our services. I agreed to help him and I have. Besides, I don't know how to contact him."

John produced a business card from his jacket pocket.

"I have his office number right here. Call him before you leave. Don't do something you may regret for the rest of your life."

Skye shrank from the piece of paper, her eyes suddenly filled with anger.

"Call him? Call him and say what? Thank you for ruining my vacation by assuming I'm a criminal? Thank you for making me an emotional wreck? I don't think so. I couldn't bear to listen to his excuses. The man is an emotional vacuum. His only interest is the marine life he studies. I have no intention of contacting him now or ever."

John felt secretly pleased by her reaction, but strove hard to hide it. Best to let her think he'd put his size twelve feet firmly into his mouth.

Soon after they'd finished their meal, they boarded the non-stop flight to London. Skye took one last look out of the window as the huge plane climbed out of SeaTac, heading northeast. The lights of Seattle twinkled below, becoming smaller and smaller as the plane gained height. Skye thought she caught a glimpse of the Space Needle and somewhere off to the right, she knew, was Walker's office.

Fleetingly, she wondered if he sat at his desk, compiling his report. Another ecological disaster safely averted, thanks to his expertise. Would he think of her and the brief time they had shared, she mused. Would he even miss her?

No, she was sure he would dismiss the whole affair as business; filing the days they'd shared and loved along with his report. Her heart squeezed in anguish. John was right. Perhaps she should have called him, but hearing his voice would destroy her. Besides, what could she say? 'Tell me you love you, and I'll stay?'

Walker's work would always come first. There was no room in his life for a permanent relationship. He traveled light and couldn't afford any baggage to slow him down. She'd done the right thing. She'd walked away with her dignity intact, knowing that by giving her expertise she had acted without malice. It had cost her personally, but in time, she would forget the pain and the hurt.

John watched Skye's inner struggle. He sighed with relief. She was back under his protection and he was going to make sure nothing like this ever happened to her again. If Walker came looking for her, he would have to get past him first. He reached across the small table between their seats and took her hand, linking his strong fingers in hers.

"Try to relax, and get some rest. I'll let you know when they serve dinner. Would you like a brandy?"

"I couldn't face another meal, but a drink would be good."

Although exhausted, her body fought against sleep, her mind a maelstrom of thoughts and memories, depriving her of the rest she so badly needed. The further the plane flew, the paler her face became, the circles beneath her eyes darkening with each passing mile.

Somewhere over Canada, Skye finally fell asleep. John covered her with a blanket, turned out the overhead light, and for the first time since seeing her with Walker, relaxed.

CHAPTER TWENTY-SEVEN

The helicopter had been circling over the *Rosario Queen's* last position for fifteen minutes, the powerful spotlight trained on the surface of the sea. McCabe's eyes burned with the effort of staring at the water, his body tense with apprehension. He was too late, damn it! Walker must be on the freighter, now miles away to the north. By the time the helicopter refueled on Whidbey, it would be even further way. He turned away from the cabin door, his expression darkening to an unreadable emotion.

The suddenly the winch man called out.

"There! About thirty yards off our port side I think I see something"

The pilot brought the large machine down into the hover. McCabe pushed his way to the port window and focused all his attention on the spot the young airman indicated.

"Can you see it? There's something floating in the water."

Try as he might he couldn't see anything out of the ordinary. He shook his head.

"Pass me those night vision goggles." He snatched them out of the airman's hand and turned his head away from the window just long enough to pull them over his head. He waited for his eyes to adjust to the eerie green light.

"I can't see a damned—" Just then the moon appeared through the clouds and cast a ghost-like shadow on the water and... yes! He could make out the shape of an object as it floated just below the surface.

"It's a damned porpoise, you idiot."

He pulled off the goggles and his headset, and threw them on the floor of the cabin. It was hopeless, like searching for a single fish in a shoal of thousands! It was an enormous area to search with only one helicopter. Without a survival suit, no one could spend more than half an hour—three-quarters at the outside—in the icy cold water and survive.

He glanced at his watch and did some quick math. The tide was on the turn. The strong current could carry Walker's body to Alaska and back before it was found. He had no way of knowing if these unscrupulous bastards hadn't tied Walker to one of the barrels before throwing him overboard, or worse, killed him. Whichever, the outcome would be the same; Walker's body would be lying on the ocean floor along with the bottom feeders.

One of the crewmen mouthed something and indicated his watch. McCabe guessed the young airman was indicating that the large machine was nearly out of fuel. He leaned closer and lifted the airman's ear protectors.

"I don't care if this damned machine is running on fumes, tell the pilot to go round one more time!"

"But, Sir—"

"DO IT!"

McCabe watched as the young airman keyed his mike. He didn't care if they had to ditch the bird in the sea. The pilot did as requested, and took the helicopter in for one more circuit of the search area. The downwash from the rotors flattened the wave tops and kicked up spray. McCabe rubbed the ache in his temples and wiped away the imaginary grit in his eyes before pulling on his headset and goggles. He took up position in front of the starboard window and stared out into the blackness.

Up in the cockpit, the co-pilot held his breath, and offered a silent prayer to the patron saint of pilots. His eyes on the fuel gauge, the indicator already well into the red zone.

McCabe had to admire the skill of the two pilots as they held the huge machine steady with nothing to guide them but the instruments. It hung in the sky, held by some invisible thread, impervious to the elements, the only controlling factors being their skill and the amount of fuel remaining.

McCabe's jaw clenched, his lips compressing into a thin line. The pilot's less than calm voice filled his headset.

"Sir, we have to break off the search *now*, otherwise we won't make it back to base."

McCabe bowed his head in defeat. Anxious for the life his friend, he couldn't justify putting five other lives at risk by continuing the search when fuel was so dangerously low.

"Break off and head for Whidbey, but I want this bird refueled and back in the air in under five minutes."

The pilot acknowledged the transmission. He gained height, and banked to the right in readiness to peel off.

"There! About twenty feet off our port side," said the airman who wore a pair of thermal imaging goggles. "There's a heat trace. It's... it's a body. Yeah, it's definitely a body!"

McCabe shoved the man roughly aside. In the powerful glare of the searchlight, he could clearly see the outline of a body in the water. He secured his safety line and stood back as the diver opened the door and clipped his harness to the winch cable before easing himself out and into the blackness of the night.

Slowly, the cable paid out, lowering the wetsuit-clad diver, until finally he disappeared from view under the belly of the aircraft. The winch man lay on the floor of the cabin, his body half out of the open doorway, his hand steadying the cable, his voice calm as he guided the diver and the pilot ever closer to the target.

McCabe hardly dared hope. The beat of the helicopter's rotors echoed inside the cabin. The winch man issued an urgent string of commands and the remaining crew leapt into action.

"What's happening? Has he reached him? Is it Walker? Is he alive? God damn it! Someone talk to me!" McCabe shouted.

His questions went unanswered. He watched as inch by inch the cable was reeled in. Unable to bear the tension, he leaned out of the doorway as far as he dare, the only thing between him, and certain death being the thin line attached to his safety harness.

In the moonlight, he saw the diver emerge from the sea, along with the unmistakable shape of a limp and seemingly lifeless body. McCabe turned away from the doorway, unable to watch the unfolding scene, fear, stark and vivid in his face.

Willing hands reached out and dragged the diver and the unconscious form into the cabin. The crew worked as a well-oiled machine, their actions honed by years of training. McCabe stayed out of their way, knowing that in this situation his presence would be a hindrance rather than of help.

Within seconds, the ropes binding the inert form's hands were cut and the body rolled on to its back. Resuscitation equipment and blankets appeared from nowhere, as the crew medic set about clearing the airway and putting a line into a vein.

The tension was unbearable. McCabe gently pushed the medic aside, so he could get a glimpse of the body's corpse-like face. He staggered backwards, blindly searching for something to hold onto.

Walker appeared to be in a catatonic state, his face gray and ghost-like. His lips were tinged with blue, and his body felt colder than an Alaskan winter. Walker didn't appear to be breathing, the heart monitor barely registering a beat.

McCabe did his best to hold his emotions in check, but failed. Tears ran down his weatherworn face. He slumped to the cabin floor and put his head in his hands, experiencing a mixture of uncontrollable rage, and unbelievable sadness.

Walker was dead. And it was his fault.

A raw and primitive grief overwhelmed him.

The crew continued to work on Walker. They stripped his body of its wet clothing, wrapped him in blankets, adding a heat-retaining blanket as a final covering.

The pilot's came on the radio. "Whidbey want to know the patient's status."

The medic started calling out Walker's vital signs. "We're bringing in a male, approximately one hundred and eighty pounds. Unconscious, pupils fixed and dilated, no discernable output, with a body temperature of less than ninety-four degrees. He has a head injury requiring a CT scan. CPR commenced. Ask them to have a full cardiac-pulmonary resuscitation team standing by, including a surgeon experienced in cardio-pulmonary bypass techniques."

"What's the point? Can't you all see he's dead?" McCabe said. A hand descended on his shoulder.

"He's still in with a chance, sir. In circumstances such as these, the body shuts down—the technical term is hypoxemia. It's similar to hypothermia. The body loses heat. The heart rate slows, as does the respiratory rate. Cold-water near-drowning can be survivable. In some cases, people who've been submersed in very cold water for as long as an hour can be fully resuscitated."

"He's dead. He's dead and it's my fault!"

"No, sir, he's not dead, at least not yet. He's in cardiac arrest, but we've commenced CPR. His body temperature has dropped a little since we've picked him up, but that's only to be expected. We call it 'afterdrop.' The doctors at Whidbey are experienced in dealing with near-drowning victims. Once we land, they'll put him on cardiac-pulmonary bypass to re-oxygenate his blood, and use other techniques to raise his body temperature. How he responds depends on how long he's been unconscious and in the water. Don't give up hope yet."

McCabe stared at the young medic. "Someone mentioned a head injury. Does it affect his chances?"

"It won't help, that's for sure. As for how serious it is—it's difficult to tell without a scan. There has been some blood loss. Whidbey has all the equipment standing by. Your friend looks fairly fit and healthy, and he's young. They're all things in his favor. Provided there's no brain injury or cardiac damage, then I'd say his chance are about fifty-fifty."

The helicopter flew low and fast over the sea, in a race between life and death. McCabe's gaze never left Walker's face. In his mind he repeated the mantra, 'don't you die on me, Walker! Hold on, help is coming. Hold on.'

Then suddenly, they were on final approach. The helicopter touched down, and the doors were thrown back. The stretcher carrying Walker was loaded into the waiting ambulance and whisked away at high speed to the medical facility.

As the endless night grayed into dawn, the doctors worked on Walker. McCabe felt helpless. He sat in the waiting area and made himself a promise. Whatever the outcome, he would find the bastards responsible for this. Even if it took him the rest of his life, he would follow them to hell and back if he had to, but pay for Walker's life they would.

CHAPTER TWENTY-EIGHT

London, Five Months later.

John put his head round the door of Skye's office. "Can you spare a few minutes?"

"Sure, I was due for a break. What can I help you with?"

He crossed the room and propped a hip on the corner of her desk. The dark circles under her eyes, which had been all too evident when they first returned from Seattle, had vanished. She was a picture of radiant womanhood—a woman whose smile held a depth that had been missing for far too long.

"Will you have dinner with me tonight?"

Skye rested her chin on her hand, a bemused smile on her lips. Hardly a week passed without John asking her to dinner, yet she always found a reason to turn him down. She owed him so much—her sanity for one thing. Without his support, she would have never got over the events of spring or got this far in her career. She had a lot to thank him for.

"I'd like that. I'd like that very much."

His mood suddenly buoyant, his mouth curved with a secret smile. He brushed her cheek with his fingertip.

"I'll pick you up at eight. Any preference what we eat? Italian, Thai, or Chinese?"

"You choose. But please, no Sushi! I've gone right off fish. Just let me know whether I need to wear something casual or smart."

"As I don't often take my business partner out to dinner, I think we should push the boat out a bit."

Skye's rich laughter filled the air. "John Ridge, you're the biggest liar I know. We had dinner last week. Admittedly, there were seven other people present, but I seem to remember you were there too."

"I want you all to myself for one evening, so that I can stare into your magnificent blue eyes and whisper sweet nothings in your ear. I can't do that with an audience or when I'm sat at the other end of the table."

"Are you flirting with me? What happened, did your latest conquest turn you down?"

He placed his hand on his heart and adopted a forlorn expression. "You wound me. My intentions are strictly honorable. Honorable that is until after I take you home and you give me coffee."

"You're incorrigible! After I give you coffee, you leave."

"You're breaking my heart."

Skye enjoyed their gentle sparring. "How many women have you been out with this week, two? Three?"

"Let me see… you'll be the third. It is only Thursday after all." She would be the first, since they had arrived back in London, but he wasn't about to admit it.

"Only three? Careful John, you'll be losing your reputation."

"Hah, Hah very funny. Seriously, when did we last have dinner together?"

Skye remained silent.

"Exactly! You can't remember anymore than I can."

"Get out of here and let me do some work, before I change my mind."

John held up his hands in mock surrender. "I'm going. Just don't stay too late. I don't like to be kept waiting." He closed the door behind him, and a heard a soft thud, followed by laughter.

Skye picked up her notebook from behind the door and sat down. She turned and stared out of the window towards Tower Bridge. She had come a long way from being the pathetic creature that had stepped off the plane from Seattle five months ago. While her memories of Walker were stark and raw, she hadn't sat around moping like a lovesick kitten. There was no point. He'd made it blatantly obvious he didn't trust her. If he really cared for her, he would have been in touch. Instead, all she had received was a check in the mail in settlement of her fee. No phone calls, not even so much as a 'thank you' note.

The new software was an outstanding success and Dunbar and Ridge Computer Consultants had gained worldwide acclaim and were now financially secure. John had rushed out and purchased a new car that was able to go from zero to death in less than six seconds. He scared the life out of her every time he roared into the car park. She would require a week of tranquilizers to regain her equilibrium after he had driven her home.

Seven o'clock and Skye emerged from the bathroom wrapped in a towel. She opened her wardrobe and wondered what to wear. Moving the hangers along the rail, she selected a long skirt and matching blouse then discarded them in favor of a trouser suit.

Ordinarily, she would have worn her favorite jade dress, the same dress she had worn on Debbie's last night at the cabin. The same night, that Walker had joined them for dinner. Skye flopped onto the bed, her legs suddenly weak.

"Damn you, Walker! You could have phoned me after all I did for you. You can't even do the decent thing and send me my suitcase. I bet you've thrown it into the sea in a fit of pique. Well, I hope you rot in hell!"

While it was inconvenient, clothes and personal items were easy to replace. A broken heart took somewhat longer to mend. Determined not to let memories of Walker spoil her evening, she held the suit up and stared at her reflection in the full-length mirror. Twisting this way and that, she held her hair up off her shoulders and neck. It was too business-like for an evening with a friend.

She riffled through the hangers and settled on a calf length floral summer dress, with a fitted bodice, in shades of yellow and gold. A little bit frivolous perhaps, but it suited her mood. She pinned her hair up on the top of her head, leaving some tendrils to fall in soft curls around her face.

The doorbell rang as she put the final touches to her make up. She collected her wrap and purse off the bed, and went downstairs to open the door.

John didn't know what to say, Skye was a vision of loveliness that quite simply took his breath away.

"You look stunning." Unable to stop himself, his hand slipped around her waist, and he softly kissed her cheek.

Taken aback by his reaction, Skye stepped to one side, smiling self-consciously.

"My, my, more compliments. You'll give me a big head if you're not careful. You don't look bad either." She said, admiring his striking appearance in a well-tailored suit. But wow! His cologne was strong enough to gas a badger. She took a deep breath. "I don't look any different to when I walked into your office as a freshman all those years ago. Only older."

"If I recall, you were wearing jeans ripped at the knee, your hair was scraped back into a pony tail and your teeth had enough metalwork to cover Buckingham Palace. The dress is a definite improvement." He gave her legs a long appraising look. "As for the rest—I'll be the one to judge how you look. Are you ready?"

Skye stared at the sleek, red Ferrari parked on her driveway.

"You are sure you can handle that thing. I'd rather like to arrive looking as I do now, not as if I've been pulled through a hedge backwards at ninety miles an hour."

"I promise I won't go over the posted speed limit, even if it makes us late for our table." He held open the passenger door. "I hope you don't mind, but I thought we'd dine out of town. I've reserved a table at a place in Richmond down by the river. It's such a lovely evening I thought you would enjoy the setting."

The leather seat felt cold against her skin. Skye watched in admiration as John lowered his tall frame into the impossibly low car. Her fingers tightened imperceptibly on her small evening purse as the engine started with a growl and the needle on the speedometer climbed frighteningly quickly. Twenty minutes later, John turned into the restaurant's car park. Skye breathed a sigh of relief. Tranquilizers for a week? Make that two and triple strength, she mentally amended, as he helped her out of the passenger seat.

The restaurant was impressive, the décor tasteful, and the lighting subdued. John smiled secretively. He'd chosen this restaurant for its quiet and sophisticated ambiance.

When a waiter appeared at their table with a rose, Skye was speechless. She accepted it graciously and breathed in its heady bouquet.

"If you treat all your lady friends this way, they must be very impressed."

"The others are lucky if they get a McDonald's Happy Meal."

Two dimples appeared in Skye's cheeks as she suppressed her giggles. "Yeah, right, and I just stepped off the boat last week. Why all this? Are you after a pay rise, because if so, the answer's no."

"If I wanted a pay rise, I'd take one. Does there have to be a reason for us to have dinner?"

"No, but this is pushing the boat way out the other side of the ocean."

"So?"

"We could have gone somewhere less expensive," she whispered.

"How do you know how expensive this is? There are no prices on your menu."

"Exactly! That's what's worrying me."

"Relax, I can afford it."

"Yes, but can I? Or is this my share of the profits you're spending?"

John's smile deepened. It was good to see the teasing laughter back in her eyes. Not only was she stunningly attractive and highly intelligent, both qualities he admired, but rarely found in a woman, she also possessed some rare inner quality that made her stand out from the crowd. He could barely stop staring and every time his gaze met hers, he felt a rush of something far more intense than just friendship.

Skye sipped her wine and agreed that John's choice of restaurant was a good one. The food was superb and cooked to perfection, the wine heady, and the company amusing.

John guided her out of the restaurant towards his car. "Once round the universe or home?"

"Home, please. Whilst I have no doubt that this car is more than capable of gravity defying speeds, I would prefer you to keep all four wheels on the road."

John merely nodded. Although his fingers held the wheel lightly, inside he was anything but calm. He maneuvered the Ferrari out of the parking bay and opened the throttle. The evening had gone well, but it wasn't over yet.

A short time later, he took Skye's key out of the lock and handed it to her, his large hand lingering in hers slightly longer than necessary. He leaned forward and gently kissed her cheek.

"Thank you for a lovely evening," said Skye. "Would you like to come in for a coffee?"

He allowed Skye's question to hang on the air for a moment before answering. "I'd like that, but only if you're sure it's not too late."

"I don't think I'll turn into Cinderella just yet. Go through, and take a seat in the study. Help yourself to a brandy. I'll bring the tray through in a moment."

John always felt comfortable in Skye's home. Of the two reception rooms, the study was his favorite. Small, comfortable, and filled with books, it had a cozy intimate feeling. It overlooked her garden, and on warm summer evenings, she would throw open the patio doors and allow the heady scents to fill the room.

"Put a match to the fire if you feel a little chilly." Skye placed the tray on the table in front of the couch.

"I'm not cold. How about you?"

"I'm fine. But I will have a brandy if you're pouring."

John crossed to the cabinet, returning with the decanter. He poured two generous measures into the crystal snifters she had placed on the tray. He took a sip from his glass; the amber liquid slid down his throat, warming the pit of his stomach.

"There's something I want to ask to you," he said, sitting next to her on the couch.

"What's that?"

Uncertain of what her reaction would be, he hesitated. He'd been rehearsing what to say for days, and now the moment had arrived, his mind was filled with a crazy mixture of hope and fear. Awkwardly, he cleared his throat.

"We've known each other what, thirteen years?" He reached over and took Skye's glass from her hand, a strange eager look flashed into his eyes.

"Fifteen, but who's counting?"

"We know each other's mood swings, strengths and weaknesses, likes and dislikes. We rarely argue. In fact, we make a darned good team."

"I suppose we do. Where are you going with this? Do you want to break up the partnership? Is that what you're saying?"

"That's the very last thing on my mind."

"Then I don't understand. Is there a problem?"

He took her left hand in his and watched her face for any sign of objection.

"What I am trying to say is this; Skye, will you marry me?" His intense brown eyes met her blue ones as he took the small jeweler's box from his trouser pocket with his free hand.

"John, I…" Skye's lower lip trembled. John's stammering voice became a buzz in her ears.

"I've loved you from the first day I saw you, but both of us were young and I had nothing to offer you back then. It's different now."

Skye stared at him in disbelief. "John, I… I don't know what to say. We've been friends for so long and I never—" The words wedged in her throat. She stared at the diamond and platinum ring sparkling in the jeweler's box. She needed time to think and with raw hurt evident in John's eyes, she couldn't do that. She went and stood by the window, her body trembling with shock.

John crossed the room and took her into his arms. Skye kept her hands by her side and tilted her head back so that she could see his face.

"All these years, I've loved you as a brother. I've never thought of you in any other way. You've always been such a rock for me, always there when I needed you. I know you've asked me in the past, but I always assumed you were teasing me."

"Teasing you?"

Choosing her words carefully, she tried hard to explain. "Yes, teasing. I've lost count of the number of times you've asked me to marry you. The first was on my twenty-first birthday, and you've done so every year since. I always… always treated it as our private joke."

"At first, it was. But lately, I've come to realize just how much I love you."

"If I gave you the impression that we were anything more than friends, I'm sorry." The disappointment and anguish she saw in his eyes was almost her undoing. "Don't make me be the one to hurt you."

A half smile crossed his face, his arms tightened around her waist and he inclined his head to hers.

"Don't give me your answer tonight. Think things over for as long as you need. We've got plenty of time. I understand you may not feel the same way about me now, but given time—" His words hung heavily on the air.

Skye leaned lightly into him, feeling the warmth of his body. She opened her mouth to say something, but he silenced her with a fingertip.

"I've more than enough love for both of us and I know, given the chance, I could make you happy. Many couples start out as friends and make a marriage work. I think we could too. When you've thought things through, I'm sure you'll agree. In the meantime, I'd be honored if you would wear this." He touched her left hand to his lips and kissed the ring he placed on her finger.

A lump formed in Skye's throat. The words wouldn't form. She rested her head on his shoulder. He caressed her cheek then gently tipped her mouth to his, whispered goodnight, and left.

Skye refilled her glass and struggled to put everything into perspective. What an emotionally charged evening it had turned out to be. A proposal from John was the last thing she had expected. His refusal to accept her assertion that they could only be friends, had left her feeling embarrassed and at a loss at what to say.

She kicked off her shoes and curled up on the couch. John wasn't classically handsome, but there was an inherent strength in his face, which was echoed in his character. A loveable rogue someone had once described him, and some even declared him to be downright sexy, although she never saw it herself. To her, he was John. Her best friend and business partner, the brother she had never had. But her husband?

Skye rotated her neck trying to ease the tension in her shoulders. The more she thought about John's offer, the more confused she became. This wasn't a decision to be made lightly. Marriage was what she wanted, wasn't it? However, marriage implied love and not just on one side.

She had no doubt that marriage to John would be safe, for he would never let her down. Confused, she wandered restlessly round the room, the chimes of the hall clock startling her as it struck one. John had left two hours ago. No matter how heavily his proposal laid on her mind, she had to get some sleep. She swallowed the last of the brandy, turned out the lights, and made her way upstairs.

With a heavy heart, she climbed into bed, but sleep wouldn't come. Somewhere in the distance, thunder rumbled. The approaching storm brought back bittersweet memories of another place—a place where she had learned what it was to love and be loved. A love so all consuming and glorious that she doubted she would ever find it again.

She lay awake, hugging her pillow. Memories of Walker filled her mind. The way he held her, his smile, his low throaty laugh, but most of all she remembered his kisses.

The storm raged, then passed on. She finally fell into a restless sleep, but the confusion in her mind remained.

The following morning, she went to work as usual. No nearer to reaching a decision, she dreaded John asking her again. When he put his head round her door to say 'good morning,' he was his usual cheerful self and never mentioned his proposal.

CHAPTER TWENTY-NINE

Seattle, the same time.

"How long before I can go back to work, doctor?" Walker asked the medic who shone a light into his eyes.

"After a serious head injury we suggest patients take it easy. How are the headaches?"

"Not as bad as they were. I get a couple of migraines now and then, but the medication you gave me usually takes care of them."

The doctor consulted his notes. "You're a very lucky man, Mr. Walker. Not many people go through what you did and survive. I understand you have your own business which necessitates a great deal of travel and that you fly your own plane."

"That's correct."

"You're making an excellent recovery. As to whether you meet the criteria for your pilots' license, that's something you'll have to take up with the Board of

Aviation. I'll see you again in a month and we'll make a final decision then."

Walker failed to hide his disappointment. "I guess you know best. I could do with a change of scene. Is it okay if I go home to Friday Harbor?"

"I don't see why not. But take it easy, you still need to build your stamina."

Walker slipped off the examination table and got dressed. He took his cane off the back of the chair and let himself out of the small cubicle. He collected his prescription for painkillers and went out to the waiting car.

"How'd you get on?" McCabe asked.

"The good news is that I can drive again. I can also return to the lodge, so long as I take the ferry. But the doc says I'm not ready to return to work."

"That's great news." McCabe glanced at his friend. Walker's tight-lipped expression said it was anything but. "I know you're feeling down, but be thankful we're able to have this conversation. I can't tell you how much hair I lost worrying about you lying in that hospital bed." He rubbed his head to emphasize his point.

Walker laughed. "Give me a break, you dick—you've been bald for years."

"Yeah, I know. It made you smile, which is better than looking at you when you're scowling. That's enough to make a whale turn tail and head south."

"That bad, huh?"

"Yep, and your temper… Jeez, most of us have been on the receiving end of that over the last few months."

"So, I'm a lousy patient. You're supposed to humor me."

"You can say that again."

"I guess I owe people a few apologies, including you." And Skye, if I can find her and she'll listen to me, Walker added silently.

"Nah, we forgave you a long time ago. When are you planning on leaving?"

"I'm aiming to catch the next available ferry. No offence, but I'm tired of this town. I've seen more doctors in the last five months than I have in thirty-seven years. I know how a lab-rat feels. I want some peace and quiet, and a chance to get some gentle exercise without being jostled by pedestrians every time I walk out the door."

McCabe pulled out to overtake a taxi. "You're not fully recovered yet. Is it wise for you to be at the lodge on your own?"

"If you're referring to the seizures, I haven't had one in three months and it's likely I won't have another. But I know the signs, so quit worrying."

"Has the District Attorney's office been in contact?"

"I gave my initial deposition yesterday and handed over my report. I'll contact his assistant before I leave and give her the phone number of the lodge."

"Well, you know where I am if want to talk to someone."

"About what?"

McCabe hesitated. "That lady computer geek—the one who gave you so much grief at the cabin. I wondered if you'd been in contact with her."

Walker almost growled at the mention of Skye's name. "Are you asking from a professional or personal point of view?"

"Both. I got the impression you two had got things together."

"That's none of your damned business," Walker replied and stared out of the window at the passing stores. A brooding expression settled on his features

McCabe pulled into a parking space outside of one Seattle's more exclusive apartment buildings.

"I'm sorry I bit your head off," Walker said finally. "It's been a long day, with all the tests and, yeah, I'm a little disappointed that I can't go back to work."

"Apology accepted."

Walker eased his bad leg out of the car and stood with the aid of his cane. Closing the door, he rested a hand on the roof of the vehicle and leaned in through the open window.

"Thanks for driving me today."

"No problem. You take care out at the lodge. You've only got two legs so don't damage the other one by falling over a tree root. And remember, your friends are here if you need them for anything, day or night."

"Yeah, I know. And, McCabe—"

"Yeah?"

"Thanks for saving my life." He turned and walked towards his building, his movements stiff and awkward.

Six days later, hot, sweating, and out of breath from the exertion, Walker limped along the beach toward the dock. He leaned on the handrail and rubbed the ache in his right thigh. It was barely a mile from the lodge to the cabin, yet he felt as if he had climbed Mt. Rainier. Until that moment, he hadn't appreciated just how unfit he'd become.

Without warning, memories of Skye came tumbling back. For it was here that he'd first seen her—a slim figure in a bright red oversized sweater. It was one of those early spring days, when the air was cool, and the sun strong, the first hint that winter was finally over. He remembered how the sun had glinted on her hair, highlighting the red and gold strands. He'd been surprised to see her, and had bitten her head off, but she'd stood up to him, her auburn hair swinging about her proud shoulders, anger flashing in her eyes.

"Damn it Skye, why did you walk out on me?" Overwhelmed by feelings of nostalgia, he let out a long exhausted sigh. He shook his head to wipe out the memory, but his mind refused to co-operate. He limped up the beach to the cabin, his right thigh and calf muscles screaming from the strain of walking over the uneven ground.

Following the investigation, not knowing whether he would survive or not, the realtor had canceled all the bookings for the cabin. He inserted the key into the double lock and pushed the door open. Inside felt cold, damp and empty, just like him. He crossed to the window and drew back the drapes, allowing the sunlight in.

The room was just as it had been on the night they had traced the hacker and flown to Seattle. A layer of dust covered every surface. Under a lamp, on the table next to the couch, he found Skye's book, the corner of a page turned down to mark her place. Next to the music center a selection of her CDs was piled haphazardly. In the kitchen sink, a cup waited to be washed, a faint hint of lipstick on the rim.

In the bedroom, Walker felt an overwhelming sense of loss. Her clothes still hung in the wardrobe. He took the jade dress off the hanger and buried his face in its soft folds.

Her clothes. That was why he was here. In her eagerness to get away from him, she had left them behind, instructing the realtor to pack and ship her belongings back to England. Unable to gain access, the realtor had inundated Walker's answering machine with demands 'to forward Dr. Dunbar's belongings to London as soon as possible.' Now back on the island for the first time in months, he was finally able to comply with the request.

He slumped down onto the bed; his shoulders hunched forward, a man on the edge of despair. He grabbed a pillow and hugged it, choking back his groans of anguish. Throughout the long days lying in the hospital bed, wondering if he would regain the use of his right leg, he thought of her. When the pain of the headaches was unrelenting, he called out her name.

But she never came.

The knowledge that she hadn't contacted him, twisted inside like a knife. If she knew what it had cost him to bring the perpetrators to justice, would it have made any difference to her, he wondered. Would she have jumped on the next plane and sat by his bedside until he came out of the coma?

During his recovery, he'd slowly come to terms with the fact that he'd lost her.

As he wallowed in his wretchedness, a plan slowly formed in his mind. He stood without the aid of his cane and hobbled crossed the room. In the corner, under the dresser was her suitcase. He dragged it out and lifted it onto the bed. Carefully, he removed her clothes from the hangers, folded them, and placed them inside with her other belongings.

In the following days and weeks, he pushed himself hard, harder than he'd ever done before. He walked, worked out and swam, and did everything he could to improve his fitness until finally the day dawned when he threw away the cane.

Exactly five weeks later, he sat in the doctor's office and waited for the verdict.

"You're fit enough to return to work, on the understanding that you seek medical advice if you develop any headaches that last longer than twenty-four hours, or if you start having seizures. You have a metal plate in your head and I don't want you taking any risks. Is that understood?"

"Perfectly."

Walker walked out of the surgery and stabbed the air with his fist, basking in the knowledge that he could finally put his plan into action.

CHAPTER THIRTY

Exactly seven months after his accident, Walker stepped off the plane into the early morning sunshine of a London autumn. The air was chilly, but no colder than when he'd left Seattle the evening before. A frustrating delay at immigration, and then he was walking though the terminal towards his rental car. He eased the sleek Jaguar out of the parking lot, filtered into the rush hour traffic, and drove to his hotel in the heart of the city.

The bellhop opened the door of the suite and handed Walker the key. Walker opened his case and took out his shaving gear, and headed for the shower. Ten minutes later, feeling refreshed, he sat down on the bed and ordered a full English breakfast—none of that continental rubbish the airlines were so fond of serving. While he waited for room service to deliver, he took the newspaper cutting from his wallet and read it again, even though he knew the words by heart.

'*A new charitable foundation is to be launched tomorrow evening with a gala dinner and ball. Set up by Dr. Skye Dunbar, it aims to help young people, who, due to unforeseen circumstances, are unable to complete their university degree course.*'

Although he had dozed on the plane, jet lag hit him hard. His neck and shoulder muscles felt stiff and a headache throbbed at his temple. He stifled a yawn, and skimmed the pages of the phone directory until he found listing for Dunbar and Ridge Computer Consultants. He picked up the phone and punched in the number. An unfamiliar female voice answered. A few seconds later, he put the phone down and looked at the address he had scribbled on the note pad. A phone call to the front desk, secured him a street map and directions. Suddenly, he didn't feel quite so tired.

An hour later, he strolled into the offices of Dunbar and Ridge. He smiled at the young woman sat behind the reception desk.

"I'm here to see Dr. Skye Dunbar."

"Do you have an appointment, sir?"

"No, I don't. But it is rather important that I see her."

"I'm sorry, sir, but Dr. Dunbar has left for the day. She's not back in the office until Tuesday."

"I've come a long way. Perhaps you could call her cell phone and ask if she would agree to see me?"

"I'm sorry, sir, I can't do that. I can see if Dr. Ridge is available or I can make you an appointment to see Dr. Dunbar next week, whichever you prefer."

"I don't wish to see Dr. Ridge, and I can't wait until next week. Could you give me her home address?"

"I'm sorry, but it's against company policy to give out personal information."

"Look, you don't understand—"

"Is there a problem, Maureen?" A male voiced shouted through an open office door.

"It's this gentleman, Dr. Ridge. He wants to see Dr. Dunbar, but she's left for the day."

John put down the paper he was reading and walked to the door of his office, almost yanking it off its hinges.

"What the hell do you want?"

"I'd have thought that was obvious, even to you. I've come to see Skye. As she's not here, I'd like her address."

"Would you, now? You'd better come into my office. Maureen? You can go for the day and lock up on your way out."

John sat down behind his desk and eyed Walker suspiciously. "I've one question," he said, getting straight to the point. "Why? Why now after all this time have you come to see her?"

"That's none of your business."

"You're wrong, it is my business. You've left it rather late to ask if she's pregnant."

Pregnant? God! In seven months, Walker hadn't even considered the possibility. "And is she?"

"No, she's not."

"Then it's not an issue, is it? My reasons for wanting to see Skye are none of your concern. If you'll give me her address, I'll not take up any more of your time."

"Do you think I'm that stupid? You've got a bloody nerve coming here. After what you did to her, I should have you arrested."

Walker grabbed Ridge's hand as it reached for the phone. "I'm not interested in what you think of me. I came to see Skye. She might be upset if she has to bail you out for false arrest. Are you going to behave like the gentleman you're obviously not, and give me her address?"

"There's something you should know."

Walker's head jerked up.

"You're not the first American to break her heart."

"Really?"

"There was someone else before you—a sailor in the Navy. He said he loved her, but in the end, he treated her like dirt. I see from your expression that has a familiar ring."

Walker made no response. An icy chill ran through his veins as Ridge told him about Michael. No wonder Skye had looked so scared the first time they met. To compound matters, he'd not trusted her and kept her at the cabin. She must have been terrified.

"There is no way I'm letting you anywhere near Skye," John continued. "I helped her pick up the pieces after Michael and I helped her rebuild her life seven months ago. I'm not going to stand by and let you, or any other man, destroy her again."

The cold knot in Walker's gut tightened another notch. "I'm sorry she's had some bad experiences, but that's life. It's never an easy ride. If I'd known about Michael, I would have handled things differently. All I want is the chance to talk to her. If she wants me to leave, I'll go, but only if she tells me to."

"What makes you think she will want to see you? You haven't made any effort to keep in touch. Why is it so important now?"

"I have my reasons for not contacting her, reasons which I'll explain only to her."

"You should know that things have changed. I've asked her to marry me."

Walker's worst nightmare had come true. "I see. And has she accepted?"

John smiled confidently. "She will."

What started as a small seed of inner torment grew and grew, until overwhelmed by jealously and anger, Walker grabbed Ridge by the shirt, pulling him across the desk.

"I'll find Skye with or without your help. Until I've spoken to her, I wouldn't book the church just yet, if I were you."

"If and when you catch up with her, make sure you ask her about Laura," Ridge shouted as a final shot. He slumped back in his chair, straightened his tie with a shaking hand as the door to his office slammed shut. He couldn't afford to drop his guard, especially now that Skye was so close to accepting his proposal. Thankfully, her phone number was unlisted and it was four days before she was due back in the office. After the dinner tomorrow night, she would be safely out of town for the weekend.

CHAPTER THIRTY-ONE

It was barely twenty-four hours since Walker had confronted Ridge. Feeling less than confident, he stood inside the doorway of the Dorchester Hotel and watched as a limousine drew up outside. A doorman stepped forward and opened the door. Photographer's bulbs flashed as first Skye, then Ridge stepped out onto the red carpet.

He couldn't bear to watch and quickly turned away. He threaded his way through the throng of waiting guests to the bar. It was empty except for an elderly gentleman sitting in a corner. Walker ordered a scotch from the underworked barman and downed it in one. It came as no surprise that Ridge was Skye's escort for the evening, but he hadn't realized what a powerful opponent the man would be. His jaw clenched, his eyes narrowed. Pain like acid burned in his chest. The doctors may have saved his life, but it was an empty shell without the woman he loved. Ridge had won, and yet—

He looked at his reflection in the mirror behind the bar, and welcomed the surge of jealousy that brought determination flooding back into his veins. He straightened his bow tie, and then strode to the door. Five minutes later, he merged with a group of people returning from the restrooms and entered the ballroom. Once inside, he took a glass of champagne from the tray of a passing waiter and wandered around smiling at couples that passed him.

At last, he saw her. Dressed in black silk, Skye's gown was simple and understated. The fabric followed her every curve until it reached her ankles, where it swirled around like a cloud. Her rich auburn hair, tied back into a neat chignon at her nape, highlighted her creamy skin and the delicacy of her features. She wore little jewelry, just a pair of diamond studs in her ears.

As the final chords of the waltz died away, he threaded his way through the throng of couples on the dance floor. His right hand descended on her shoulder and he spun her round.

"I believe the next dance is mine," he said, as the orchestra played the opening bars of a dreamy song.

Shock siphoned the blood from Skye's face. She moved away, but tripped on the hem of her gown and would have fallen if his arm had not tightened around her waist.

She gave him a hostile glare. "Just who do you think you are barging your way in here? This function is strictly invitation only, and I don't recall placing your name on the guest list."

"Whatever happened to *hello, Walker, nice to see you?*" Beneath that touch-me-not exterior, he saw the longing in her eyes.

Skye masked her inner turmoil with a deceptive calmness. "Sarcasm doesn't suit you, nor does it impress me. I'll ask you one more time. How did you get in here, and why have you come?"

Her body took on a will of its own, picking up the tempo of the beat as he whirled her around the dance floor. Walker looked so handsome in his black evening suit and crisp white shirt that her breath caught in her throat. Her emotions swirled, like the fabric of her gown. She felt shock and excitement, and the heat of desire where his hand rested against the bare flesh of her back, then anger and pain.

"I'll answer your question. I waved my checkbook at the guys on the door. They were more than happy to accept my donation and offer me a glass of champagne. As for why I'm here, God damn it, Skye, you walked out on me and I think I have a right to know why!"

"I walked out on you? That's rich coming from the man who couldn't even thank me for helping him."

Deliberately, she brought the heel of her shoe down on his foot. He didn't even blink.

"Nice try, but I'm not letting go until you and I have talked. Are you going to play nice and ask me about my donation? It was very generous."

"What was it, Walker, a need to salve to your conscience?" Skye shot back and feeling him tense under her hand, she knew her barb had found a home. "The Foundation doesn't need your money."

"You always did have a temper, and a sharp tongue. It's about time someone tamed you." He lowered his lips to hers, his intent plain for her to see.

In that instant, she wanted to lash out and hurt him as much as he'd hurt her and she didn't care who heard her.

"Don't-even-think-about-it!" she warned.

"Perhaps you're right. This isn't the place. I prefer a more intimate setting when making love to a woman, but then you know that."

Skye's head snapped back. Her cheeks flooded with color. She glared at him, stunned by his bluntness. "Go away, Walker. Go away and leave me in peace."

"Sorry, Skye. You don't get rid of me that easily. I *will* talk to you, and you *will* listen," he said. "We can either have our conversation here, where we stand a good chance of being overheard or on the terrace, it's up to you." When she didn't respond, he abruptly caught her by the elbow and firmly escorted her from the ballroom.

Skye hurried to keep up with his long strides. "Bullying tactics again, Walker? Do you get your kicks by giving women bruises?"

He stopped dead and jerked her round to face him. "Be careful, push me any further and I'll forget we're in polite company, and give you the argument you're looking for. All I want is a few minutes of your time."

Twin stains of scarlet appeared on her cheeks. Heads turned to watch them. Skye's embarrassment turned to raw fury. Damn the man if he wasn't right. She couldn't afford a scene, at least not here.

"Five minutes. After that, you walk out of here and out of my life—for good."

"Still issuing stipulations? Sorry, sweetheart, I'll leave when I'm good and ready and not before."

"Damn it, Walker! I made my terms perfectly clear back at the cabin. You've settled my invoice, there is nothing further to discuss. Please just go back to the States or wherever it is you came from."

"Yeah, you did. I even recall agreeing to some of them. You high tailed it out of Seattle so damned fast you didn't wait to find out if we caught the guy responsible for dumping the chemicals. Were you that desperate to get away from me? Aren't you the least bit curious as to why I've waited seven months to come after you?"

"No."

"I don't believe you. Just as I don't believe things are over between us." Something intense flared in his eyes. He stroked her back and felt her pulse quicken beneath his fingers. "Don't deny it, Skye. You want me as much as I want you." His gaze traveled across her bare shoulders to the curve of her breasts.

Skye's fists bunched at her sides. She had no intention of falling under his spell once more. Yet, despite her determination, a delicious shudder heated her body igniting the desire.

"I'm staying at the Savoy. I'll expect you for lunch." He let her go. "Dr. Ridge, I wondered when you'd make an appearance."

Ridge's face was like thunder as he acknowledged Walker with barely a nod of his head. He turned to Skye.

"Are you okay?"

Twin stains of scarlet appeared on Skye's cheeks. "You remember Mr. Walker. He's very kindly made a donation to the Foundation." She gave John's hand a warning squeeze in the hope that he would follow her lead. The last thing she wanted was for the evening to turn into a bar room brawl.

Ridge's eyes narrowed. "Is that so? I'd say that's the least he can do. Never heard of bank transfers, Walker?"

"Yeah, I've heard of them, but some things are best done in person. Besides, Skye and I have a lot of catching up to do."

"I've already told you—any business you had with Skye is finished. Now unless you want me to call security, I suggest you leave."

"What is it with you, Ridge? You always want to call for help. What were you, the playground wimp?"

Ridge's mouth tightened.

Skye stepped between them. "That's enough! People are beginning to stare. You will not ruin this evening, is that clear? I said is that clear?"

Walker thrust his hands into his pockets. He wanted to punch Ridge on the nose, but Skye was right. There was too much at stake, and stooping to Ridge's level wouldn't earn him any brownie points.

"John?"

"Perfectly."

Skye let out a long sigh of relief. "Good. People are starting to leave, I think you should go back inside, I'll join you in a moment."

"Only if you'll let me show him the door first."

Skye frowned. "I can handle this, John. Now please, go and see to my guests."

Ridge glared at Walker and then pointedly lifted Skye's left hand to his lips and kissed it. He turned on his heels and left.

Walker raised his eyebrow questioningly. He caught Skye's hand before she lowered it to her side.

"Very touching. That's quite a rock you're wearing. I assume there's something significant behind it."

Skye blushed; all the hurt and anger she had suffered at his hands came flooding back. She held her head up high, her blue eyes boldly meeting his.

"John's asked me to marry him, and I've agreed. Are you going to congratulate me?"

"I'll be damned if I will. You know you don't love him, not in that way." Walker bent his head, his mouth seeking hers.

No longer worried what people might think, Skye twisted in his arms and tried to push him away. The more she struggled, the more demanding his lips became. His arms held hers tight by her side as his tongue traced the soft fullness of her lips, sending shivers of desire racing through her. Suddenly, her lips parted of their own volition and she returned his kiss.

Abruptly Walker let her go. "Don't forget Skye. Lunch. Tomorrow. Twelve-thirty at the Savoy. Don't be late, otherwise I'll come looking for you."

Shaking, she watched him walked away.

She paid little attention to John on the drive home, until he asked the one question that had been on her mind ever since Walker had tapped her on the shoulder.

"—How he got by security is a mystery. Without an invitation, security should have stopped him at the door. When I get into the office on Monday, I shall make a formal complaint. The man is a menace! I hope you didn't give him any encouragement to stay."

"Oh, Walker. I have no idea why he came." She had done nothing but consider the reasons for Walker's unexpected return. She rested her head on the cold glass of the window and tried to concentrate on what John was saying, but the combination of a little too much champagne and Walker's demanding kiss had left her mind and emotions reeling.

"Skye? Are you even listening to me? I asked if you'd given him any encouragement."

"What do you mean encouragement? If you think I rang him up and said 'Hi! I'm throwing a party, and you're invited,' think again."

"Then I don't understand why he chose tonight of all nights to turn up, do you?"

"Do we have to talk about this right now? It's been a long evening. I'm tried, my feet hurt, and I just want to go home."

"I'm sorry, love. I've been a fool. I should have realized that he was the last person you wanted to discuss. So how did you get rid of him in the end?"

With a long and exhausted sigh, which she hoped would be recognized for what it was she turned and faced John in the semi-darkness of the limousine.

"You know, you're right. I don't want to talk about Walker." Whatever her feelings for him were, she wanted to keep them to herself.

John rambled on incessantly until the limousine came to a halt in her driveway.

"If it's all the same to you, I'd rather you didn't come in. It's late and we're both tired."

"Are you sure?"

Skye merely nodded.

"At least give me a goodnight kiss."

She hesitated, and then leaned across with the intention of kissing him on the cheek, but at the last moment, John turned his head, so that her lips brushed his. She quickly moved out of his grasp before he could deepen the kiss. Suddenly, the thought of him touching her was repugnant. She stepped out of the car and hurried indoors.

It took several seconds for her eyes to adjust to the darkness. It was only when her limbs stopped trembling and she felt sufficiently calm that she climbed the stairs to her bedroom. She undressed in the moonlight, climbed into bed, and pulled the blankets up to her chin.

Sleep was slow in coming and try as she might, she couldn't banish Walker from her thoughts. His face haunted her. Smiling, serious, or thoughtful, he filled her dreams. Her last coherent thought as she drifted off to sleep was that her life had gone from order to chaos, and the man who responsible for that change, was once more back in her life.

***

Walker stood by the window of his hotel room and nursed a glass of bandy in his right hand. Far below, the lights of the city twinkled in the darkness. Memories of another night in another city came flooding back—the night Skye had located the hacker. He had no doubts that what they had shared back at the cabin was real. It was something that only came around once in a lifetime. Only he had been too stupid to see it at the time.

It was obvious that Ridge had kept the details of their encounter the previous afternoon from Skye. Was Ridge that unsure of himself, he wondered? And if he was, why had he boasted about their engagement? And who was Laura and why was she so important?

At least he'd managed to feign surprise when Skye admitted that she had accepted Ridge's proposal. But something in her eyes had convinced him she was saying it for effect. It was as if she wanted to hit out by telling him, and was challenging him to contradict her.

Ridge might be in love with Skye, but Walker wasn't in the least bit persuaded it was reciprocated. That's why they hadn't gone public on their engagement, he decided. When Skye looked at Ridge, she looked at him as a friend, not a lover. She wasn't the type of woman to play with a doubled sided coin. She was strictly a one-man woman and whether she realized it or not, she was his.

He tossed back the last of his Scotch, undressed, and got into bed.

CHAPTER THIRTY-TWO

After a long and troubled night of soul searching, Skye drove into town the following morning. Although unhappy at the prospect of seeing Walker again, she knew their relationship had to be resolved. He'd been out of her life for seven months, yet hardly a day passed without her thinking about him. A war of emotions raged within her. Why couldn't he have just said what he had to last night and left?

She stopped her car in front of the hotel and handed the keys to the parking attendant. Taking a deep, unsteady breath, she paused by the revolving door, uncertain whether to enter or not. Walker sat in one of chairs in the lobby. He looked relaxed despite his closed expression, his presence as compelling as it had been the first day they had met. Even now, she could feel the tangible bond between them and couldn't tear her gaze away from him.

Walker stood as she approached. He placed a hand on her arm and kissed her cheek.

"I'm glad you came."

The touch of his hand made her pulse leap with excitement. Her mouth curved into an unconscious smile. "If I recall, you didn't leave me much choice."

"I am glad you came, all the same. I hope you don't mind, but I've ordered lunch in my suite." He guided her towards the bank of elevators.

Skye hung back. "I'm not sure that's a good idea."

"Relax. I only want talk to you without the risk of interruption."

She hesitated, her head swirling with doubts. She'd come this far, she couldn't back out now, not without making an utter fool of herself. She stepped into the crowded elevator. Although the ride took only seconds, Walker's nearness was overwhelming as he stood behind her in the confined space. When he casually rested his hand on her shoulder, it took all her will power not to lay her cheek against his hand.

Walker's suite was on the top floor with a fine view of the river. Two sumptuous leather couches stood either side of the fireplace with a coffee table in between. A small dining table stood in front of the large window and was laid for lunch.

Skye took her time admiring the view then focused her gaze on him. "Was it purely a coincidence that you turned up last night? Or are you here for a specific reason?"

"It was no coincidence. The way we left things back in Seattle… you didn't give me chance to explain. There are things that need to be said."

"I said all I had to back at the cabin."

He regarded her from beneath heavy-lidded eyes. Today, she wore brown trousers, a green roll neck sweater, and tweed jacket. Her thick, auburn hair hung loose in waves framing her face. He felt the hot flood of desire and longed to pull her into his arms.

"You don't believe that. If you did, you wouldn't be here today. However, you are, and that tells me a great deal. Don't you want to know why it's taken me so long to come after you?"

"Not really. My life doesn't revolve around you."

"It doesn't, at least, not at the moment. But it does concern me."

The implication of his words sent her pulses racing, but she couldn't allow him into her heart again. "It shouldn't."

"There's the matter of an impending court case, for one thing. You're an expert witness, or had you forgotten?"

Skye raised her chin stubbornly. "I'm more than happy to give a statement."

"But that's not sufficient."

"Says who?"

"I do. I want to ensure those responsible are put behind bars for years, and the only way I can do that is if you give evidence in person."

Two deep lines of worry appeared between her eyes. "No way!"

"That's one of the reasons I'm here. To take you back to the States with me. I knew if the DA wrote to you,

you'd find some excuse not to come or just plain ignore the letter."

"I am not going anywhere with you." She picked up her bag and walked towards the door. He reached out and spun her round to face him.

"Wrong again, sweetheart. You have no choice in the matter. Either you come willingly or the DA issues a subpoena. Either way, you will attend or go to jail, it's your choice."

"Bullying tactics are becoming a habit with you."

"Yeah, but they work, don't they?" He led her to the couch. "If you want the truth, the court case is just an excuse. I'm here because I wanted to see you and apologize. We said some harsh things to each other back in the cabin."

"I've told you—"

"For once, will you just listen to what I have to say?"

Skye clamped her mouth shut and waited. The tense silence between them lengthened.

Walker cleared his throat and began to tell her what happened after they had located the hacker. Skye listened first in astonishment, then in horror to his words. The color drained from her face and she shook as the fearful images built in her mind

"I woke up in a hospital bed three weeks later, bandages everywhere, drips in both arms. I'd been in a coma. Of course, by then, you had already left and I was in no fit state to follow you. When the doctors finally said I could travel, I booked myself on the first available flight to London. I went to your office, but your fiancé refused to let me see you. I'd read an article about the Foundation, and well, you know the rest."

"No one told me. I never knew." Tears blinded her eyes and choked her voice.

"How could you? McCabe had his suspicions about us, but he didn't know for sure. He contacted the hotel, and the receptionist told him you had checked out. He figured that as you were already on your way home, you weren't interested in knowing."

Skye felt utterly miserable. Just thinking about what he had endured tore at her heart. A sob rose in her throat and she swallowed hard. She looked into his eyes, but her gaze clouded with tears.

"It was touch and go for a time, or so I'm told. Every day I lay in that hospital bed I thought about you. I promised myself that if I ever got out of there, I would come after you."

"You're okay now, though? I mean—"

"Physically, yes."

"I'm glad," she said softly.

"Are you?"

"What sort of a question is that? Of course I am. John never told me you'd been to the office."

"Yeah, well that doesn't surprise me. The guy's a regular Rottweiler where you're concerned. But if he had told you, would you have agreed to see me?"

Skye stirred uneasily on the couch. "Yes. I mean no... I'm not... Oh, I don't know."

"And your engagement? It's a bit sudden, and somewhat surprising. I guessed Ridge was in love with you, but I got the impression that you viewed him as nothing more than a friend. What made you change your mind?"

"I have my reasons."

"Do you love him?"

Skye turned away, unable to meet his gaze. "Yes, I love him." But not in the way I love you, she added silently.

"I don't believe you. I've held you in my arms and felt you tremble when I kiss you. I've seen the passion in your eyes when I caress you. Tell me, do Ridge's kisses and caresses make your pulse race? When he makes love to you, do you ache for him as you ache for me?" Walker lifted his hand, stroked the soft skin at her wrist, and felt her pulse kick.

Skye flushed scarlet as her embarrassment turned to raw fury. "My relationship with John is none of your business." As she said the words, a terrifying realization washed over her. The harder she tried to ignore the truth, the more it persisted. Walker knew. He knew she loved him and always would.

"If you marry Ridge, you'll make the biggest mistake of your life! After all, it's a high price to pay for security. It's not easy living with someone you don't love. Oh, I daresay you will convince yourself it's the real thing, but as the years pass, you'll regret it. Then what will you do?"

Alarm and anger rippled along her spine. She freed herself from his gasp, her blue eyes blazing. "Stop it! Stop it! I don't want to hear anymore. You have no right to talk to me like this."

"I think I do."

"Why should I believe you? You couldn't even trust me, for God's sake!"

His voice was quiet, yet held an undertone of authority. "I'll admit for a time I didn't trust you, but as soon as I found out that I was wrong, I apologized. You gave yourself to me. You wanted me as much as I wanted—want you."

She knew he was telling the truth. He hadn't forced her into doing anything she didn't want, but she would die rather than admit it.

"You're just like every other man."

His eyes narrowed and hardened at her accusation. "I assume you're referring to Michael."

Skye stared incredulous, her heart pounding. "Who told you about him?"

"Ridge seemed to think it was his duty. I guess he told me because he hoped in some perverse way, that I would be too ashamed to face you and leave. But his ploy didn't work."

All her anger drained away. The mention of Michael's name brought a twisted smile to her face.

"I should have learned my lesson the first time round," she said in a choked voice.

Walker flinched at her words. "I never meant for you to get hurt."

"No? At least I know John loves me, and will treat me with respect, which is more than can be said of you."

"How do you know, Skye? You won't give me a chance to put things right between us. I know I should have been honest with you, but there was so much at stake that I couldn't take the risk. However, it never altered my feelings for you."

She walked to the window and looked out at the cloudy sky. Would things have been different if she'd stayed, she wondered. She had accused him of not trusting her, but she hadn't trusted him either. She had assumed he was just like Michael, another of life's takers.

Turning, she faced him. "What do you want, Walker?"

"I want to spend the rest of my life with you, but you've got to want it too. No half measures—it's all or nothing, I won't accept anything less."

Walker went and stood next to her. He wrapped his arms around her waist. When she didn't push him away, he brushed his lips against hers.

"Come back to Seattle with me. Let me prove to you that what we shared at the cabin, we can have again."

Skye saw the heart rendering tenderness in his gaze and quickly turned away, wearied by indecision. It was too much to take in. She needed time to think.

When she failed to reply, he released her and stepped back.

"My flight leaves Heathrow tomorrow afternoon at two. I'll see you at the airport. If not, then I hope you and

Ridge have a happy life together." He kissed her cheek once more, and walked into one of the bedrooms.

Skye let herself out of the suite and left the hotel. Too distraught to drive, she walked along the street and until she found a coffee shop. She sat down at one of the small tables, lost in her own thoughts and impervious to the glances of staff and customers alike.

She lost track of time. It was only when someone turned out the lights that she paid the bill and left. Somehow, she found her way back to the hotel and collected her car. It was dark when she parked outside a row of smart town houses in one of the London suburbs. Walking briskly up the path, she knocked sharply on the door. The music coming from within paused and John opened the door. His hair was a mass of unruly curls, and there was the faint shadow of a beard on his chin.

"Why didn't you tell me Walker came to see you?" Skye pushed past him into the hallway.

"It must have slipped my mind."

Skye raised an eyebrow. "Don't lie to me."

"Okay, I deliberately didn't tell you. Walker had the effrontery to come to the office looking for you. But I told him to go sling his hook, that he wasn't wanted here."

"You had no right to do that. Just as you had no right to tell him we are going to be married."

"What do you mean I had no right? I'm your fiancé."

Skye stiffened and glared at him. "You are not my keeper, nor do you get to decide who I see. As for marrying you, I think my response at the time was I would think about it. Well, I've thought about it and have decided that I can't marry you."

John ran a hand through his hair and frowned. "What do you mean you can't marry me? I know you were upset by Walker's unexpected appearance last night, but there's no need to take this stance."

"I'm sorry, but I don't love you, not in that way." She pulled his ring off her finger and placed in on the hall table. "You're my friend and always will be. I told you that the night you proposed. Besides, you've always been happy with your life, playing the field, not tied to one woman."

"But, Skye, I've waited for you for years. I can't allow you to marry someone else. I love you, even though you've been with him."

"This isn't about sex. It's about love, and I can't love you the way you want me to. You'll end up hating me and I couldn't bear that."

"It's him, isn't it? You're still in love with him. Forget him, he's no good. He'll only hurt you again. He's just like Michael."

Skye flinched, and pressed a hand to her throat. "You've said quite enough. I won't change my mind." She opened the door and ran down the path towards her car. Visibly shaking, she fumbled with the keys. Mercifully, the engine fired before John reached out and tried to grab hold of the door handle. She gunned the engine. Her last sight of him was as he stood on the curb watching her drive away, a glazed look of defeat and utter despair spreading over his face.

CHAPTER THIRTY-THREE

Walker took his time packing. If he hadn't betrayed Skye's trust, she would be with him. The emptiness he'd felt during the last few months was nothing compared to torment he now felt. He took the airline ticket he'd purchased for her from his wallet, screwed it into a ball, and tossed it into the waste paper basket.

He'd made his pitch, but it wasn't good enough. She had made her choice and it wasn't him. Twice he'd allowed her to walk away, but this time he knew it was for good.

He phoned the lobby and had the rental car brought round to the front of the hotel. He paid the bill and checked out.

The events of the last twenty-four hours had left him in a foul mood and the heavy London traffic did nothing to improve it. For reasons he failed to comprehend, returning the key of his rental car became a major undertaking.

The queue at first class check-in was minimal, and having completed the formalities, he checked his luggage. He walked through the terminal to the nearest bar and ordered a large scotch on the rocks. It tasted like gall, and he pushed the glass away in disgust.

He hated commercial flights. The three-hour check-in always seemed a ridiculous waste of time, and the hours dragged more slowly than usual. Rather than going through to the departure lounge, he wandered the terminal aimlessly, until he couldn't delay any longer.

"Hey, miss, you can't leave your car here!" The parking attendant shouted at the auburn haired woman as she abandoned her car outside the main terminal building. She didn't care whether they towed it away or not. She glanced at the slim gold watch on her wrist and started running toward the glass doors.

Breathless, she pushed her way through the crowds of travellers. She scanned the listings on the departure board. There was only one flight to Seattle showing. Gate thirty-seven; right at the far end of the terminal building. Even if she could bluff her way through security, she would never make it in time.

Her lungs burned with effort as she ran the final yards towards passport control. The queue was longer than she'd anticipated. She stopped in dismay, her breath coming in ragged gasps. Her sense of loss was beyond tears, the only things left to her were the raw sores of an aching heart. She scanned the faces, tears welling in her eyes. Hastily, she brushed them away and hurried towards the desk.

Walker waited impatiently in line with his fellow passengers. Time had run out. He had no alternative but to take that final step, and pass through passport control and security screening.

Above the noise of the crowd, he thought he'd heard someone call his name. He turned to look, but there was no one he recognized, just the usual melee of travelers in a rush to get to their destinations. Disappointed, he handed his passport, along with his boarding pass, to the immigration official and waited for clearance.

"Walker! Wait!"

There it was again, someone calling his name. He stepped out of the queue and turned. Looking back towards check-in, he saw her, a slim figure in an oversized red sweater running towards him.

"Skye? Skye. Oh, my God, you came."

"I couldn't let you leave. Not without telling you—" She paused to catch her breath.

He held her at arm's length. "What is it you want to tell me?"

Taking a deep, unsteady breath, she stepped back and lifted her eyes to his. "I don't love John. I lied when I told you I'd accepted his proposal."

"We can't talk here." With her small hand held protectively in his, he led her through the concourse towards the exit.

"What about your flight?"

"There's another tomorrow and the day after that. Come on, let's go. Where did you leave your car?"

"It's probably been towed away by now for being illegally parked."

He laughed. "Well, let's go and find out, shall we?"

An embarrassing twenty minutes later, having paid a hefty fine and received a stern talking-to, Skye drove away from the terminal building towards the airport hotel with Walker sitting by her side.

They found a table in a quiet corner of the lounge and ordered coffee.

"Better?" Walker asked, as Skye replaced her cup on the saucer.

"Yes, thank you. I'm sorry you missed your flight. It was the traffic—"

"Don't worry about that now. There's something I need to ask you."

Skye took a deep breath and tried to relax. "Yes?"

"Who is Laura? Is she Michael's child?"

Her head shot up. There seemed no point in hiding the truth. "She has absolutely nothing to do with Michael! She's my daughter. It was a long time ago, during my second year at university. I stupidly believed that her father loved me, but he walked out of my life the day I told him about the pregnancy. I agonized over what to do, and eventually decided to have a termination only I couldn't go through with it. I started skipping lectures because of the morning sickness, and John found out.

Without his support, I would have dropped out of university."

"Which explains your closeness to Ridge and why you set up the Foundation. Where is she now?"

Her faint smile held a touch of sadness. "I don't know. I gave her up for adoption. A decision I have regretted it every day of my life. She will be sixteen this year."

"And Michael?"

"I wish I'd never met him. He found the only photograph I had of Laura, and accused me of lying. He kept me locked up in a hotel room for a week, and used the information to blackmail me."

Walker flinched, her admission cutting him to the core. "Which is why you ran from me, when I stupidly kept you at the cabin?"

"Yes."

Suddenly, it all made sense to him. She had gone to the cabin to re-build her life. When she opened her heart and soul to him, he'd thrown it in her face, sending her back to the one man she felt she could rely on—Ridge.

"Why? Why did you come today?"

Skye bowed her head. "I wanted you to know that I never accepted John's proposal. I said that to hurt you. I shouldn't have done."

Walker reached for her hand. "And that's the only reason you came?"

"Yesterday, you told me that if I married John I would be committing myself to a loveless marriage."

"Yes, I did."

"You also said you wanted me, but wanting someone isn't the same as loving them. And a relationship implies both."

"I guess it does."

Skye was crestfallen. She snatched her hand out of his. "Then I can't come with you."

The silence stretched until finally Walker said, "Why not?"

"Because wanting me in your bed isn't enough."

He sat back, rebuffed. "Damn it, Skye. I thought... I hoped that by coming here, you'd decided you wanted to be with me."

"I do. But I we have different goals in life." Skye bit her lower lip to stop it trembling.

Walker leaned forward in his chair, rested his arms on his thighs, and stared at his hands. After a while, he raised his head and studied her.

"I love you, Skye. I have loved you since the first day I saw you. Once I had held you in my arms, I couldn't bear to be away from you. I lay in the hospital, and all I could think about, was you. You see, I rather thought you loved me."

Skye's heart was beating too fast for comfort. She wiped away a tear with the back of her hand.

"You love me?"

Walker stood and gathered her into his arms. His kiss was slow and thoughtful. Lifting his mouth from hers, he gazed into her eyes.

"I want you as my wife. As the mother of my—*our* children. Skye, will you marry me?"

Skye smiled. "How soon can you book another ticket?"

The smile in Walker's eyes burned with a sensuous flame.

"Shall we go and find out?"

THE END

About the author

Victoria Howard is the author of three romantic suspense novels; *The House on the Shore*, (a 2009 Joan Hessayon Award finalist), *Three Weeks Last Spring*, and *Ring of Lies*. She is also the author of several short stories, including the Kindle short, A Little Protection.

Born in Liverpool, Victoria trained as a medical secretary, and subsequently worked for the National Health Service. She spent twenty years living on a croft in the Highlands of Scotland, managing a company involved in the offshore oil and gas industry.

During those rare times when she isn't writing, Victoria can be found curled up with a book, gardening, designing knitwear, walking her Border collie, Rosie, or travelling the world.

Victoria is also a member of Romantic Novelists' Association and The Alliance of Independent Authors.